M000311576

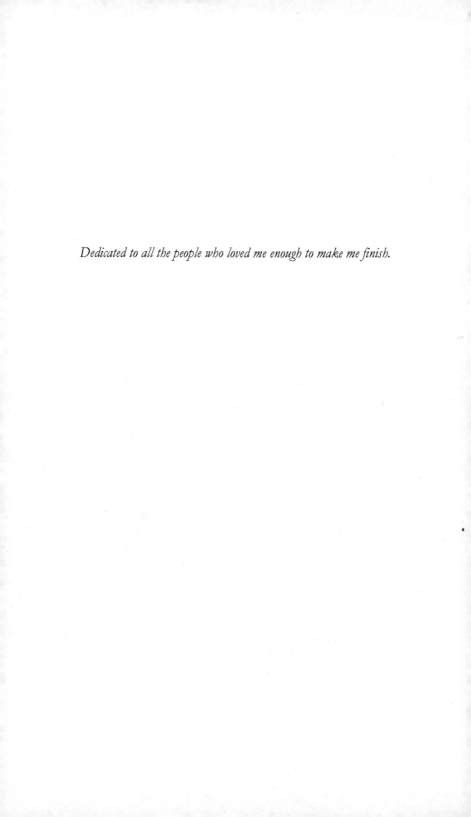

Dedicated to all the people who loved me enough to make me finish.

CHAPTER ONE

Brittany had always chided Tom for his bad memory—now he wished it was worse so he didn't remember her. He was steaming the milk for a white chocolate mocha when Tom remembered his window. Water streaked down the large front windows of The Cup, and everyone was complaining about the rain. It had rained every morning all week, but he'd remembered to close his window until today. He'd been looking for his other brown sock and wondering if his car would start. Twice recently it hadn't, and he'd ridden his bike to work; consequently, he'd arrived dripping, and squashed around in his brown loafers all day. Today his car started at the expense of his memory, and the window stayed open. Tonight his bed would be soggy. Last time, he'd draped his comforter over the refrigerator, but it had taken two days to dry and still smelled like wet dog.

Mrs. Donahue broke his reverie.

"How are you today, Tommy?" She was the only person who called him Tommy; said he reminded her of her grandson.

"I'm fine, Mrs. Donahue. How are you? How's your knee in this rain?" She was a regular, but she never ordered the same drink two days in a row.

"Oh, my knee. It aches and pains. It's going to rain forever. My geraniums are delighted—green as my grandson on Bob's sailboat. The rain missed the summer, but it's here now. Do you think it'll be a snowy winter?" She looked at him briefly, but he knew from experience it didn't matter if he replied. "No matter. Bob always hires the boys next door to shovel. I hope they do better than last year; there was a slippery spot and I almost broke my legs. Both of them." She sighed.

Mrs. Donahue was cheery and effervescent, wrinkled, gray, and crazy. She liked to talk about her garden, her grandsons, and her husband Bob. Tom enjoyed her. She talked a lot. He just had to remember the easy things—like geraniums—to get her started. Other people needed more coaxing, but he enjoyed the challenge, even when unsuccessful. When a sad-eyed blond came in on Monday, she hadn't even looked at his face. Tom finished making the mocha, and Mrs. Donahue wandered to a front table where she could "keep an eye on the rain, to make sure it doesn't misbehave."

Tom glanced at the clock as he wiped the counter. 9:30, four hours left. Tom had never wanted to be a barista. When he was younger he'd dreamed of being a firefighter or a doctor. But making dreams happen is hard work, and Tom's dreams faded quickly. After everything happened with Brittany, he dropped out of college and moved back in with his parents. His residence there was short, as he tired of their opinions about his life and moved to Denver. Now he lived in a small flat and worked at The Cup, an independently owned and very popular coffee shop.

Four years later he knew most customers by name. A few people were rushed and harried every day, but others came in leisurely, to talk to Tom, and get coffee. Sometimes they forgot about the coffee. His patience and kindness made him a gentle audience, so once people started talking to him they struggled to stop. There was no end to the aches and pains he listened to. Everyone hurt over something, and everyone wanted to be heard. Not wanting to talk about himself, he became a listener.

He had grown up on a farm in Idaho. As the youngest of five, he'd always felt overlooked. At school he was smart, but not exceptional. In sports he was neither bad nor good. He didn't excel in anything during college, and after he dropped out he felt like a failure. While nothing distinguished him from anyone else, his siblings were always in the spotlight. Mary wasn't married, but the rest were. Elizabeth had two daughters, Matt had a daughter and a son, and Jake and his wife lived in Chicago. When people asked him about himself, he responded cheerily, "I just grew up in the country and wandered into the city to see if the rumor about not seeing stars was true." Then he sidetracked, asking them about who they were and where they'd been. He had found that people will talk about themselves as opportunity presents; being listened to is rare—feeling heard even more so.

The girl was an enigma. She wouldn't make eye contact, and she didn't smile back. She was strangely unresponsive to his sunshine. The bell above the door interrupted, and Mr. Peterson walked in for his daily cup of coffee. The shop was always in a lull right after 9. Mr. Peterson was the sole exception; he came in and talked to Tom, for as long as he was allowed. He complained about everything from his hip replacement to his poor tomato crop, but he had a dry sense of humor that made his complaints interesting instead of tiresome. Tom liked him, for he saw his loneliness. Mrs. Peterson had died of Alzheimer's three years before, declining until she didn't recognize him, and screaming and trying to hit him every time he came close to her. The day that Mr. Peterson told Tom the story, he hadn't known how to respond.

Today Mr. Peterson was railing on restaurants.

"I walk up to the counter for my food, and some half-asleep kid stares at me through his piercings. There is absolutely no self-respect anymore. Or respect in general." He 'humphed.' "The only place I still get good service is Francie's Diner. Her girls actually know how to serve. She just hired a new one. Sweet little thing. What about all this rain? I bet Sherry is happy about her geraniums..." All this before he'd reached the counter. Tom's heart cheered up, and he started pouring the coffee he knew Mr. Peterson wouldn't remember to ask for. He talked about Mrs. Donahue, and how he hadn't talked to her husband for a while. As an afterthought he added,

"How are you, Tom?" He peered at Tom, as if remembering for the first time that he was there. Mr. Peterson's life had been hard, but it had made him kind. Tom smiled.

"I'm doing fine, Mr. Peterson. Just back here making coffee, as usual." Mr. Peterson eyed him up and down, taking in the brown-tan plaid flannel, blue jeans, brown apron, brown curly hair, and brown eyes.

"You look awfully brown today, son. Looks like you coordinated your eyes and your hair and your shirt and your shoes and your apron. Spend lots of time on that?" He laughed at his own joke, and wandered over to his favorite chair in the center of the shop. Every day he looked through the same picture book of famous landmarks that was on the table beside the chair. Tom imagined he was thinking of all the places he wanted to go.

Tom spent the rest of the lull tidying, restacking cups, straightening chairs, and wiping tables. The lunch rush started a little before twelve, and Tom loved it. He raced with himself to stay ahead of the line, even if it wasn't long. When more than four people were lined up, he felt like he was losing a game. The faster he could serve people, the happier they were; when his customers left the shop happy, he felt like he was winning.

Tom looked around the shop to make sure everything was in order. It was a long room, with six tables, each a different size, surrounded by random chairs. Some were white, some brown, and some black, all unique. Scattered among the tables were pairs of overstuffed chairs, each made cozy by a small coffee table placed between the two. Three walls were covered with a pale wood paneling, and the fourth was painted a deep sage green. Bookshelves lined the entire right wall; the lower shelves were cluttered with children's books and small games, and the upper shelves held works of science and philosophy and history, and random knickknacks that people brought Phil Kohle back from all around the world, for his shop. On the green wall hung an eclectic collection of paintings. One of them was the famous picture of

The Cup

A NOVEL

ANNELIESE RIDER

a man and woman in a diner at night, and every time he looked at it Tom imagined the story it told.

The floor was wood, originally stained a deep brown but worn and scratched over the years. The shop used to be a small ballroom dancing studio; after it had gone out of business and stood empty for several years, Phil bought the place and switched the wallpaper for wooden paneling, breathing new life into the tired room. He kept the odd chandelier and covered the floors with randomly patterned throw rugs. Phil was an odd man, and he liked to run an odd shop. 'Character makes people love a place,' he'd tell Tom, running his hand along the long wooden bar. Regardless of oddity—perhaps because of it—the cafe got more business than any other coffee shop in its section of town. Phil knew almost everyone and was always telling people to stop by. Tom's friendly manner instantly won them over and convinced them to come back.

The bell over the door rang. Rinsing something in the sink, Tom chimed,

"Good morning, welcome to The Cup!" He glanced at the clock, which like everything else in the shop was non-traditional. Seven read "rush," eight read "frenzy" and nine read "lull". Right now it was almost eleven, and the hour hand was halfway between 'Lull-ish' and 'Lively'. Drying the cup and looking up, Tom saw the girl who wouldn't smile setting her bag at one of the overstuffed chairs. She straightened and walked towards the counter, eying the big menu on the wall. Tom spoke.

"How are you today?" He half smiled, which Mrs. Donahue told him made him look nervous, not charming. Without looking at him, the girl replied,

"Fine."

"How 'bout all this rain?"

She shrugged, put her hand on the counter, and said,

"I'll have a large Chai Latte."

"Wonderful."

He rang her up, gave her change, and moved to start her drink.

"I don't like rain." He looked up as she continued, "Well, I like it when I'm warm and cozy and dry. But last night I had my window open and the rain came in and my bed got all wet." He thought about his wet bed.

"I'm really sorry. That's awful." She looked at him, surprised that he didn't have more to add. He asked,

"Have you lived here long?"

"No." She didn't seem inclined to say more, so he remained silent for a moment, then asked,

"Oh. Welcome. Do you like it?"

"It's nice. I like the weather, when it's not raining." She sighed.

"It's been a rainy fall, it's not usually this wet." The hissing of the steam wand in the milk filled the silence. "Where did you move here from?" She replied somewhat stiffly,

"New York."

"I've always wanted to go to New York." She raised her eyebrows. "Do you miss it?"

"No."

Almost defiantly, she lifted her chin.

"Oh." He cleared his throat, placed her mug on the counter, and slid it across to her. "Here's your chai."

"Thanks."

"You're welcome. Enjoy your afternoon."

He smiled brightly, but she didn't. As she walked away, he added, "I hope your bed is dry tonight." She didn't acknowledge him, but placed her mug gently on a table and reached for her bag.

The clock gave a tiny chime to indicate eleven, and three people came in. He'd speculate about the girl later. He hoped he could talk to her again, but she finished her drink, read for a while longer, and left.

Tom got off at 2. On his way home he planned to buy dinner. He never bought much, because he didn't have much money and he didn't like to cook. He usually ate breakfast at The Cup, brought a peanut butter and jelly sandwich for lunch, and scrounged something for dinner. Yesterday when he'd opened his cupboard, there sat a lonely can of expired green beans, and half a box of bran that his dad had bought when he'd come to visit Tom three months ago. He'd eaten the beans.

CHAPTER TWO

The rain was slowing down as Tom left work. He always parked his car, a beat up old Buick from his great grandma, a few blocks away. It worked relatively well most of the time—it was just ugly. It was brown maroon, and rust spots gave it a rattletrap air, as if it might suddenly disintegrate. His nephew Flynn had affectionately named it Whitaker when Tom had brought it home, and the name had stuck. Tom sauntered down the street, enjoying the fresh air. The smell of coffee lingered on his clothes and skin, and the brisk autumn crisp was refreshing. Reaching his car, he tricked the door open. At some point in the car's past, the lock had broken and it took a special trick to jiggle the lock and unlatch it. Sometimes it worked on the first try; sometimes it took a half dozen tries. Brittany had always teased him about Whit, but he was attached to the car. He claimed it was family.

Tom didn't like shopping—there were too many people and too many decisions. He walked down the same aisle four times before choosing a bag of frozen tater tots, and one of chicken nuggets. He could shop again tomorrow.

His apartment was eight miles from The Cup. As he drove home in the rain that had resumed, he noticed a car he didn't recognize stopped on the side of the road. It was an Oldsmobile, he guessed from the 80's. It was dirty blue, not baby enough to be cute, not green enough to be perky. Tom always stopped to help people if he wasn't in a hurry, so he pulled over behind the car, and waited till the woman inside got off the phone before he walked over. Peering through the window proved difficult, as the sky reflected against the wet glass, so he didn't fully recognize her until she opened her door. The blonde girl stared up at him. He smiled, unbidden.

"Oh, hi. I didn't see it was you. Everything alright?"

Obviously not.

"My car died."

She looked at him. He didn't compliment himself by assuming it was for his looks. She had nothing better to look at.

"While you were driving it?" Obvious again. "It just died?"

She nodded.

"It made a funny sound, then turned off and I coasted to the side. I was thinking about looking in the hood but I didn't want it to fall on my head."

Grinning, Tom too slowly realized she was completely serious. He cleared his throat and said,

"That's smart. How long have you had it?"

He motioned towards the vehicle.

"I think it's an '87? I'm not sure. My neighbor sold it to me last week."

"Did you check the oil?"

"No."

"Okay. If you could find the button that pops the hood, I'll take a look."

Tom walked over to the hood of the car and looked in. It hadn't been very well cared for; most of the metal was rusty, and the belts were old and worn. The oil was low and dark, but not dry. Nothing was visibly wrong with the car.

"Have you gotten gas recently?"

She looked up at him.

"No."

"I think you might be out of gas."

She sighed, then said,

"Nothing blinked or dinged."

"Sometimes it doesn't in older cars."

"Oh." She sighed.

"Are you on your way somewhere? I can bring you if you're late."

"No. It's my day off."

"Good. There a gas station not far from here—we can go pick up some gas."

She hesitated at the offer, frowning as she thought.

"I just called my boss, and she said her husband could come get me."

"I'll take you, really it's no problem." She looked at him skeptically. "Really. I'd love to take you. I just got off work and I'm not in a hurry."

For the first time, she considered his offer.

"Well…" A pause as she thought, then, "Okay. I'll call her back and tell him not to come."

He smiled.

"Great."

He closed the hood, walked back to his car, and for the first time realized he didn't know her name. Sliding into the driver's seat he reached over to the passenger's side and swung the door open for her. For the first time she almost smiled.

"Thanks."

He grinned, and said,

"I just realized we haven't officially met. I'm Tom."

"I'm Janelle. Nice to meet you. Thanks for all your help."

Janelle. Tom liked the name Janelle. It reminded him of his third grade math teacher, Miss Jane. She always smelled like cinnamon and wood.

"No problem, I'm just glad I came past."

"Me too."

Tom let the words hang in the air. He didn't want to overwhelm her if she didn't want to talk—but he didn't want to make her uncomfortable with silence. His squeaking windshield wipers filled the stillness. Not only did they squeak, they left streaks. He laughed nervously.

"Sorry about my wipers. I should change them."

He usually grew more and more frustrated until he stopped using them completely, preferring the silence of a blurry windshield to the mind numbing drone of the shrieking rubber.

She shook her head, and said,

"It's fine. They sound just like mine." She paused, deliberating. "Sometimes, I imagine they're singing a song and I try to sing along." Tom laughed. Realizing his laughter might hurt her, he said,

"I'm not laughing at you. You're just more patient than I am."

She said,

"Oh?"

He shook his head, said

"I'm nowhere near that calm."

He looked over at her. She was wearing pale blue jeans, a massive teal sweater, and white lace up shoes. Her big, dark green glasses were almost the same color as the bike Tom's brother had given him for his twenty-first birthday. She worked a silver ring back and forth around her middle right finger, and occasionally rubbed her snub nose with her finger.

She knocked her knees together, keeping an odd rhythm with the ring-twisting and the squealing wipers. Tom felt she was listening to a song that he couldn't hear, and almost expected her to begin singing. He asked,

"Do you like music?"

"Yes! I do."

There was a hint of real feeling in her voice.

"Do you make it or listen?"

He chastised himself for the awkward wording.

"I had piano lessons when I was younger, but when things got complicated, I stopped. Now I just sing. I've never had lessons though. I like to listen."

She kept twisting her ring.

"Anything in particular?"

She didn't seem to mind his questions.

"I like almost everything. I don't listen to country, or heavy metal, but that's all."

Tom turned the radio on, and soft classical music filled the air. He liked classical music for early mornings, because it put him in a good mood; he wasn't a morning person by nature, but one crabby barista makes a lot of crabby people, so he'd learned to be cheery early in the mornings. Janelle started humming along with the song, which was an obscure piece that Tom didn't recognize. She stopped long enough to say,

"I like classical. This is good."

Tom looked over at her again, and asked,

"How long have you been here?"

"Huh? Oh. Yeah. I moved from New York."

She seemed completely oblivious that she'd answered the wrong question. He didn't try to ask again, instead commenting,

"Wow. That's far."

"Yeah."

She nodded.

"Do you have a good place to live?"

She nodded again and said,

"I'm in a tiny apartment on West Elm."

"Really? I live on West Oak! What's your address?"

Elm and Oak were two streets apart. He went down Elm some mornings on his way to work.

"You do? Wow. 217. The little brown house. I live in the attic apartment."

"I live in 429! We're almost neighbors."

He grinned at her. Shyly, she barely smiled back, but tapped her fingers to the music as he hummed. The rain continued, and with it the whining wipers. When he was little, his dad told him the rain was God's sweat. It had fascinated him; he always wondered why it didn't smell funny if God was sweating. And if it was sweat, why wasn't it salty? As a seven year old he'd pondered this as he watched the rain race down crooked tracks on the window.

His father was a fine furniture carpenter, and he'd taught Tom much of his trade. When he was little, Tom sat on the top step of a stepladder and watched his dad. A self-proclaimed perfectionist, Mr. Bailey didn't mind making plain solid pieces of furniture, but loved crafting pieces with complicated designs and intricate patterns. He'd measure and re-measure, then carefully cut and sand until all the wood felt as soft as velvet. After they were perfectly smooth, he'd carefully chisel out intricate designs, then assemble the piece and stain it in whatever shade the customer requested. Tom loved watching patterns take shape under his father's careful hands. He always told Tom exactly what he was doing, and how to do it. He'd wanted Tom to be a carpenter, but Tom didn't like all the pressure of perfection that following in his father's footsteps would mean. He liked carpentry as a hobby, but didn't want it as a job.

Janelle seemed content to look out at the rain and tap her knees with the music. Tom asked,

"You said you called your boss—where do you work?"

"Francie's Diner."

"Really? Francie is wonderful. Do you like it there?"

She stopped tapping her knees.

"It's good. I'm training, so it's a lot right now. But I think when it settles down I'll like it a lot."

He nodded.

"I remember training. You learn one thing, then mess something else up, right?"

"That's exactly what it feels like. I was a waitress in New York so I know how to serve, but everywhere is a little different."

"I can imagine that."

"You like being a barista? I always wanted to be one."

Tom nodded. He tried not to answer too eagerly in his delight at her seeming interest in conversation.

"I like it most of the time. People are strangely transparent with you when you're behind a counter. They feel like you're safe and you won't invade on their lives, because there's a barrier. So people talk to me a lot. I like that."

Janelle made a noise in agreement.

"It's not quite like that for us, but I do understand. Does it ever get tiring?"

Tom cocked his head. People didn't often ask him about his job.

"Some days it feels long; but the way people cheer up when you listen to what they have to say is worth it." She nodded, and he added, "I like my boss. Once he had me rewrite the menu in Spanish. Just to confuse people. Another time he flipped the pictures on the wall upside down, and left them that way for a month. He loves to do things a little differently."

She smiled.

"That's funny." They were almost to the gas station, and Janelle continued, "What are we going to use to carry gas?"

"I'll see if I have something in my trunk, and if I don't can buy something."

There wasn't much in his trunk—a blanket, some jumper cables, a football, and the muddy pair of cleats Tom wore to play soccer some Saturdays.

"Looks like we're going inside, which is fine. We should also pick up some oil for your car."

Tom opening the door of the store for Janelle. It was rudimentary chivalry that his sisters had drilled into him when he was young. There were three aisles of odds and ends that were completely unrelated and unpredictable. The walls were lined with fridges, mostly full of alcohol with the occasional juice or tea. They looked for something that would hold gas, but there were no empty containers. They were about to give up, when Tom noticed a gallon jug of iced tea.

"Do you like iced tea?"

She looked confused.

"I guess. Why?"

"There's a gallon jug here that would be perfect."

He opened the fridge and lifted it out.

"Can't we just pour it out?"

He shook his head.

"I really don't like wasting things. I think we should drink it."

She raised her eyebrows, and said,

"All of it?"

"All of it."

She shrugged.

"I'll drink some of it, at least."

He bought the tea and a quart of oil, and they walked back out to the car. It was just cold enough to sit inside Tom's car, instead of standing by the pump. Tom held the jug in his lap and unscrewed the lid.

"It would be better if we had cups. Oh well."

He lifted the jug to his mouth and began drinking. Janelle sat in silence and looked out the window, then back at him. He tried to look suave as he drank, thinking about this unfortunate first impression. He gulped a few more swallows, then said,

"Ready?"

He held out the jug, and she took it. It was heavier than she expected, and she dropped it a little bit and it bumped on her legs. As she tilted it to her lips carefully, Tom said,

"Careful—it's a little heavy."

She nodded, concentrating on not dropping the heavy jug or dripping any tea on her sweater. She didn't drink as fast as he had, but her slow gulps slowly brought the amount down. Just as she was getting ready to lower the jug, a bird flew smack into the windshield, thumping loudly and skidding onto the roof of the car. Tom and Janelle both jumped, and Janelle lost her grip on the tea. The mouth of the jug slid off her lips and tea began to pour onto her sweater. She yelped and flipped the jug up, but not before quite a bit of tea had spilled. It began to settle into the wool, turning the bright blue into a muddled blue-brown. She groaned.

"Ohhh. Oh no. It's going to be stained. And I love this sweater."

Tom, unsure of the appropriate response, simply said,

"Oh my." She was looking down at her sweater disconsolately, and Tom's brain kicked back into gear. He continued, "Go wash it in the bathroom. The stain should come out. Here's my jacket."

She shook her head.

"I couldn't take that."

He looked at her.

"Take it. It's fine."

She nodded and pulled the sweater off. The white t-shirt she wore underneath wasn't too wet. She was skinny underneath her bulky sweaters, and on her arms were large fading bruises. Tom didn't think anything of them. While she was inside cleaning her sweater, Tom soaked up any tea that had spilled on her seat, then got out of the car to look for the bird. It had apparently inflicted more damage on Janelle than itself, for it had flown away. Tom had lost his appetite for tea, so he poured the rest out and filled the jug with gasoline. By the time Janelle came back out he was ready.

"How does it look?"

He motioned to the sweater, not dripping but very visibly wet.

"I think I got it all out. It just needs to dry."

He nodded, and said,

"Good. I filled the jug with gas, so if you're ready we can go back to your car."

"Cool."

She sat quietly, her sweater bunched up in a tight ball on her lap. Tom poured the gas into her tank without spilling too much, as she watched.

"Try to start it?"

She turned the key, and after a moment of sputtering, the engine turned over and on.

"If you're just going home, I'll drive behind you and make sure you make it okay." He paused, then added, "Maybe you should stop and get gas."

"Okay. Thank you so much for your help."

"You're welcome—it's what I'm here for."

She nodded and closed her door, and through the raindrop-covered window, she smiled at him. A real smile. He grinned back, hoping it wasn't as big and cheesy as he felt.

CHAPTER THREE

The next morning, Tom slept in and ate leftover nuggets and tater tots for breakfast. The only other option was the three month old box of bran. He stood in the middle of his apartment with his coffee, wondering how he should spend his morning. His apartment was one big rectangular room on the second floor of a three-flat house. The front (and only) door opened into a small section of tile floor that was usually dirty, because he'd spent too much time washing floors for chores as a teenager to care if his floor was always sparkling clean. To the right of the door was a coat closet where his only coat would be hanging if Janelle didn't have it. He kept his bike wedged into the closet as well, squeezed in diagonally. Past the coat closet was the kitchen area, separated from the other half of the room by a long bar. In the back corner behind the kitchen was the bathroom, and in the opposite corner of the room, pushed up next to the wall and under a window, was Tom's bed. His bedspread was draped over the refrigerator drying, because when he'd gotten home last night it had been soaked from all the rain. The apartment smelled damp and musty.

His bed was tall, a mattress on a long high dresser. In the front corner by the door was a brown overstuffed chair and tiny table, and against the wall between the chair and the bed was a desk that the previous renter had left. It was painted white and had become chipped over the years. Tom planned to strip the paint and re-stain the desk into a natural brown, but he never seemed to find the motivation to do it. The walls were a cream tan, and mostly bare. He had two pictures; one a large print of a wave breaking around a lighthouse, and the other a smaller family picture from several years before. His guitar was propped in the corner by the overstuffed chair, and hanging above the chair was a clock with only 12, 3, 6, and 9 on it. Sometimes it stopped working, but when he tapped it with a finger it would start ticking again. Sometimes he thought about putting more art on the wall, but he never got around to it.

He'd considered getting a cat, but he would rather have a dog. His landlord was an old man, Mr. Gordon, who had a wrench in his hand whenever Tom saw him. He wasn't meticulously strict, but he didn't like dog hair, and he didn't like when his tenants complained about barking. Tom didn't mind not having anything to take care of, so he didn't try to argue it.

Finishing his coffee, Tom pulled his bike out of the closet to make another trip to the store for groceries. On his ride back he planned what to eat for lunch. He liked avocado and egg sandwiches— his Aunt Mildred made them for him when he visited. She had recently sent him a box of socks. She had a knack for sending the most unusual presents, but they always ended up being exactly what he needed. Like socks. As he rounded the corner onto West Elm, debating between scrambled or sunny side up eggs for the sandwiches, he saw Janelle in her driveway. He slowed to a stop, and pulled over to talk to her.

"Good morning."

She was preoccupied with what appeared to be a pine cone in her lap, and she jumped when he spoke.

"Oh! Hi, Tom. You scared me."

"Sorry about that. What're you holding?"

She held her palms up to him, and nestled among the brown spikes were two beady little eyes.

"This is my hedgehog, Marvin."

Tom leaned over, reached a finger out, and ran it down the spines of the little animal.

"I've had him since I was nineteen. Do you want to hold him?" Tom nodded, and parked his bike in the grass next to the driveway. He crouched down in front of her, and Janelle tipped the prickly ball into Tom's hands.

"He's tired, I just woke him up. He sleeps a lot."

Tom nodded.

"He's very nice."

He used a thumb to stroke the spines, and looked at the half open little black eyes. After a moment he moved to give Marvin back to Janelle.

"Here, I don't want to drop him."

She grinned up at him, and took the hedgehog, tucking him close to her sweater.

"I think he likes you."

Tom laughed, and straightened.

"I have to bring my food home and go to work, otherwise I'd stay and visit for longer."

He picked up and mounted his bike, as she said,

"Stop by anytime, really."

She waved as he rode off. He hummed all the way home.

After lunch, Tom went to work. He drove, because it would be a late shift and he planned to check his mailbox at the post office on his way home. His dinner shift today was with Jimmy, who had a wild imagination. Every time Tom worked with Jimmy they made up stories about the customers. Today there was a man wearing a blue velvet hat and a woman in a large yellow sweater. The stories that they told each other were as eccentric as the clothes. Right before dinner, a man in a tailored black suit came in. Tom recognized him from the early mornings, but he'd never talked to him because he always looked like he was in a hurry. Today he looked more relaxed, although he was still rocking back and forth from heel to toe, which Tom had noticed was one of his habits.

"How are you today, sir?"

The man blinked in surprise and cracked his knuckles before answering.

"I'm fine, thanks."

He reached into his pocket and rattled some change.

"I'm Tom. I see you a lot."

Tom realized he might sound creepy. The man evidently did not think so, because unfazed, he replied,

"Mike. Pleasure. I love this place. Best coffee in Denver." He nodded to himself, then continued, "I wish I had more time, I would come here just to sit. Unfortunately, I have a meeting tonight at Francie's."

"That's a bummer," Tom said, then continued, "I hope it goes well. What did you want to drink?"

"Oh, yes. Just a large black coffee. Nothing fancy. Just enough caffeine to keep me awake in case this meeting goes till two like it did last time." Tom raised his eyebrows, and Mike nodded. "Sometimes people just get carried away. We ordered dinner twice." He laughed at this comment, and Tom smiled, then said,

"That's a lot of sitting. I wouldn't be able to do it."

Mike shook his head, saying,

"I can barely do it."

Tom handed his coffee across the counter, and Mike said, "Thanks! I'll see you around!" As he turned away, Tom said,

"No problem, have a great meeting."

* * *

Her third day in Denver, Janelle's landlady Mrs. Lincoln had suggested Janelle apply to Francie's Diner. Janelle enjoyed the food industry, and she didn't mind working something she was used to until she was adjusted to living in a new place. Francie was one waitress short, and the interview was fairly simple. It was evident that Janelle had experience, and Francie liked the way she smiled shyly from behind her large glasses. She had started a week ago. Francie was kind, and the small staff of waitresses was glad to have one more person. The regulars tipped generously, and the good management made up for the occasional cranky customers.

Today, Saturday, she was scheduled from three till closing. The diner was set up like a classy old dining room, with tables scattered throughout. The smaller tables sat against the wall and seated two people, while the larger tables held anywhere from four to twelve people. Each waitress got one or two big tables per night, and four or five small tables.

Tonight at her small tables, Janelle was serving two couples, a family of four, and two college aged girls. Her big table was a group of businessmen having a meeting. In New York she'd worked at a diner called Smithies, as one of five servers. She'd worked there for years, and they'd become like family. When she told them she was leaving, Sarah and James Smith, the owners, had cried, and their grandson William Christopher had sat on her lap begging her to stay.

As she took orders from her large table, one of the men looked at her as if he recognized her. He was clean cut, in his mid-thirties, hair neatly trimmed. He wore a classic black suit, and stared at her from brown eyes behind rimless glasses. His face was ordinary; proportional, symmetrical, and kind. His chin was even, his mouth was pleasant, and the bridge of his nose started right where it should. He continued to stare at her as she brought orders and drinks out, but Janelle didn't recognize him. His vigilant presence flustered her, and she brought the wrong dish to several customers. The more nervous she felt, the more mistakes she made.

Mid-evening she was running orders of macaroni and cheese to the toddler, and carrying a tray of refills over for the meeting. She stepped into the aisle but didn't see a purse strap that had fallen off of a woman's chair. She was thinking about how it was time to offer dessert to the two girls, and how the couple at the table next to her looked unhappy—the woman looked unsatisfied with her meal, the man just looked like he didn't want to be there. Janelle didn't realize that her toe had caught the strap as she walked. She stumbled forward as the leather went taut, and the tray started to tip. Reaching up with the plate of macaroni, she tried to correct the tilt, but she overcompensated, and as if in slow motion, she watched the glasses slide off the edge of the tray, and crash to the ground. What had been a clean aisle was now a sorry mess of ice, fizz, broken glass and red straws. The restaurant was silent, and five dozen pairs of eyes were trained on her, standing in front of the mess, still holding the pasta that had miraculously stayed on the plate, although it was floating in a puddle of iced tea. The rosy pink of exertion in her cheeks burned into a deep scarlet, as she bent and picked up the largest pieces of glass and the tray. A woman at the table next to her spoke, saying,

"It's okay, honey. When I was younger I spilled a tray of spaghetti all over a man's tuxedo."

There was a general groan of compassion, and Janelle nodded at her, attempting a smile. She straightened and marched the tray and broken glasses back into the kitchen, and asked Joe, the bus boy, to clean up the mess.

"Sorry Joe—I dropped my drinks."

He looked at her sympathetically, and said,

"You'll laugh about this later, I'm sure. It's okay. I'll go clean it up."

He walked out with his cleaning supplies, and Janelle started re-pouring the drinks she'd lost, and put in a new order of macaroni. She walked out with the trays, stopping at the family table first. The toddler was coloring crazily with the red crayon on the paper menu, while the mother burped the baby.

"I'm so sorry about the wait. I had your macaroni, but," she motioned towards where Joe was now mopping the aisle, and continued, "I didn't want to serve you macaroni with iced tea in it." The mother nodded and smiled, and the father said,

"That's absolutely fine. We understand."

Janelle smiled gratefully.

"It should be out very soon."

They smiled at her, and she continued with her tray of drinks to the large table.

"Sorry this took so long. I had a little accident."

There was a general murmur of sympathy. The man who was watching her, clearly higher up in the chain of command, nodded, saying,

"It's just fine, ma'am. Just fine. We didn't mind at all."

They all nodded.

The rest of the evening went more smoothly. The man stopped staring at her, the talkative lady assured her everything was just fine, and her customers all left her generous tips. The business men lingered, talking through eleven, twelve, one, one-thirty. Janelle couldn't finish her shift until they left, so after she'd cleaned up all her other tables she sat in the back and waited. They had ordered dinner, then dessert, then more appetizers.

Francie's closed officially at two AM, although people rarely stayed that late. At 1:45 Janelle heard the scraping of chairs as they pushed back from the table. She looked out from the doorway of the kitchen, and the man who had been looking at her motioned her over.

"Sorry we took so long. You've been great."

Janelle nodded, smiling.

"My pleasure. Have a good night."

The men all nodded and smiled at her. She'd cleaned up their plates earlier so she didn't have much to do. Janelle picked the stack of bills they'd left her as a tip. There were mostly fives and tens, but there were also two twenties. Ninety dollars. It was the biggest tip she'd ever gotten. She stared at the handful of green, then smiled. Maybe the man had recognized her from somewhere—or maybe he was just sympathetic.

On Saturday nights Janelle parked her car by the post office across the street, because Francie's parking lot was small. As she walked to her car in the still quiet of the night air, she noticed a letter on the ground. She bent down to look at it, and realized that it was addressed to Tom Bailey, 429 West Oak Street. Tom was her friend. The handwriting looked like a woman's, but the return address didn't have a name. Without thinking about it, she picked it up and put it in her bag. $225 of tips, and saving a letter for Tom. What a good night. When she got home, she crawled into bed without washing her face.

CHAPTER FOUR

Monday morning found Tom speeding down his street at 5:45, trying to flatten his mussed hair with one hand and his wrinkled shirt with the other, one knee on the wheel. After he'd gotten off work on Saturday, he'd gone to the post office to get his mail. He only picked it up every few weeks, so there was always a lot. He'd been shocked to see a letter from Brittany in the pile when he was flipping through it, but he'd decided to wait until he got home to open it. Without realizing it, he'd dropped it while he was fumbling with his keys to unlock Whit. After he'd torn his apartment apart, and gone back to his parking spot to look for it, he gave up. He'd gone home and sat on the edge of his bed for most of the evening, staring at the rest of the mail that he'd scattered about the table in his search for the one piece that he wanted. This morning he woke up late. He'd been in the middle of a dream about losing his can opener, and suddenly all of his food was in cans and he couldn't open any of them, and he was getting desperately hungry, and he couldn't find anything to open them with. He slept through his alarm and only woke up because he tangled his arm tightly in the sheets and it couldn't move. He picked up the nearest clothes he could find, which were on the floor, and ran out the door.

He was only four minutes late. There were a lot of engineers who came in early, and if they had to wait for their coffee, they got cranky. While prepping the brews he caught glimpses of his reflection in the tall carafes that kept the coffee hot. His hair was messy, and there were circles under his brown eyes. John was opening with him, but he was also late this morning. Thankfully, so were most of the early customers. John was a morning person, which Tom usually didn't mind. When he arrived, he bounced in and greeted Tom cheerily:

"Good morning, Thomas!"

He was the only person who ever called him Thomas, and persisted even when Tom didn't respond because he wasn't used to it.

"It's a beautiful day, isn't it? Ahh. I love mornings."

"Good morning."

At this point, John actually looked at Tom.

"Wow. You look awful. Is everything alright?"

Tom didn't talk about his personal life to anyone, so John had no frame of reference to ask about. Per usual, at the question, Tom sidetracked John and got him talking about himself.

"Yeah. I didn't get a lot of sleep last night. Busy day. How was your weekend?"

He never really lied; he just didn't tell all the details of the truth. John sighed sympathetically, saying,

"Oooh, that's a bummer," then in the same moment and breath, his eyes lit up and he started bouncing back and forth, "My weekend was great! My little brother came and visited me, and we went hiking and camping and…" He told Tom every detail of their adventures, ending with his brother's broken toe (canoes are heavier than they look) and a doctor visit. Tom listened and laughed at the right points and asked about the little brother's toe now. John unlocked the door and switched the large wooden sign over so that "Enter at Will" faced out, and "We're Bone Dry" faced in. Phil had such eccentric taste even his open sign was odd.

Around six o'clock people started streaming in. Tom knew most of the men by name, and usually talked briefly to each of them as he poured coffee and made drinks. This morning he didn't have much energy. When anyone asked how he was, he answered with the routine, "Not too bad, thanks," or, "Fine, just fine." That was how he always

35

answered, so no one expected anything different. Sometimes he'd wondered what people would do if he told them his day was awful. He'd never done it. He didn't like to dwell on his awful days, so he never said anything. Around seven, as Tom was making a drink, he glanced up and saw Mike. As he stood in line he rocked back and forth, heel-toe, heel-toe. After ordering his drink, he stood by the bar and continued to rock. Tom spoke.

"Good morning, Mike."

He'd learned a long time ago that addressing people by name makes them feel known, and people long to be known. He made it a point to remember and use names consistently.

"Good morning…" Pause while he looked for a name tag, "… Tom."

"How're you this morning? How was that meeting Saturday?" Mike bounced his hands on the counter, looking surprised.

"I'm fine. The meeting was a mammoth. Went until almost 2 a.m. We were the last ones in the restaurant." Tom thought the meeting had been at Francie's, but he wasn't sure. "Francie is really good about letting us stay late."

He was still bouncing his hands on the counter. Tom said,

"Wow. That is late."

Mike nodded.

"You're telling me. My wife used to get so annoyed that I was out so late for meetings. I think she started to get jealous of my coworkers."

He said it with humor, but behind his wry smile was the faint shadow of emotion. Tom noted it, but made no comment, and handed Mike his coffee with a parting,

"Well, I hope you don't have to work that late today. Have a great morning."

"Thanks. Tom, right? Thanks, Tom."

Mike kept rocking, heel-toe, even as he walked out.

Later, during a lull, as Tom wiped the counter for the fourth time in twenty minutes, Mrs. Donahue walked in slowly, humming. Sometimes it took her five minutes to get from the door to the counter, because she was so easily distracted. She seemed to have an uncanny knack for observation.

"Good morning, Tommy. You're looking awful today."

He laughed.

"Good morning, Mrs. Donahue. It's good to see you too."

She plunked her hands down on the counter and peered up at the menu from behind her thick rimmed gaudy gold glasses. They had rhinestones on them, and tiny little elephants marched up and down the frames between the jewels. She kept them attached to herself on a long gold chain that was segmented by big glass beads of all different colors, and sometimes when she took them off she would drop the mess on a table and say, "Well! It's a pain to be so classy." Today she ordered a pumpkin spice latte, because they'd just gone back on the menu for fall.

"What'd you do this weekend, Tommy? I went out on Bob's sailboat with him, and we stayed out for hours. I was wrapped in a blanket the whole time—it was so cold! Then we came back and had hot chocolate. And yesterday at church there was a potluck dinner, and I ate my body's weight in food. Then Bob and I went home and sat on the couch staring at each other all afternoon."

Tom chuckled, and she giggled.

"But really, Tommy. How are you? You look awful. Did you sleep at all last night?"

Sometimes she wouldn't take his aversion for an answer.

"Not much. I lost something important yesterday, and I spent a long time looking for it."

He sighed, and looked down at his feet, which had started to ache, which was unusual. Staring up at him from the bottom of his legs were two shoes: a brown suede lace up, and a worn tan leather loafer. He laughed, and added,

"In fact, I was in such a hurry when I woke up this morning that I put on two different shoes."

Mrs. Donahue slapped the counter and said,

"Oh, Tommy. You need a wife."

Tom laughed at her comment, but with some reserve. Brittany. And I'll never know what the letter said. He looked back down at his feet in their mismatched packages.

"Well, thanks, Mrs. Donahue. Maybe someday. She'll have to be pretty patient to deal with me."

He started preparing her latte, and she prattled on about what a lovely fall it was, and how she loved the colors. She asked if Mr. Peterson had come in yet today, and when Tom was going to ever take a day off. By the time he'd finished her drink, Tom had heard about every major event that was transpiring in town in the next month. He handed her the latte, and she took it in one hand, grasping his hand with her other.

"Thank you, Tommy. You're a dear."

She pushed her glasses back up her nose, turned, and hummed her way over to her table by the window. It was a sunny Monday, and she smiled as she rested her chin on her hand and tilted her face toward the sun streaming through the window. Tom stood behind the counter and watched her. He'd never expected to hear from Brittany again. He looked at his mismatched shoes and wondered what the letter had said. Now it barely mattered.

CHAPTER FIVE

Monday morning found Janelle as relaxed as Tom had been frenzied several hours earlier. She didn't work till 3, so after a slow breakfast, Janelle drove to The Cup to read for the morning. When the bells over the door clinked as she walked in, Tom looked up to do his routine greeting. When he saw her, his face lit up.

"Good morning, Janelle!"

He grinned. She couldn't help smiling at his enthusiasm.

"Hi Tom. How are you?"

She asked before she'd even reached the counter, and he paused before he answered.

"I'm fine. Just fine."

She raised an eyebrow. He didn't look fine. His hair was flat to his head on one side like he'd just woken up, and his shirt was wrinkled, as if it'd been in a pile on the floor before he put it on. She didn't comment on that, instead saying,

"I brought your jacket back for you. Thank you so much for letting me wear it. My sweater didn't get stained at all."

She held his jacket up, neatly folded. He motioned to the hooks off to the side of the counter. His backpack was on one of them.

"Thanks, you can hang it there if you don't mind."

She complied, then came back to the counter and ordered a drink.

"How was your weekend?"

She looked at him openly, hoping for an honest answer.

"It was fine. I worked and relaxed. How was yours?"

Hands on the counter, she said,

"It wasn't too bad," then added, "Work was pretty awful, actually. There was a meeting at my big table, and I spilled a tray of drinks in the aisle." Tom winced as she continued, "It was embarrassing."

She sighed, remembering the shame. Tom moved around behind the counter preparing her drink, and after a moment of silence, he said,

"I remember the first time I spilled a drink. I had just made a large latte for a woman wearing a suit, and as I passed it over the counter and she reached for it, my coworker Jenny dropped a glass on the floor and it shattered. Both of us were so surprised that I almost threw the cup at her. It ended up all over the front of her suit coat and skirt. She was gracious, but she was not pleased." The way he told the story made Janelle feel better, and he added, "It's okay. Now that you've got a big spill out of your system, you'll never need to do it again."

She nodded, and he passed her mug across the counter.

"Thanks, Tom."

He nodded and grinned, and she walked over to her chair, eagerly anticipating her book. She reached into her bag for it, and saw Tom's letter. She'd forgotten about it. She fingered it and looked over to where Tom was flipping mugs top-side-up and back again, looked under each one as he did so, like a little boy looking for Santa Claus. He seemed distracted. She moved over to the counter, sliding the letter back and forth between her fingers, watching him. He didn't notice her, and jumped when she cleared her throat, holding the letter out,

"Sorry to startle you. I found this outside of the post office Saturday night."

He looked at the letter as if it was a brother he hadn't seen for a decade. His mouth hung open as he stared. After some time, he spoke.

"Oh." It fell flat. He added, "It's mine. Thank you."

He took the envelope, and nonchalantly put it in his backpack. Janelle walked back to her seat wondering what the letter said. Whoever it was from, he cared a lot.

When Janelle held out the letter, Tom's heart had stopped for the second time in so many days. His joy at being reunited with the letter was tempered with a knot in the pit of his stomach about what it might say. Brittany. He finished work as well as he could, mentally absent. He took his time walking to his car, watching the orange leaves in the trees and the squirrels yelling at each other from tree to tree. He wiggled his key in Whit's keyhole, but today the car was feeling recalcitrant, so it took Tom multiple tries to free the lock. He wondered why he bothered locking the rusty old rattletrap. Most people knew it was his, and the ones who didn't certainly wouldn't target it for theft. After finally tricking the lock, he dropped into his seat and took the letter from his bag. The envelope was cream white, and inside was a neatly folded piece of soft stationery. His address had been written with a fine pen, in neat cursive. Brittany had always had beautiful handwriting when she chose to put the time and effort into it. The paper smelled faintly of her perfume. He slowly unfolded the paper. A cream colored card tumbled onto his lap. It was her business card, and on the back she'd written a phone number, marked as "My Cell." Tom stared blurrily at the paper and the envelope, finally letting his eyes focus on the words.

Dear Tom,

It's been a while. I guess you probably didn't expect to ever hear from me again. I've been having a lot of conversations recently with old friends. Remember Mrs. Johnson? And Professor Winsley? And Kimmie, and Tim. They've all made me think a lot. I got your address from Tim.

I live in Dallas now—wanted to get out of the cold. I'm sorry for how everything happened between us. I was clumsy, young. You don't have any obligations towards me, but I would be delighted if you would call me. I'd love to talk to you. My cell is on my card.

I hope you are well today, my friend.

Brittany

He put the letter down and looked outside. The leaves were still falling, the sunshine was breaking through the trees, and cars were passing. Everything was exactly the same, but everything was exactly different. The pit of his stomach was questioning him, as it did during the climb on a roller coaster, or the time he'd crashed his dad's pickup truck into a tree and had to go home and tell his parents. He turned the key, and Whit rumbled to life. Tom pulled into the street without looking either way. He drove to the graveyard, disregarding all his errands. Whenever he had to do serious thinking, he went there and wandered aimlessly, his mind jumbled in confusion.

Brittany. They grew up together. Her family moved to his town when she was six, and they were in the same class in school and church. It was a small town, and everyone knew each other. And everyone knew that Brittany and Tom were the same age. As soon as Tom was an acceptable age for romance, everyone teased him about Brittany. Valentine's Day meant three weeks of hearing about who should receive his attention. Both families wanted it, the whole town expected it, he took her to the school dances every year. She was smart and a little sassy, he was clean-cut and kind, a perfect masculine match for her femininity. Through most of high school they were just good friends (his mother's idea), but Christmas of their junior year he'd asked her to be his girlfriend, and she'd said yes. Everyone instantly started planning their wedding. Tom and Brittany had laughed it off—their parents told them they were still young, to enjoy life. Even so, Brittany went to college at a state school with a very specific vision; she wanted to go into the fashion industry. Tom wasn't sure what he wanted to do, but he wanted to be with Brittany, so he went to the same school as an unspecified major. Everything seemed to be going well, besides the occasional fretting over his future. He didn't have plans for his life—he just wanted Brittany in it.

At the beginning of their junior year, while he was entertaining visions of proposing, Brittany was having doubts. Their relationship started going downhill. She pulled back gradually, but when he asked her about it she denied it, kissing him on the cheek and telling him how much she loved him. Her reassurances gnawed at the back of his mind, but he did his best to silence the doubts. He bought a ring, and began making an elaborate plan to propose exactly where he'd asked her to be his girlfriend four years before, their hometown in Idaho, a pretty bridge over a bubbling stream in a local forest preserve. His planned proposal was even the same date, during their winter break. The morning of, everything was perfect. Tom calmed his nerves, then called Brittany and asked her to take a walk with him. She agreed. When they came to the bridge he told her all the things he loved about her, then dropped to his knee and held up a ring. But instead of the delighted reaction he had imagined again and again, she shook her head violently, started to sob, and told him she couldn't marry him. He was shocked, but she couldn't explain. When she tried she just cried harder. Finally she managed to choke out her conviction that they weren't going to work, and she asked him to take her home. She sobbed the entire way, and he sat silent, numb with the slow-dawning reality that she didn't want him. It had stopped his life. He dropped out of school and moved home, but home was full of memories and opinionated family—so he moved to Denver to get away.

And now this. He'd never understood what had changed—she'd seemed to love him so much. He kicked a pine cone between the gravestones, watching it spin crazily across the grass. There was no explanation. The sun had been sinking slowly, and it had been getting chillier, but Tom in his flannel was too preoccupied to remember that his jacket was in the car, and even if he had remembered he wouldn't have cared. He circled the tombstones, kicking pinecones, asking God why. He'd grown up with the solid belief that there was a God, but started to question Him when He'd grown silent in Tom's grief. He'd slowly let his beliefs go, and when Brittany rejected him, he'd dropped any idea of believing in God completely. But he did believe, when something big happens, whether good or bad, one must acknowledge God. The sun dropped gradually, and it was then that Tom realized just how long he'd been walking. His shadow had lengthened and faded in the dusk, and he was beginning to get cold. He walked faster and faster, growing frustrated at the weather, at Brittany, at God. He'd never done anything to deserve what she'd done to him. He had been able to suffocate the feelings, giving himself the instant remedy that, "It'll be okay. I'll be fine." This had worked at the time, but it never let him heal. Instead of a simple scar, his pain had stayed fresh, although he worked to ignore it. He walked quickly, stalking up and down the rows, and before long it was completely dark. He realized this because in his frustrated marching he walked right into a small gravestone and fell headlong. He lay on the ground, face in the prickly cold grass, one shoulder resting on a flat tombstone, and the other crushing an expired bundle of flowers left by some sad relative. The grass started to make his face itch, so he stood up slowly, fingering his car keys.

He navigated the tombstones more carefully, back to his car. He hadn't locked the door on Whit, so he climbed in and turned the key. Whit clunked to life, sputtered for a moment, and died. Tom turned the key again, and after a feeble scraping sound, there was silence. Tom put his head on the steering wheel and groaned, then used the feeble glow from his cell phone to scrutinize the engine. It was too dark to see any problem. Tom sighed and sat on the curb next to his lifeless vehicle. He could call someone for help—but it was around dinnertime, and everyone was probably eating, and he didn't want to bother anyone. He scrolled through the contacts on his phone, then chose not to call anyone. He didn't want to be trouble. He was six or seven miles from his apartment, so he decided to walk home and bring his bike the next day after work to see if he could figure out the problem. He set out. The walk back to his apartment would be long. He was hungry, tired, and his feet hurt from the two different shoes. He walked in the grass next to the street, hands in his pockets, head down, pondering the irony that he had gone to the graveyard to think and now all he could do was think. He walked through the dark grass, thinking about his car and the letter and Brittany, and wishing that he didn't have to open in the morning. Cars passed him, but none of them stopped, and when one slowed down, Tom pulled his phone out of his pocket and pretended to be talking. He didn't want to be trouble, and he was embarrassed that he couldn't keep his car in good enough condition, because he was so poor. No one knew how little money he actually had. He had only just finished paying college debts for a degree he hadn't gotten, and had little money for anything, including car repair.

The walk was long and dark, and Tom's feet were sore and dew-soaked when he got home. He ate toast with jam, and a can of baked beans while he sat in his bed. When he finished, he turned the lights off and put his head down. The letter, the car, and Brittany chased each other around his mind, relentlessly pestering him. It was close to the middle of the night when his weary mind finally rested, and he slipped off to sleep.

CHAPTER SIX

The next morning Tom's head felt like a foggy, jumbled mass of memories—everything from Brittany and high school, to receiving the letter yesterday. He felt like his mind was a film and the tape was on repeat. As he got ready for work his brain was blank, broken from all of the thinking he'd done.

Heavy-hearted, Tom rode his bike to work, grateful that it wasn't raining. He was opening with John again, John who was so dependably cheery in the early mornings. Tom looked to him to provide the early customers with their first fifteen minutes of interaction, and as his mind slowly woke up, Tom tried to smile more. As he grew accustomed to the idea of general cheer, Mike came in.

"Good morning, Tom! How are you?"

He spoke, almost hollered, as soon as he walked in, disregarding the line of men quietly enjoying the early morning peace.

"Hi Mike, good to see you! I'm fine."

I'm almost fine. That counts.

"How are you?" Mike rocked back and forth in line, heel-toe heel-toe, behind four men who stood solidly two-footed on the ground.

"I'm great. Hey, were you out walking last night? I thought I saw you."

"Uh, I did walk yesterday."

Mike continued bouncing, moving closer to the counter.

"It was you? Around seven? Maybe a little later? I was coming home from work early. It was along 6th Street. Hands in your pockets, looking at the ground?"

Tom laughed as Mike moved closer to the counter and continued to rock, the people in front of and behind him looking at him skeptically.

"Sounds like that was me."

Mike's eyebrows shot up as he rocked, stretching his face out like rubber.

"Cool! What were you doing, anyway? It was an awfully wet night for a walk."

Tom sighed slightly. There was no evading it. Mr. Cliffe and Mr. Toban were both paying attention now.

"Well, my car broke down, so I was walking home."

He rushed through the phrase, hoping maybe they wouldn't catch all of it. Mike eyed him, now only one person away from the counter.

"Oh."

Tom waited. Mike, mid-rock, stopped.

"Did you ask for help?"

Tom looked at his hands, pouring coffee for Mr. Toban, then back up at Mike.

"Uh, well, no."

He hoped that would be enough. Mike's gaze was part disapproval and part interest.

"What's wrong with your car?"

He had reached the counter. "A large coffee, black."

"It was too dark to tell. I drove it to the cemetery but when I tried to leave it started then died, and wouldn't start again. I couldn't see anything in the hood. I'm planning on going back today."

"How did you get here?"

Tom cringed. Too many personal questions.

"I rode my bike."

Mike started rocking slowly again. Standing still seemed to be take more effort moving.

"You're riding over after work?"

Tom nodded.

"It's not a big deal. Did you say you wanted cream and sugar?" Tom knew the answer, Mike had said it when he'd ordered his drink, and he always took his coffee black, but he wanted to stop the questions.

"No. Black. If you need any help, call me."

He pulled a business card out of his wallet, and wrote something on the back.

"This is my cell."

He shoved the card over the counter towards Tom.

"Thanks, Mike. I appreciate it."

Mike nodded, turned and walked out. John began to prattle to the customers, and Tom made drinks in silence, contemplating. People didn't usually care.

* * *

When she gave Tom the letter, it was as if a switch had flipped in his behavior. Instead of seeming sad and aimless, he'd become hyper. At work that afternoon, Janelle replayed the situation in her mind, wondering who the letter was from and what it was about. The delicate handwriting meant it was probably from a girl. On her way to The Cup the next day, she thought about asking him, not sure if it would be badly received. She settled on listening if he chose to tell her, but not prying where it wasn't her place. When she walked into the shop, Tom was talking to an older lady wearing a very unattractive floral blouse. A massive beaded chain dangled from her glasses. He looked up at her when the bells clinked, and instantly smiled.

"Excuse me, Mrs. Donahue. Good morning, Janelle!"

She grinned self-consciously.

"Hi Tom."

He motioned at the lady standing next to him.

"This is Mrs. Donahue, have you met?"

Janelle recognized her from Francie's, but they hadn't met.

"No, I don't think so. I'm Janelle."

Janelle proffered her hand, but Mrs. Donahue looked at her for a moment, then grasped her shoulders and pulled her into a firm hug.

"Well hello dear, it's so nice to meet you. I'm Sherry Donahue. Tommy always calls me Mrs. Donahue, but you can call me Sherry if you want. Your choice. Are you new in town?"

Janelle had to smile. The woman spoke as if she had a secret, and treated her like they'd been friends forever. It was pleasant.

"Yes, I am. I'm from Ne—"

Mrs. Donahue cut in.

"Ah, wait! You work at Francie's! She was telling me she just hired a new girl."

The comment didn't demand response, so Janelle just nodded. "Do you like it here?"

"Yes, I think it's really gr—"

Mrs. Donahue interrupted again.

"Yes, isn't it? We don't have too much to boast of, but what we have is the best. Like The Cup, and even Tommy here."

She reached across the counter and patted his cheek. Tom stood sheepishly, turning red.

"Well, it's been really lovely talking to you both, nice to meet you Janice, but I need to go watch the world go by."

She picked up her mug and marched over to her table by the window. Tom and Janelle watched her walk down to the front of the shop. Tom broke the silence.

"Sorry about your name. She'll get it right eventually."

Janelle laughed.

"It's okay. I'm used to it. My grandma called me Jeanette until I was seven. My mother didn't have the heart to tell her I wasn't named after her until one day I signed my name in a card for her. She's been sorry ever since."

Tom smiled, and she added.

"How are you?"

She looked closely at him.

"I'm great."

She looked at him disbelieving, as he paused, then added,

"How are you?"

"You look tired."

She didn't answer his question. He blinked.

"I am a little tired."

"Oh. Why?"

He looked at her, and she evenly met his gaze. She knew from her own experience that he was deciding whether or not to tell her. People who have been hurt don't expect to be listened to.

"My car broke down so I walked home."

He sped up the second half of the sentence, as if it wasn't true.

"Oh. I'm sorry. I wish I could have helped."

Tom laughed a little as if he didn't believe her. She frowned slightly.

"No, really. I wish I could have helped you."

"It's okay. How are you?"

She let it go.

"I'm fine. I'm reading Pride and Prejudice."

"Really? I read that in college for a literature class. Do you like it?"

He was genuinely interested.

"It's good. I'm not too far yet."

"You'll have to let me know what you think."

He showed earnest interest.

"I will!"

There was the pause of a moment as both wondered what to say, then she asked,

"Oh, can I have a large chai latte?"

It was colder today, and she wore a big brown sweater with her tan jeans. She loved big sweaters; not only did she feel protected, but they hid her arms. It didn't matter anymore, but the habit was hard to break.

"Absolutely. And because I want to thank you for giving me my letter back, it's on me."

He said this with finality as he shifted his balance from one foot to the other.

"That was no big deal. Anyone who knows you would have given it back. I can pay for my drink."

But he was determined, and nothing she said would change his mind. Acquiescing, she said,

"Thank you. I appreciate it."

He began to fix the drink, and she stood at the counter, wondering if she should try to talk to him or sit in her chair and start reading. He solved the problem.

"How was work yesterday?"

He wasn't looking at her, instead watching the milk he was steaming.

"It was much better than Saturday. I didn't spill any drinks."

He nodded encouragingly, saying,

"That's good."

They both stood there, his hands busy with the drink, hers resting one on the other on the counter. He asked,

"How's your car?"

"It's okay. It makes a lot of funny noises, but it hasn't died again."

"That's good. I'll still look over it if you want me to."

She didn't remember his first offer.

"I would appreciate that a lot, actually. When are you free?"

"Thursday and Saturday mornings? And afternoons the rest of the time."

It was a seniority privilege, being allowed to open that many days in a row and only close twice. She said,

"I close every day except Wednesday, and I have Saturdays off for now. How does Thursday morning sound?"

He had finished her latte and placed it on the counter.

"That's great. How does 10 sound?"

She would have to get up earlier than usual, but it was worth it.

"Ten sounds great. Enjoy working. Get some sleep. Fix your car—wait, how'd you get here this morning if your car is broken?"

His eye twitched. She'd heard that was a sign of stress.

"I rode my bike."

"Oh. How long does that take you?"

"Not too long. Maybe like twenty or twenty-five minutes."

"You must have to get up early. No wonder you look so awful!"

She threw her hand over her mouth as soon as she said it. He laughed shallowly as she tried to save herself.

"I mean, you don't look that bad, you just look really tired. I mean, that's not a bad thing, you just look like—well, you should sleep more!"

She fumbled for a while trying to rectify her blunder and only making it worse. She felt the blush rising in her cheeks, and Tom said,

"It's fine. Really."

He nodded sincerely, and she smiled through her burning face.

"Thanks. I'm going to read now."

She picked up her drink and walked over to her table, careful not to spill her latte.

"You're welcome. I'll come by Thursday at 10."

Occasionally she could feel him watching her, but when she looked up he wasn't looking at her—he was staring into space right where she sat. He was troubled.

Later that day at work, the man in a black suit was at Francie's again for a meeting. He didn't watch Janelle as much as he had the first time he'd seen her, but when she brought the table the bill, he addressed her.

"Excuse me, do I know you from somewhere?"

She shook her head.

"I don't think so."

He stared at her, perplexed.

"Where are you from?"

"New York. I moved here recently."

He looked straight into her eyes, like a critic examines a painting.

"I could've sworn I've seen you before."

"Interesting. I don't think so."

She had no interest in the conversation, but she'd been taught the guest was always right, and he was the guest.

"I've been in New York on business quite often."

"Maybe we passed in the street."

She doubted he would have noticed her in street clothes. The white collared shirt and black slacks that Francie's girls wore were very different from the massive sweaters and skinny jeans that Janelle usually wore. And she wore her contacts to work, even though she didn't like them as much. Glasses were annoying to keep pushing up on a sweaty nose.

"Maybe. I'll keep thinking about it."

You do that. Meanwhile, she smiled, handed him the check, and collected the dessert platter and plates on the table. That night when she got home, she racked her brain, looking for the man. She didn't recognize him at all. Maybe he had seen a picture of her—maybe he knew her father. The thought froze her heart.

CHAPTER SEVEN

When Tom got off work, it was drizzling. He sighed as he walked out of The Cup, for biking in the rain was a wet and grimy business, and he had to ride over to the graveyard to check on his car. He rode slowly, occasionally wiping the water out of his eyes. Faithful Whit was still there, parked crookedly as testament to Tom's hurry the previous day. He parked his bike under a big tree, thinking somehow that would keep the seat dry, and propped the hood open to examine the engine again. Nothing looked wrong. He tried to start it again, but every time he turned the key, all he heard was a nasty scraping. He would need to get it towed. And he didn't have the money for a tow or a new battery right now. He sighed and leaned against the bumper.

He could leave it in the parking lot for a while and risk a ticket. He could call a tow truck and pay money he didn't have. He could call the junkyard and see how much they would pay him for it. Deciding on the first, he stood, closed the hood, and walked back to his bike, seat now wet in the drizzle. The tree hadn't helped much. He sighed, wiped the seat clean with his sleeve, and rode home. Brittany. The car. Sometimes things were just too much. That night he tried to watch football, but he kept catching himself staring past his computer screen. After drinking a cup of tea, he crawled under the covers and tried to focus on anything besides his car and his heart; his car was broken yet again, his heart had never healed.

Thursday morning, Tom arrived at Janelle's house a few minutes after 10. Her ugly old car was parked in the driveway, and Janelle was sitting on the porch steps wearing a sweater that was big enough for several people to wear simultaneously.

"Good morning, Tom! Thanks for coming over!"

She seemed like a morning person.

"Good morning, it's a pleasure."

She smiled. He gestured towards the car.

"So it's making a funny noise?"

"It's clunking. It clunks the most when I press on the gas. But it's always clunking the rest of the time."

Tom opened the hood and poked around. Then, he crawled underneath the car and looked up from the bottom. The car hadn't been taken care of well, and had been out in the weather. It was rusty. There was, however, no impending disaster, though a few parts would need to be replaced soon. He rolled out from under the car. Janelle had grown tired of standing and was sitting on a large rock next to the driveway. She asked,

"What's the verdict?"

"Well, there's nothing obviously wrong, but with clunking it could be a number of things. You'll want to bring it to a mechanic before too long."

It was going to take a lot of time to get the car in good condition, and at least a thousand dollars for all the parts. It could be done gradually, as nothing pressed for an immediate fix. He told her all this, and she stood there with her arms crossed and her lips pursed together like she was trying to solve a math problem.

"Okay. It may be a while."

He nodded, and said,

"It should be okay for the time being, but the sooner you can get it repaired, the better."

He wiped his greasy hands clean on his grungy pants.

She was shifting back and forth, and looking at her ugly blue car, as he gathered up the tools he'd brought, just in case anything needed an instant fix. It was almost lunchtime.

"Do you—I mean, if you want—well, do you want to stay for lunch?"

She stumbled through the sentence, looking up through her massive green-framed glasses.

"I'd love to."

He finished cleaning up his tools and put his backpack by his bike in the grass.

"Great! Come on in."

It was an old house and she lived in the attic apartment. To reach it, he followed her up three flights of steps. When they reached the landing in front of her door, she paused, reached into her pocket, and pulled out a key.

"Sometimes I get paranoid, and lock my door even when I'm right outside. I like to know I'm the only one in my apartment."

She spoke almost apologetically.

"Welcome to my little home."

She fumbled with the key as she tried to unlock the deep blue door. Tom remained silent, waiting patiently behind her. She finally tricked the door open, and waved her hand to welcome him in. It was all one room, with the ceiling slanting down on either side. A twin bed was under the ceiling in one corner, and low bookshelves lined the other wall. The far wall was a little kitchenette, with sink, fridge, and oven. Next to the fridge was a door, which he assumed was the bathroom. A little table and two chairs were pushed up against the close wall, and an old looking purple velvet reclining chair sat next to the bed. Tom had thought his apartment was sparse and small, but hers lent a new meaning to the word. The only windows she had were four panels in the slanted ceiling, two on each side of the slope. Janelle spoke:

"It's not much, but it's cozy, and I like it."

Tom nodded.

"What do you want for lunch? I was going to make peanut butter and jelly."

"It's nice. Size doesn't make too much of a difference, really." She looked at him gratefully, as he added,

"Peanut butter and jelly sounds great. Can I do anything?"

"Sure. Get the peanut butter? It's in the cabinet over the oven." She pointed.

"Do you want one sandwich or two?"

"One is fine."

"Great. I'll make them, you can sit down."

He sat at the tiny table, watching her. She hummed as she spread the sandwiches. After a few moments, he broke the silence.

"Do you have brothers or sisters?"

She looked at him over her shoulder.

"I have three."

She didn't volunteer any more information, and he didn't ask.

"Cool."

Seeming to remember her manners, she returned the question.

"Do you?"

"I have four. I'm the youngest."

She brought the sandwiches to the table on paper towels.

"I always wanted to be the youngest. I'm the oldest. Here's your sandwich."

"Thanks. Looks good."

She sat to eat, and he added,

"What's it like being the oldest? Do you like it?"

She shrugged, nodded.

"I guess. I never knew what it was like to be anything else."

He nodded, and said,

"That's true."

They silently munched their sandwiches. Janelle reached for her mug, and said,

"I hope you don't mind drinking out of mugs. I don't have any glasses."

Tom shook his head.

"That's fine. I like mugs. I work with them all the time."

She put her elbows on the table.

"My mom used to tell me it was improper to drink anything but hot drinks out of mugs."

"Do you miss your parents?"

He asked without thinking. She looked at her sandwich.

"No. Not really."

She looked like she could've added more to her comment. He waited as she decided, but her next comment was unrelated.

"I saw my landlord yesterday. He asked me if I wanted another window in my apartment. I didn't know that was an option. He said certainly, and told me to pick a few places where I'd like one and let him know, and he'd put one in."

Tom raised his eyebrows.

"That's nice of him."

She nodded.

"Apparently it sat empty up here for a long time before I came. I think I remember him saying his last renter left eight years ago. They thought it was too much work after that, but now his wife wanted some of her own spending money, so here I am."

He looked around, considering the different possibilities for windows.

"Well, there's not a spot at either end for windows, but there is room on both sides."

He pointed to different spots on the walls on either side, and she nodded.

"I'd like one over close to my bed. If he's only giving me one I'll give him a few options."

"That's a good idea."

They had finished their peanut butter and jelly, and were now surveying the small room closely. She mentioned a few more places she'd like a window, and he affirmed each idea. Then, with a glance at his watch, Tom stood.

"Thanks for the sandwich. I'd better go home and get ready for work."

She nodded, said,

"Thank you so much for looking at my car. I appreciate it."

"It was no problem, really. I'm happy to help."

She smiled gratefully, and he walked lightly down the steps, whistling.

He had some time before work still, after he'd gotten ready, so he sat in his overstuffed chair and looked at the letter from Brittany on the little table next to him. The business card was next to it, and he picked it up and ran it through his fingers, turning it from corner to corner, looking at her name printed in big fat black letters, and the printed number across the back. He hesitated, then reached for his cellphone. As soon as he dialed her number, he wished he hadn't. He hoped she wouldn't pick up. He thought he was in luck, but at the end of the fifth ring, she answered.

"Hi this is Brittany."

She sounded calm and confident, just like she always did. He paused. There was still time to hang up. Then he heard Matt in his mind telling him not to be a wimp, like he had their entire childhood. He sighed quietly, and sat up straight in his chair.

"Hi Brittany. This is Tom."

She didn't answer for what felt like forever. When she did, her voice carried a note of subtle excitement.

"Tom! Hey Tom! I'm so glad you called. How are you?"

"I'm doing fine. I got your letter."

He waited.

"Oh…"

Another long silence.

"Thanks for calling me."

"You're welcome."

Pause.

"So…"

She'd always been good at talking to people, and he assumed she should still be, if she put her mind into it. After some time, she continued.

"What'd you think?"

Not much to work with, but she was trying. As good as she was at talking to people, she was bad at talking about feelings.

"Well, I was surprised. I didn't expect to hear from you."

She didn't seem to know what to say after that, so Tom finally asked,

"What should we do?"

She cleared her throat twice before answering.

"I just really started to miss you and feel really sorry, and I wanted you to know. I care about you a lot."

Her voice started to quiver, and his heart jumped. He didn't know what to think. After all these years. She had been so good about saying she cared. She hadn't always acted like it, but she'd always said she did.

The "Oh" escaped from his lips half-word, half-gasp for air, and he added,

"I don't know what to say."

She waited a moment, then said,

"Well. I guess we could just talk for a while. How have you been?"

He paused before answering, thinking about what to say. His carefully crafted walls hadn't been expecting this invasion.

"I've been well."

Pause.

"How are you doing?"

"I'm alright. I'm working in Dallas as the marketing manager for a clothing company. Tim said you're working at a coffee shop?"

Tom wondered how much Tim had told her about him. He only talked to Tim a few times a year, but when they did talk they talked through everything.

"I'm a barista at a little local place. It's a great job."

"That's really cool. I never saw you doing that."

This pricked. They hadn't talked for four years, closer to four and a half. They didn't have many points of connection based on circumstance any more, although they had plenty based on past. She continued,

"I bet you're good at it. I'm sorry to say, but I'm at work, so I need to go. But thanks for calling me."

He sighed.

"Okay, sure. Talk to you later."

Tom hung up, and stared at the plate he'd left on the counter last night. He didn't know what to think. After work tomorrow afternoon he would call Tim.

CHAPTER EIGHT

Tom had almost forgotten about Whit, abandoned in the graveyard. Friday afternoon after work, he rode his bike down to the cemetery. From a distance, he saw a bright pink square on the window. As he rode nearer, he realized it was a ticket. He sighed, and left it there. Whit would be fine until next Tuesday, when he got his paycheck and could get it towed to the shop. Rather than the traditional bi-monthly Friday paydays, Phil Kohle paid his employees every other Tuesday.

Sitting on a large tombstone in the graveyard, Tom pulled out his phone and called Tim. He answered on the second ring.

"Hey Tom!"

Tim was one of the few people who had bothered to stay in touch with Tom after college. After catching up on a few brief details, Tom filled him in on Brittany's letter and call, then asked,

"She said you gave her my address—what'd she say to you?"

Tim was quiet for a moment.

"She called me about a month ago. Sounded like she'd been crying, and maybe still was. She asked a lot of questions about you, like where you were, what you were doing, if you were married."

"Wow."

Tom asked,

"Did she talk about herself?"

"Not very much. She's in Dallas, and she's been thinking about your relationship and how it ended."

"Really?"

"She said she has a lot of regrets. Misses you."

Tim said the last part quietly, and Tom received it just as quietly. After some time, he said,

"Oh."

"Yeah."

Tim had always told Tom that Brittany was perfect for him, and that it was something else that made her refuse him, and in the end she would come around. There was the slightest note of triumph in Tim's voice now. Tom let the realization sink in. Brittany. He'd loved her so much. He still did. The acknowledgment made his heart ache. When he spoke again it was almost a whisper,

"Did she say anything else?"

"Not really. Just that she was going to send you a letter and see what happened. I need to go man, my wife needs something. It's good to hear from you. Take care of yourself."

Tom nodded, realized that Tim couldn't hear him, and said,

"Okay. Will do. Thanks, Tim. You too."

He watched the golden and red leaves. They looked like little pieces of sunshine that had dripped off the sun. When Tom was little, he'd play in the leaves with Matt. They'd collect dozens of leaves and pretend they were gold, and bury them in the yard in all different places. Then they'd come back and dig them all up, searching for them as if it was a pot of treasure. Once they'd gotten in trouble for digging a big hole in the middle of their mother's bed of pansies.

That night, Tom dreamt he was wandering around a graveyard. He kept hearing a woman calling out for help, but he couldn't recognize the voice. He ran faster and faster, searching for the source of the cries. In his frenzy, he tripped over a tombstone and fell, face pressed into the earth. When he tried to stand, he couldn't. There was a weight pressing him down. Laughter began to ring out all around him. He woke up clutching the sheets. He hadn't had nightmares since college.

* * *

Saturday was the coldest day of fall yet. Francie's was slow, and at work that evening, Janelle was busy thinking about all of the things she planned to do during fall. Around ten, after the dinner rush had slowed, Tom walked in and sat down at one of the small tables against the wall. There were dark circles under his eyes, and his shirt was wrinkled, like he'd worn it three days in a row. He'd sat down at one of Janelle's tables.

"Hey Tom, welcome to Francie's!"

He looked up at her.

"Hi Janelle. Thanks."

His eyes stared past her into the distance.

"Well, it's nice to see you here. Can I get you something to drink?"

"Water's fine."

She nodded, and handed him a menu.

"I'll bring that right out to you, and take your order whenever you're ready."

As if actually realizing she was there for the first time, he smiled, and said,

"Thanks."

She walked away, wondering what was bothering him. He hadn't seemed so upset when she'd seem him at The Cup yesterday morning. She peeked at him out of the kitchen. He was playing with the ketchup bottle abstractedly. She brought his water out.

"Here's your water."

He looked up, startled.

"Oh. Thank you."

"Pleasure."

He went back to his distracted fiddling, as if forgetting she was there. After a moment of silence, she said,

"Are you ready to order?"

His menu was exactly where she'd placed it minutes earlier. He looked down at it, surprised, as if he hadn't known it was there. He opened it, sighed, and closed it.

"Meatloaf and potato wedges?"

She scribbled it on her yellow pad of paper, and said,

"That should be just a few minutes."

He nodded, staring at the ketchup. When she brought his plate out a bit later, he was running his finger along the fork, as if trying to shine the brushed metal. He didn't notice her.

"Tom."

He jumped.

"Are you okay?"

"I'm just thinking."

He ran his fingers through his messy hair.

"Let me know if you need something."

Tom nodded, and Janelle set the plate down and walked off. She kept an eye on him as the night continued. He ate slowly, working the food around in his mouth each time he took a bite. He dropped his fork on his plate once and jumped at the sound. Once, his phone rang. After a somewhat lengthy conversation, he hung up stared at his half-eaten plate of food.

"Tom, what's wrong?"

Janelle had grown tired of his attitude of misery. He looked up at her, brow wrinkled, staring intently at her face as if he were evaluating her.

"I have a question."

The same distracted air.

"Yes?"

"Can you sit down at work?"

Not the question she'd expected.

"If it's slow it's okay for a few minutes."

Tom shoved the chair across from him out with his foot, and motioned towards it with his hand.

"Have a seat."

She complied, smoothing the little black apron she wore and fixing the corner of the tablecloth which had flipped over onto the table.

"Have you ever loved someone?"

Also not the question she'd expected.

"Like, my little brother?"

He shook his head.

"Someone outside of your family."

He paused, then clarified,

"A man."

Janelle ran her finger along the edge of the tablecloth and scrunched her nose.

"No."

"Oh. Well if you had and you ended it, would you have explained why?"

She had never been asked such a thing. She remembered when her mother would try to explain to her father that she was leaving him, but he was always too drunk to listen and she always lost her resolve. It was the closest relationship model she had.

"I suppose I would try."

He nodded, then asked abruptly,

"Would you cry?"

"If I were sad. Which I probably would be."

Janelle remembered the times her mother had cried in front of her father. Once, he'd been drunk and picked up a kitchen chair to swing at Janelle, but her mother had stood in front of her and begun to cry pitifully. Janelle's father had looked confused and frustrated, but he'd put the chair down.

"You would."

It wasn't a question, just a statement.

"Yes, I think so."

"Okay."

And after a long moment of looking intently at her face, he looked down at the ketchup, which he was still rotating slowly. She stood, mentioning how she should get back to work. He didn't respond.

After serving coffee and pie to several couples, and bringing two checks, she went back to the kitchen to get coffee and pie for Tom, and brought it out for him.

"I brought you pie."

She clanked the plate in front of him, and poured coffee into the mug that had been sitting on the table.

"It's on me."

He looked up gratefully, for her tone would bear no disagreement. "Thanks."

"You're welcome. Let me know if I can do anything for you, okay?"

He nodded, and she walked away, worried.

Tom sat at the table picking at his pie and slowly drinking his coffee until Janelle was sure both were cold and unappetizing. When it was quite late, he stood up and walked out, waving at her on his way. There was a twenty on the table, and a note on his napkin:

Janelle - Thanks. Have a good night. - Tom

She smiled and pocketed the note, wondering what was eating at him. She didn't know much about him. He didn't pry deeply into her life because she never let people in and he seemed to understand that. In return, she didn't ask about him, because he didn't seem to be open and she didn't want to be obnoxious. Janelle realized, as she walked to her car in the crisp chill, that this was no way to be friends with someone. She determined to ask him more about who he was. She wanted to know him.

* * *

The next morning was Sunday, and as his coworker John had asked to switch shifts with him this week, Tom had the morning off. He slept in. When he was younger, he'd always had to wake up to go to church. Now, since he ruled his own life, he did other things with his Sundays. He lounged around, and sometimes went on long walks or bike rides to the nearby foothills. This Sunday, after a late breakfast, he packed a lunch and got on his bike. The ride into the mountains took several hours, but Tom enjoyed the sensation of struggle when he had a lot to think about. He panted and pedaled and suffered all the way up the foothills, sweating in the chill fall air and wondering what Brittany was thinking and feeling. He missed her; not just because he had loved her so much, but because, although he would never admit it to himself, he was lonely.

He rode hard, climbing higher and higher, letting the wind in his face clear away his rattled emotions. Stopping for a mid-afternoon lunch, he sat on a large boulder, from which he could see the city and some lakes, and he watched two hawks fly, diving and soaring and gliding along, as if they were children playing. Everyone had thought Brittany was his perfect match. He'd thought Brittany was his perfect match. After their relationship ended, he never thought they'd even talk again; it had ended so messily.

Climbing off his boulder, he mounted his bike and turned downhill, to head back to town before dark. The downhill ride was much easier and faster. He stopped at the store on the way home and bought food for dinner, and when he got home, he showered. It wasn't until later that he pulled his phone out of his backpack. He had multiple missed calls and voicemails from his older brother Matt. He listened to messages while he was cutting a green pepper.

"Hey, Tom? Call me back as soon as you get this."

He sounded worried. The next four messages were all similar, Matt almost pleading with Tom to answer his phone. Tom's mother had also called, and his sister, Elizabeth. Tom stopped preparing dinner and called Matt back. He picked up on the first ring.

"Hey, Matt? It's Tom."

Matt started talking before Tom stopped,

"It's Mary. She's in the hospital. She got hit by a car."

His heart froze. After a moment of shock, Tom asked,

"Is she okay?"

Tom almost didn't want to know the answer.

"You should probably come home."

Silence filled the air, punctuated by heavy breaths, Matt's. He was crying.

Tom was still holding the knife he'd been using to chop green peppers. He stared numbly at it. Mary the oldest, he the youngest, they were years apart, but still close. When she came home from college, she always made a point to spend special time with him, and as he grew older, she paid attention to him consistently, always watching out for him. She was short and her eyes were always crinkled at the corners, as if she was always laughing at some secret joke. Now, she lived in a little apartment in a neighboring town to his parents. She was the head librarian at the local library, and kept a German shepherd that seemed almost as big as she was.

"Matt?"

Tom was drawn out of his thoughts by the realization that Matt was still on the other end of the line, crying quietly.

"Matt? I don't have enough money for tickets."

It hurt to say.

"It's okay. Maggie and I will pay for it. Just come home."

Matt and his wife Maggie still lived in the town they'd grown up in.

"I'll come on the next flight I can get on."

"We'll pick you up from the airport."

Tom stood at the counter mindlessly after the call was over. Mary in the hospital. She might not be okay.

He bought a one way ticket for Boise the next afternoon after work—Phil told him he could take off as long as he needed to. Tom planned to go straight from work to the airport. He didn't sleep much, tossing and turning, his muddled and confused dreams all involving Mary's injury and death.

When John got in that morning, as he was putting on his apron, he said,

"Good morning To—wow. Is everything alright?"

Halfway through his statement, he'd looked over at Tom. Tom hadn't looked in the mirror before he left. If he had, he would have seen the gray circles under his eyes, his mussed hair, and his wrinkled shirt. Although this was becoming a token look for him, there was a note of panic in his eyes that was unusual.

"My sister was in an accident yesterday. She's in the hospital."

John stopped mid-movement, and said,

"Oh man. I'm sorry. Is she okay?"

"I don't know. I'm leaving for Idaho this afternoon."

John sympathetically and awkwardly patted him on the back.

"I hope she's alright."

"Me too."

They continued in silence. When the shop opened, John took register, which required more interaction with people. Tom gave brief answers to the customers, not unfriendly, but not trending towards conversation. Mike came in around seven, rocking heel to toe as usual. Four people from the counter, he spotted Tom.

"Hey Tom!"

Tom had been pouring coffee. He spilled a little on his hand, startled when Mike spoke so suddenly, and he swore under his breath.

"Good morning, Mike."

He said it wearily. Mike, bouncing, responded.

"It's going to be a beautiful day!"

When he was rushed Mike was almost brusque, but in a good mood he was effervescent.

"Looks like it."

Answering with little fervor, Tom continued to pour coffee.

"Is everything alright?"

Mike seemed to have noticed his marked lack of enthusiasm.

"Yesterday my sister was in an accident, and she's in the hospital."

The words hung in the silence between them, and for the first time since they'd met, Mike stopped rocking.

"Oh. I'm really sorry."

He stood, flat footed. The people in line before and after him also expressed their sympathy with sighs and groans, and Tom looked at his feet, uneasy as the center of attention. After standing silent for a moment, Mike spoke.

"Why aren't you there?"

"I'm flying out this afternoon."

Tom's mind was a muddle of details.

"Do you need anything?"

Mike noted the bewildered look. Tom mastered his greater urge not to ask for help, and said,

"I need a ride to the airport. My flight leaves at four."

Mike took the coffee he'd ordered from Tom, saying,

"Four. Should I pick you up here or your house?"

"I get off work at two. Here?"

"Two it is. See you then."

Coffee in hand, Mike turned to go.

"Thanks."

Tom couldn't think of anything else to say. The morning continued as usual, Tom working on autopilot. He kept bumping into corners and knocking over empty (and some full) mugs with his distracted hands. After he brewed a bag of tea in a cup of coffee, John stopped him, patted him on the back and directed him to a seat.

"Just sit for a while. We're not busy."

Phil had asked John to stay all morning with Tom. Tom sank into one of the wingback chairs, and thought about Mary. Her slow smile, contrasted with her firecracker laugh. Her big personality, and friendly manners. It was a family joke that if there were no people around, Mary would make friends with the rocks and the birds. She was winsome and kind, and often forgot herself helping someone who needed it. The last time he'd seen her was right after Matt's wife Maggie had their second baby. Tom had gone home to see his new nephew, and Mary had let him stay at her apartment. He'd slept on the couch, and they'd talked long into the night, about college, about Brittany, and about Denver and The Cup. She understood him as no one else in the family did, and she cared for him even when big events were going on for someone else. He knew his whole family loved him—but sometimes Mary was the only one who remembered to remind him.

Just then, Janelle walked in. Lost in his reverie, Tom didn't notice her. He had been staring abstractedly at the painting of the man and woman in the diner. When she saw him, she came over and stood in front of him. He didn't notice her, and after a few moments she cleared her throat. He swung his head over to focus on the disruption.

"Oh. Hi."

She smiled, but when she saw his face, her smile faded.

"Hi Tom. Is everything okay?"

She looked at him.

"My sister's in the hospital."

Janelle's eyes got bigger.

"Oh. What happened?"

Tom rubbed his right thumbnail with his left thumb, staring at the toes of his shoes.

"I don't know. I'm flying home today. My brother Matt didn't say much."

"Oh, wow. I'm so sorry."

She patted him on the shoulder. "Can I do anything for you while you're gone? Watch your apartment?"

"I think it will be fine."

He sighed.

She stood there staring at her scuffed white shoes. He didn't have the energy to assure her it would be alright. He wasn't sure himself.

Breaking the silence, she said,

"Call me if you think of anything I can do."

He looked up gratefully, saying,

"Sure."

She put her bag down in the seat next to him.

"Oh. Let me give you my number. You don't have it, right?"

He shook his head. She found a pen and an old envelope in her bag, and she scribbled out her cell number. He folded the paper, putting it in his pocket. She ordered a drink and sat down with her book in a chair near him. He stared out the shop windows mindlessly, hoping that it was just a bad dream from which he would soon wake.

Mike came to pick him up at two, and as Tom swung his backpack into the back seat and buckled up, Mike spoke.

"How you doing?"

"Fine."

His voice was flat.

"Thanks for picking me up."

They drove in silence for a while before Mike spoke again. When he did, it was to ask,

"Do you know what happened?"

"No. My brother called me last night just to tell me to come. He was crying too much to say what happened. I have no idea."

Tom closed his eyes as if to hide everything his brain was imagining. Mike looked over at him, then said,

"I'm so sorry."

Tom remembered driving with Mary when he was having a bad day in high school. She would pick him up from school or sports practice or home, or wherever he was, and they would just drive. Tom had loved it, the slow of going nowhere in no hurry. It'd always calmed him down, because Mary was silent until he wanted to talk—which sometimes wasn't for a very long time.

Mike interrupted his reverie:

"Tell me about your sister—"

He interrupted himself with sudden silence, then added,

"That is, if you want to."

Tom looked at him, and Mike, eyes quickly going back and forth between Tom and the road, leaned forward slightly, tapping the steering wheel with his thumbs. Tom assumed he did this because he wasn't able to bounce up and down while driving. With the invitation, Tom realized he hadn't told anyone in Denver about his family. Suddenly, he was very lonely. He took a deep breath, and began.

"I'm the youngest of five kids. Mary is the oldest, and she's always been the one who took the most care of me. Growing up, she watched out for me. She made my lunches while I was in elementary school and middle school, and she would always put a little note in with the sandwich. I never realized how much I appreciated it until she left for college when I was 12. It seems like I was too young to even be friends with someone in my family, but Mary has a knack for making friends. She can talk to someone and within five minutes, they've fallen under her charm and they want to tell her everything. All the things that make them cry, and all the things that make them laugh."

Mike nodded as Tom continued.

"My dad used to say that Mary could woo a recalcitrant king into giving her what she wanted, if she wanted to. I always wanted to be like her. She looked out for all of us, but especially me. She always paid attention to me, especially when something big was happening in my family and I might get overlooked. The year of my 16th birthday, my older brother got married the same week as my birthday. Everyone else in the family kind of forgot that it was my birthday, but Mary remembered and brought me a present and took me out for dinner. She was never too busy to talk or listen, and she always remembered how much I needed her, because she was always there for me."

He looked over at Mike. He had been listening intently the whole time, giving affirming "hmms" and "ohhs" at all the right places. Tom was quiet then, and Mike drove on.

As they neared the airport, Mike spoke,

"She sounds wonderful."

"She is."

A brief silence, then Mike, ever pragmatic, asked,

"When are you coming back?"

"I'm not sure, but I'm not planning on staying more than two weeks."

"Your car is still in the graveyard?"

Whit had been sitting at the graveyard for almost a week now, and had only gotten one ticket. Tom was hoping that the extra time wouldn't make a difference. He nodded, saying,

"That's where I left it."

He didn't tell Mike he didn't have the money to tow it or fix it, but Mike seemed to know. If Tom had been able to see his face straight on he would have noticed a twinkle in his eyes. And he wouldn't have given Mike the keys when he asked.

"Do you have the keys? I'll keep an eye on it while you're gone and make sure nothing happens."

Tom reached into his pocket and pulled out the keys.

"His name is Whit, and he's got a lot of problems."

They were pulling into the departure lane for the airport, and Mike looked over at him.

"Call me when you're coming back, and I'll pick you up."

"Thank you so much."

"It's the least I could do. I hope Mary's okay."

Tom swung his backpack over his shoulder and walked into the airport, fervently hoping the same.

CHAPTER NINE

Seeing Tom in the morning had cast a shadow over Janelle's day. As she drove home slowly that night, she couldn't stop seeing his face in her mind. He'd looked like a little boy who'd watched his first toy fire engine get destroyed with a bat. But there was something deeper than just disappointment on his face. Janelle couldn't name it, but she understood it. She remembered when her little brother Joe had broken his leg and needed surgery. She'd hurt all the way to her toes, and been sick to her stomach. More than that, she remembered Alex. Even though she'd been young, she still felt every instant of the terror. She had blocked it from her memory for a long time, but as she drove home in the dark she relived that afternoon on the lawn.

She'd just turned four and he was almost five. They were playing with a new yellow rubber ball their neighbor had given them—it was bright and bouncy and lots of fun. Their mother was pregnant and she was inside napping. Usually she sat on the porch and watched Janelle and Alex play, but today she'd been too tired, and just admonished them to be safe. They tossed and rolled the ball back and forth for a while, but eventually, as usual, it turned into Alex's favorite game of hold and wrestle; he held, Janelle wrestled. As they played, shrieking and laughing, he held the ball and ran down the sloping front lawn towards the street. Alex was looking backwards for her quick pursuit as he tripped down the grass, and she yelled for him to stop—but he thought she was kidding. He didn't see the SUV come barreling down the road, or the curb quickly approaching his loose shoe. His toe caught on the edge of the curb, and he flew face first into the street. The SUV was going too fast to stop.

The tire had gone over his chest, and Alex laid pale and silent. Janelle ran inside screaming to wake her mother, and they called an ambulance.

He'd died soon after of massive internal hemorrhage. In the pale blue hospital room as she sat near Alex and held his hand and listened to her mother cry, Janelle's four year old heart felt fully responsible. Her father's drinking problem had started after that. He stayed later and later "at work," until Janelle almost never saw him. He'd get home in the middle of the night, bang around a little bit, and go to sleep. Around when she was ten, he became more abusive. Although Janelle's mother tried to stop it, her father was strong and didn't listen. Janelle and her mother lived in fear. When she was younger, she tried to run away and hide, but it just made him angry, and he was always worse angry.

Because Janelle's family kept to themselves, most people didn't notice or think about what was going on, and she became good at coming up with stories for the bruises, or hiding them. Even though her mother had three more children after Alex died, Janelle bore the brunt of her father's drunken anger. After she graduated from high school, she stayed home and worked, because her mom was scared of being alone with her husband and her younger children. When her younger brother Jack got big enough to stand up for them, Janelle's mother told her to run away. So she had. To Denver.

As the car hummed along, Janelle sighed. Back at her apartment, she sat down in her purple chair and fingered her book of pictures. It was one of the only items she'd brought from New York. Her mom had made it when Janelle was younger, so she would remember Alex. It was mostly pictures of the two of them; one in the bathtub, another at Janelle's third birthday as they sat staring at the camera, faces covered in chocolate frosting. Janelle didn't remember very much about Alex, but she remembered him through the pictures, and she often wondered what her life would have been if he hadn't died. The morning sunrise found her still in her purple chair, slumped over onto the arm, a still damp patch under her cheek from her tears.

Sunday, Janelle was working lunch at Francie's. Sunday lunches were one of the busiest and most stressful times of the week, but today Janelle appreciated the hassle that kept her mind from wandering. A young woman came in and sat at a table by herself in Janelle's section.

"Hi, welcome to Francie's. I'm Janelle and I'll be your server for the day. Can I start you with something to drink?"

"Oh, hi! Do you have any specials?"

"Francie makes our peach iced tea herself, and it's a city classic."

The woman nodded.

"That sounds delicious. I'd love a glass."

Janelle came back moments later with the tea, and set it on the table. The woman glanced up from her menu and said,

"Thank you."

"You're welcome. Are you ready to order, or would you like a few more minutes?"

Turning the page of the menu over and sighing, the woman said,

"I'm not very good at decisions, and I've never been here before. Do you have any suggestions?"

"Well, everybody loves our meatloaf. But if you're not interested in that, some of our soups and salads are highly recommended."

The woman looked down at her menu, then up at Janelle.

"I love meatloaf. What does it come with?"

"It comes with potato wedges, and a choice between a side of coleslaw or a fresh garden salad. Our salad today is fresh baby greens with cranberries and almonds and a light vinaigrette."

"That sounds delicious."

"The meatloaf with the potatoes and salad?"

The woman nodded.

"Yes please."

"Anything else?"

"That's all for now."

She smiled winningly up at Janelle and handed her the menu. Her smile warmed Janelle.

Janelle kept an eye on the woman, hoping she was enjoying her meal. When she was halfway done with the meatloaf, she stopped Janelle, who was carrying a tray of refills, and said,

"This meatloaf is better than any I've eaten since my mom's. My highest compliments to the cook."

Janelle smiled, agreed, and continued past with the glasses. When the woman finished, she pulled a notebook out of her large purse and began to write and sketch in it. People sometimes came to Francie's alone, but most of them didn't finish their food and start taking notes in large leather books. The woman seemed undisturbed by her own disregard for the norm, and wrote feverishly on into the afternoon. Around four, she was the only guest who had been there since lunchtime, and she was still marking busily in her notebook. Janelle was setting tables for dinner, and noticed the woman was working on what looked like a list. She stopped Janelle.

"Excuse me, ma'am?"

"Yes? How can I help you?"

The woman looked at her sheet of paper, then back at Janelle.

"I'm not from around here, and I'm wondering what sort of coffee shops are nearby."

Janelle had noticed that she wasn't from the area by her accent. She spoke with a familiar cadence; Janelle recognized it, but she couldn't place it.

"Well, there are a few. The best one in town is called The Cup. It's a few miles north. The coffee is excellent and the shop is welcoming and comfortable."

As she said "The Cup," the woman looked up at the ceiling like she was trying to remember something. Janelle was holding a stack of plates topped with silverware, and she shifted their weight as she stood. The woman asked,

"Where exactly is it?"

Janelle gave her directions, and the woman scribbled them down in her notebook, then spoke again.

"You're not from around here, are you?"

People frequently noticed.

"No Ma'am, I'm from New York."

The woman raised her eyebrows.

"That's far. Do you like it here?"

Janelle nodded, and responded,

"Yes. It's beautiful, and the people are friendly. Are you just visiting?"

The woman was picking at the edge of her notepad with her maroon painted fingernails, and took a moment before she answered,

"Yes. I'm on a business trip of sorts, and I have a friend who lives here. I haven't seen him for a while, so I thought we might catch up."

Janelle made an obligatory comment, and the young woman giggled nervously. Janelle guessed she was probably only twenty-five or six.

"Do you—"

She stopped herself, and looked at her hands, and tried again.

"Do you know Tom Bailey?"

The woman looked nervous that Janelle would, and when she nodded, saying,

"Tom? Everybody knows Tom. He works at The Cup!"

The woman's eyebrows flew up.

"Oh. Wow. Okay."

"Is he the one you came to see?"

The woman nodded.

"He is. How's he doing?"

Janelle wondered how well they had known each other, and if she knew anything about his family. She didn't seem to know about Mary, and Janelle didn't want to be the one to tell her.

"He's doing just fine."

The woman nodded, looking at her list and running her fingers through her hair again.

"Wow. Well, that's good to hear. You say he works at The Cup?"

"He does."

Janelle nodded along with her own voice.

"Thank you for telling me. And thanks for lunch, it was delicious."

Janelle smiled, then, on a whim, said,

"What did you say your name was?"

"Oh! It's Brittany."

"Brittany. I'm Janelle. It's nice to meet you. If you need anything while you're in town, you know where to find me. Any friend of Tom's is a friend of mine."

The woman looked her up and down, and gathered her belongings together. When she stood, she was a good six inches taller than Janelle. Her suit was a deep gray, and her large black handbag completed the 'I'm quite confident, thank you,' look.

"Thank you very much. I'll remember that."

Janelle watched her as she exited the restaurant and walked over to a cute red car. She'd never heard Tom mention a girl in his past besides his sister, but then Tom never talked about himself.

* * *

Tom's flight to Idaho seemed to last forever, even though it was less than two hours. The Boise airport wasn't very large, and Tom had memorized most of the details about it. He was friends with some of the staff because it was so small, and although he didn't come home often, many of them knew his family.

Walking out of the security area, he looked around. A mother with two small children stood waiting, and an old man with a cane leaned against a pillar, watching hopefully. Tom wandered past the seats, hoping Matt was waiting outside. In the bright autumn sunlight, he looked right and left, but didn't see any cars that he recognized. He sighed and took himself and his bag to a long green bench.

Forty-five minutes later, when he finally called Matt, Matt answered.

"Hey Tom, I'm really sorry, I got held up. I'm on my way now. I should be there soon."

Tom nodded, remembered Matt couldn't see him, said,

"Okay, that's fine."

Tom sighed.

Twenty minutes later, Matt pulled up.

"Hey Buddy, sorry I'm so late!"

"It's okay."

"We were just all at the hospital with Mary, and I lost track of time. She woke up!"

He said it like it was very big news.

"Oh, good!"

He paused, then said,

"Matt, what happened?"

Matt sighed.

"She was coming home from work, walking because it was nice out. She must have been looking at her phone or thinking about something as she crossed the street, because she stepped out in front of a car. Even though the driver tried to stop, he couldn't. He wasn't going very fast, but she still flew a few feet and hit her head on the pavement. The leg on the side that got hit is broken, and her arm where she tried to catch herself. She's pretty banged up. The doctors say she has a concussion and probably some brain damage but they're not sure how bad it is."

Mike said all this in one breath. Tom looked out the window at the quickly moving colors of fall, and tapped his knees with his fingers.

"Wow."

Mike nodded.

"We were all pretty excited when she woke up. She only opened her eyes, but at least it was something."

When Tom walked into the pale pink hospital room, his parents, and Maggie and Elizabeth, were huddled around the bed. Elizabeth saw him first, and quickly hugged him. His parents and Maggie followed suit, and when they turned back to the bed and Tom saw Mary, his breath caught in his chest.

Her usually pink cheeks were pale, contrasting strongly with the deep purple marks along one side of her forehead. A cast all the way down her leg made her appear much larger than she was. She hugged the blankets with both arms, one of which was also in a cast. Her eyes were closed. Tom's mother spoke.

"She woke up for the first time earlier. She didn't say anything, but she blinked. The doctors think she might have brain damage, but they haven't told us anything for sure yet."

Her voice quivered near the end of her statement, and Tom's father put his arm around her. Taking Mary's hand, Tom squeezed gently. His mother interjected,

"They say that she can hear when we talk, even if she doesn't respond."

Leaning in, Tom whispered,

"Hey Mary. It's me. I came to see you."

His mom started crying, with her head on his dad's shoulder. Tom sat and watched Mary's face, thinking about the faces she used to make when she read to him. All of the bright animation was gone, replaced by a flat dull expression. She looked like how Tom felt when he woke up from a nightmare.

They sat in the hospital room for the rest of the evening while Mary slept. Tom's dad wanted his wife to go home and rest and shower, but she wouldn't leave, insisting that if Mary woke up she would want to see a familiar face. Tom's dad gave in, insisting she must go home and nap the next day. The rest of them left. Tom drove with Matt and Maggie. While they drove, they talked about Mary.

"How bad is she, really?"

Tom hadn't wanted to ask in front of his mom, or Mary, in case she could actually hear what they were saying.

"She's bad. Chances are she's got brain damage, and they think she's got internal bleeding too. They think she'll live, but she'll never be the same. Her behavior shouldn't change very much, but they're not sure if she's going to be able to read or write, and she'll probably have headaches often. Mom's pretty upset—well, I guess you could tell."

Tom nodded. When he was little, his mom sometimes cried when he scraped his knees. She didn't like seeing her children in pain that she couldn't fix. He imagined what she must be feeling right now, and wanted to cry himself.

That night, sleeping on Matt's living room couch, Tom had another nightmare. He was working the morning rush. The line was long, almost to the door, but every time anyone ordered a fancy drink, all he could serve was drip coffee. Each customer became increasingly more upset, but plain coffee was all that he had. He tried to fix the machines, but nothing he tried worked. He called Phil but it cut straight to his answering machine. Tom reached for another cup, and knocked a loosely lidded brewing carafe onto the floor, spilling coffee all over the shoes of the customer first in line.

He woke up with his blanket tangled around his ankles.

* * *

Janelle woke early on Monday and went to The Cup with her book. The atmosphere was different without Tom; people weren't as cheerful. Janelle sat and watched the other baristas interact with people, wondering why everyone liked Tom so much. He didn't dress better than anyone else—he had a nice face, but he wasn't overly attractive. There was nothing flashy about him; an objective observer would call him basic. But Janelle thought of the way he treated people, the way he made eye contact and remembered names and asked specific questions, about your wife or your dog or your trip last week. He always showed genuine interest in people, and did or said things to make them feel known. He leaned in when he listened. His eyes sparkled when the person he was talking to was happy, and his face fell when they were sad. The first time she'd ever seen him miserable for himself was when he got the news about his sister. And suddenly Janelle realized she didn't know the name of Tom's sister—she hadn't asked, and he hadn't offered.

She didn't know anything about Tom. Every time she talked to him, he intentionally guided the conversation away from himself, and brought it back to her. She'd never noticed in the moment, because she was caught off guard by the novelty of being heard. Now she wished she'd tried harder to know him.

A puff of air riffled the pages of the book she'd forgotten about, and the sound of heels walking towards the counter brought Janelle back to the present. She looked up, just in time to see the side of Brittany's face as she passed. She walked with confidence, in her perfectly pressed dark blue pinstripe suit. Even from the back, her brown hair was neatly placed and her posture would have made Francie proud. Janelle heard her order a soy latte. After she paid, she stood still for a moment, as if trying to make up her mind. Then she spoke. Janelle couldn't hear all of what she said as the barista steamed the milk, but she caught the last of it.

"…working?"

Brittany seemed to be a young woman of authority, someone who didn't mind working hard to make things happen. But Janelle liked her. She seemed calm, if maybe slightly controlling, but that seemed to be force of habit rather than a character flaw. She possessed a certain charm that tempered her strength into gentleness. Now, she was swaying slowly from side to side, something Janelle only did when she was nervous. As the girl behind the counter answered, Brittany leaned forward to hear. Janelle did as well.

"Oh, he's out of town. I'm not sure when he's coming back."

Brittany straightened, saying,

"Oh. Well, thanks."

Still waiting for her drink she stayed at the counter, but she turned and faced the windows, looking down at her manicured nails. Janelle looked back at her book before she got caught staring. Brittany sat down at a table by the window and took out the same notebook she'd written in at Francie's, and began to write and sketch.

From time to time Brittany put her pen down and looked out the window, focusing on nothing in particular. After some time, Janelle's hand slipped as she was putting her mug on the table, and Brittany looked over and saw her for the first time. Janelle smiled shyly, and Brittany smiled back. She hesitated, then stood and walked over, and said,

"It's good to see you!"

"Hey Brittany. How are you?"

Brittany sat down in the overstuffed chair across from Janelle and crossed her legs.

"I'm doing well. I'm so sorry, but remind me of your name?"

"Janelle."

"Oh yes! Janelle. Okay. I'll remember this time. Do you come here often?"

"Yes. I really like it."

"It seems very nice."

She paused, looking around at the bookshelves and the pictures on the wall and the sparkling chandelier that was more for effect than lighting.

"Just out of curiosity, does Tom work a lot?"

"Yes, usually. He's out of town right now."

She didn't want to volunteer any more information to the woman.

"Oh, that's right, the girl working told me that! Where is he?"

She leaned forward, folding her hands across her knees. Janelle looked down at her book, and her heart sighed. She'd been at a climax. She wondered if Brittany didn't like to read herself, or just had never been interrupted in the middle of a good story. Regardless, Janelle did like Brittany, so she slipped the bookmark into her page in case she needed to close the book.

"He went home."

Brittany didn't say anything, as if she knew there was more to it. Janelle waited, perfectly content to let Brittany wonder. She couldn't wonder silent for long.

"What for? He doesn't like going home anymore."

She'd been looking at the toe of her boot, but at this comment Janelle looked over quickly. To whatever degree she had known him

86

before, it was well enough that Brittany knew about his family trouble. Janelle had only guessed that it was hard for him—he'd never actually told her.

"How did you say you knew Tom?"

Brittany's placid composure rippled.

"We grew up together."

She shifted in her seat.

"Oh. You must have been pretty good friends, to come see him now."

Brittany cleared her throat and rubbed one thumb on the other.

"We were close for quite some time."

She paused.

"We even... well. We spent a lot of time together for a while. I enjoy his company very much."

She paused again, considering, then said,

"You must too?"

Brittany looked searchingly at Janelle.

"We talk some. He watches out for me."

Janelle smiled, and Brittany grinned nervously.

"He was always so nice to everyone."

"Yes. He is."

Janelle looked straight into Brittany's eyes, and Brittany looked down. Janelle was looking back at her book, finding her place on the page, when Brittany asked,

"Why did you say he went home?"

"I didn't say."

Janelle paused.

"His sister got in an accident. She's in the hospital."

Brittany's face fell.

"Oh no! Which sister? Is she okay?"

"I don't know. He was pretty shook up when he found out, and I haven't heard from him since he left."

Janelle sighed and fingered the pages of her book. Brittany uncrossed and re-crossed her legs, looking at her lap.

"Nobody knows when he's coming back?"

It was a statement more than a question.

"I'm not even sure if he knows. I'm sorry."

"That's okay. Thanks."

Brittany uncrossed her legs and prepared to stand, as Janelle said,

"You're welcome. Are you enjoying your stay?"

Brittany nodded.

"Yes, I am. It's a different pace than Texas, and a different climate. I like it very much."

"Good. I hope the rest of your visit goes well."

Janelle smiled, but faintly. She was still thinking about Tom's sister.

"Thank you. It was good to see you!"

Janelle nodded in response, and watched Brittany as she walked out of the cafe. They grew up together. Probably they dated, she seemed quite attached to him. She was nice, Janelle could see why Tom had liked her—she wondered what had happened.

* * *

He'd been home for three days now, and Tom was beginning to remember two things. He loved his family very much, but he was reminded of why he'd left. The atmosphere was a combination of focused and constant care and concern, but sometimes the care was a little overwhelming.

Mary had woken up briefly a few times in the past days, but she hadn't spoken; just opened her eyes and blinked. She was intubated, and Tom missed the sound of her breathing. The doctors said because of all the trauma her brain had been subject to it would take a while for her breathing rhythms to get back to normal. Tom's parents weren't sleeping. His father had gotten gray hair, and his mother looked ten years older. This morning Tom brought breakfast to the hospital, and as soon as he hugged his mother she'd started to cry. Now, several hours later, the occasional tear still found a path down her cheek. Mary had woken up several times during the day.

88

The first time had been like all the times before; her eyes had blinked open, she'd slowly looked around, then sighed and closed them. The second time Tom had been talking to her, telling her about being a barista. The nurses said she could hear even if she wasn't responding. She opened her eyes and stared right at him, first at his shirt then at his face. Her eyes came into focus, and when he smiled, the corners of her lips came up and she smiled back.

"Hey Mary. It's me. Tom."

"Tom."

It came out as more of a whisper. Mary's voice was scratchy from silence. Tom's mother had been drifting in and out of sleep in the chair in the corner, but when she heard Mary's scratchy voice, her head jerked up and she jumped from her chair over to the bed. With one hand Tom was gripping Mary's hand, and with the other he smoothed her hair from her face.

"How are you feeling?"

She groaned softly, and moved her arm. Tom's mother squealed; because she'd been completely limp since she'd been in the hospital, the doctors and the family were worried that she'd lost muscle control. She inhaled, then in an effort to speak, opened and closed her mouth several times. But when nothing came out but scratchy air, she closed her mouth and looked up at Tom, then closed her eyes again.

Tom's mother circled the bed and began to cry on Tom's shoulder. Through her tears, she whispered.

"She's okay. My girl is going to be okay."

Tom patted her back,

"Yes. She's going to be fine."

The next day Mary woke up and tried to speak again, and this time managed to ask what happened. When Tom told her she'd been in an accident, she frowned. She didn't remember, but at least she wasn't comatose. She could remember other things, and apparently hadn't lost her memory. The doctors were amazed.

That evening, Tom and his parents sat with Mary. She went between wakeful attempts at speech, and peaceful rests. The rest of them took turns between gentle conversation and contemplative silence. Tom's mother said,

"Tom, how's work? Going well?"

"It's going really well. I love people."

His father said,

"How much do you work?"

Tom's dad had been upset when Tom left school, and had always wanted him to go back and finish so that he could get a 'real job.' After Tom moved out he talked about it less, but he'd still try to sneak in comments about Tom doing a job that would last him for a long time, rather than something short term, as he called it.

"I work full time hours. Sometimes more, and rarely less."

"And you make good money?"

The same conversation every time they were together; the only thing that had changed were Tom's expectations. He no longer expected his father to understand that he enjoyed his job. His father wanted him to have a 'man's job,' get married, and have kids. He always said that being a barista wouldn't support a family.

"Yes, I do, actually. I make two dollars above minimum wage because of all the raises I've gotten, and I make twenty or thirty dollars by tips every day."

His father smiled, patronizingly, and Tom remembered how hard it'd been to convince him that it was a good idea to move to Denver in the first place. His mom chimed in.

"That's great, sweetie. Your dad and I are so proud of you."

She looked warningly at his father, and Tom sighed. His mother always took his case, and his father always took convincing. He knew his parents loved him, but knowing that they expected more from him ate away at him. It was worse when he went home. After he'd left college, when he was living at home, his dad talked to him about jobs and work almost daily, and Tom had grown used to the constant gnaw of not feeling insufficient. His father always talked about how proud he was of Matt and Jake, and the respectable jobs that they did. Even Elizabeth, before she'd had kids, was an accountant. Mary's job as a librarian pleased Tom's parents because it was intelligent, something that required a degree. Sometimes Tom wondered if they equated being a barista with flipping burgers, something they'd never wanted him to do because they said it took no skill.

That night his parents both went home and slept, and Tom stayed at the hospital with Mary for the second time. She shifted and murmured in her sleep, where before she'd been completely still and silent. He sat and watched her until he could barely keep his eyes open, then he shoved the chair next to her bed, and fell into an exhausted slumber.

CHAPTER TEN

As the days went by, Mary slowly began to recover. After six days, she could talk in complete sentences, and hold a brief conversation. The doctors were starting her physical therapy to keep her muscles from atrophying, and they all agreed that she was on the mend. None of them could believe she'd had no evident brain damage, and Tom's mother kept saying it was because she'd prayed so much for her baby girl. Everything had returned to almost normal, and on Tuesday Tom bought tickets to go back to Denver the next morning. The doctors said Mary would be discharged soon, if her head kept looking good.

Tuesday night Tom sat on the edge of the bed holding Mary's hand. Now she laid awake most of the time, and said she'd gotten so caught up on sleep she wouldn't need to rest for a year.

"I'm glad you're getting better. We were all so worried about you." She smiled.

"It takes more than a car to kill me. I still have to watch you get a career."

Tom's smile ended in a sigh.

"I doubt that'll ever happen."

Mary looked at him searchingly. Her accident hadn't damaged her perception.

"What's wrong, Little T?"

She'd called him Little T when he was little, and the habit had stuck.

"The parents think that I should get a real job. It feels like they disagree with my life."

He sighed, and paused, thinking. Mary said,

"Spit it out."

"Brittany wrote me a letter."

Mary raised her eyebrows.

"She apologized and she misses me and it sounds like she still has feelings for me."

"Wow. I didn't see that one coming."

"I certainly didn't. I didn't expect to ever hear from her again. It sounds like she's doing well."

Mary patted his knee.

"And what are you thinking?"

She had a way of asking the relevant questions like they weren't important, in such a way that made Tom feel like she was asking him to pass the butter or open the door. It set him at ease.

"Well. I was surprised. I didn't realize how much I still cared about her. I thought I was over her, but it's almost like hearing from her woke up my heart again and made me remember what it feels like to be cared about."

He thought of when they were dating, and how she'd cared for him so much. And he'd convinced himself that even when it felt like she didn't care, she did.

"Do you have many friends?"

He wandered through town mentally, thinking of who he would consider his friends. Janelle came to mind, with her big sweaters, green glasses, and quiet style.

"There's this girl named Janelle that moved to Denver from New York maybe two months ago. She's really nice. I've helped her out a few times. She moved to Denver suddenly, and doesn't seem to miss New York. I don't know exactly what her story is, but something about it fascinates me."

He realized he knew a lot of surface things about Janelle. He knew that she had a hedgehog named Mike and sang along with her windshield wipers, but he didn't actually know her story.

"She sounds like an interesting person. What's she like?"

He thought about it.

"She was really shy at first. She wouldn't smile at me the first few times we talked, and even now I don't know much about her. She's kind, but she has a scared manner. I don't know what she's afraid of. When she first moved here she had bruises all up her arms."

Mary raised her eyebrows.

"Oh?"

"I don't know what they're from. Maybe she's just really clumsy."

"I doubt it."

Mary worked with a lot of children from troubled families, and she said herself she was hyper suspicious of abuse.

"Everything started happening with Brittany right around when I met Janelle, so even though I think she's great, I've been distracted by Brittany. And my car."

Mary sighed. Brittany wasn't her favorite person. He added,

"I know what you think of her."

Mary nodded, then said,

"I trust you. Janelle sounds wonderful, but maybe Brittany has changed. What are you going to do?"

"I don't know. I haven't seen Brittany, I only talked to her once. Maybe I'll call her when I get home."

"Please be careful."

Concern drew Mary's eyebrows together.

"I will. And I'll still be friends with Janelle."

Mary nodded.

"Good. Thanks, Little T. Thanks for coming home to take care of me. I love you."

She squeezed his hand as she spoke.

"I love you too."

The knot in his stomach rose when he thought of what could have happened. Forcing it down, he asked,

"When are you going back to work?"

"I might be able to go after a few weeks, it depends on my leg. The library said I could take as long as I needed. Do you work tomorrow?"

Tom hadn't thought very much about work while he'd been home, besides about his father not liking it. The mention of it excited him.

"I don't think tomorrow, but I'll definitely stop by. I miss everybody. And they'll all want to hear about how you're doing."

"That's sweet."

She paused, looking down at her hands and rubbing her thumbs together.

"Have you considered finishing school, Tom?"

From almost anyone else, it would feel like an attack. From her, it was just a question. He relaxed.

"Sometimes."

It was true. He hadn't minded school to begin with, but he liked his life now, and didn't want to go back to the pressure and stress.

"How many credits do you have left?"

"Forty."

"Do you think it might be worth it?"

She looked out the window. As if she had asked him if he liked orange juice or apple better. No pressure. He was silent for some time, tracing the outline of her hand on the bed. He'd always done that when she came home from college when he was little. His mother wouldn't let him wake her, and she would sleep for hours after he'd gotten up.

"I guess so. I just don't want to give up my freedom. It's nice to do whatever you want."

To himself, he admitted this was an overstatement—between his only partially functional car and his college debt, he didn't have much freedom.

"Have you looked into community college? You could knock out those credits in two years and still work full time. It wouldn't be too much extra time, and it'd be easier to pay for."

He considered this.

"That's true. Maybe I'll look into it."

Mary smiled.

"To me, it doesn't matter. I think you're amazing whether you have a degree or not. Mom and Dad think so too—Dad just cares more about credentials. He wants to be sure you'll be able to take care of your family. They love you a lot, you know."

Tom sighed. Everyone always told him how much everyone else loved him. Maybe he'd gotten so used to it that it didn't make a difference anymore. Maybe he didn't quite believe it.

"I know."

He said it without any conviction. Mary narrowed her eyes.

"You don't believe me."

"I do, I do!"

She raised her eyebrows.

"Not really. But it's true. Everyone loves you so much. And we're all so proud of you. We really are."

He sighed.

"I dropped out of school and now I'm working a minimum wage job and nobody really cares what I do with myself or how I spend my time, and I'm just me. Nothing special."

"You just think you're plain because you can't see yourself. You're amazing. We wouldn't be the same without you."

Tom rubbed his right fingers on the back of his left hand.

"Thanks, Mary."

His words filled the air, and hung there for a moment. Mary reached her unbroken arm over and patted his shoulder. They sat in silence until Mary asked,

"How's Whit?"

He laughed, and told her about how Whit was sitting in a graveyard right now, but not because he was dead. They talked about Whit for a while, then other things; his job, his eating habits, her job, her church, the men in her life. Tom couldn't imagine someone being good enough for his big sister, although she'd had plenty of relationships. When they finally stopped talking, it was only a few hours before Matt would be swinging by the hospital to pick Tom up and bring him to the airport.

After making himself comfortable enough in the hospital easy chair, Tom slept. But Mary stayed awake, watching her little brother and wondering where he would go with his life. She'd always understood that he had great potential, but he'd never seen it in himself. She thought of the oddity that everyone should know someone is amazing except the person himself.

When morning came, bringing Matt with it, Tom was still asleep. Mary motioned for his silence, and they watched him. Mary whispered,

"He's great."

Matt nodded, said,

"I think so. I'm so proud of him."

"Me too. I think we sometimes forget to tell him."

Matt looked at her.

"Really? I assume he just knows."

"I don't think he does."

Tom shifted, and slowly opened his eyes. Matt walked over and patted him on the shoulder.

"Good morning, little brother. You about ready?"

Tom rubbed his eyes, mumbling,

"Sure."

He turned over to go back to sleep. Mary laughed.

* * *

The Friday before, Janelle had gone to The Cup early to read again, and was embroiled in her book when someone tapped her shoulder.

"Hi, excuse me?"

She looked up, and saw Mike standing behind her. He was rocking back and forth from one foot to the other, and in her subconscious Janelle wondered if he ever stopped moving.

"Hi, Mike. How are you?"

He looked surprised that she asked.

"I'm good, good. How are you?"

"Fine."

"Good, good, that's very good. Hey, you're friends with Tom, right? I think I've seen you talking to him once or twice."

She laughed. In a world where just talking to a person constituted friendship, she was friends with everyone.

"Yes, we're friends. He's gone—"

"I know, I know."

He wasn't annoyed, just excited.

"I brought him to the airport. I just have two questions: First, when is he coming back?"

Janelle shook her head.

"I don't know. I haven't heard from him since he left. I think he wanted to stay for a week or ten days, but I'm not sure. I think it depends on his sister."

"Hmm. Okay. Interesting. The second question is: are you a good driver?"

Before she could stop herself, Janelle said,

"Ha!"

Then she covered her mouth with her hand.

"Oh dear. I'm sorry. Yes, I'm not a bad driver. Why?"

Mike started bouncing faster, and smiled.

"Because Tom's car is broken, and I'm getting it fixed for him, but I need a second driver to follow me in my car when I pick it up from the shop. It's there now, but they said it'll be ready on Monday morning. Are you free?"

Janelle smiled.

"Yes. I don't work until three on Monday."

Mike took an excited slurp of coffee.

"Excellent. I can pick you up at your house? Or here?"

"Which is more convenient for you?"

Janelle's mother had always taught her to ask. The habit had stuck.

"Oh, it doesn't matter. The Cup might be a little closer to the shop."

"Here's great. What time?"

Mike pulled his phone out and looked at it briefly.

"It says in the email that it'll be done between nine and twelve on Monday morning. To be on the safe side, shall we leave here at eleven-thirty?"

Janelle nodded.

"Sounds great. Then we can bring it back to his apartment. Will you bring me back to The Cup, so I can pick up my car?"

"Yes, absolutely."

He looked at his watch hurriedly.

"I've got to get to work. Have a good day!"

He walked hastily towards the door, and Janelle had just looked back to her book when he spun around and came back.

"Have I given you my card?

You should probably have my number in case anything goes wrong."

"No. That would be good. Thank you!"

Mike pulled out his wallet with his free hand. It was fat with cash as well as cards, Janelle guessed. Every time she'd seen him he was wearing a different suit.

Monday, Janelle went to The Cup at ten so she could read for a while before going to pick up Tom's car. Mike came bouncing in a few minutes before half-past eleven, ordered a coffee, and stepped briskly over to Janelle.

"Good morning, Janelle! Are you ready to go?"

She closed her book and stood.

"Good morning. I am."

As they drove to the car shop, Mike asked,

"You still haven't heard from Tom?"

"Nope. I haven't. I'm hoping he comes home soon. He's been gone for almost a week and a half. What was wrong with his car?"

"I'm not sure exactly what was wrong with it. I just took it to my mechanic. He's really good. I told him to fix everything, and gave him the limit of how much I'd pay. He's very fair, so I know if he charges me up to that much it'll all be fixed."

Janelle asked,

"How well do you know Tom?"

He laughed.

"Not very well. I just think he's great. He's very unassuming, and he's always doing something for someone else. I want to help him out. His car is also a hazard to himself and everyone around him, and I don't want that thing on the streets with our next generation."

"That's very nice of you. He's going to be so grateful."

Mike brushed off the compliment, and they arrived at the shop. A man wearing a greasy jumpsuit came over to Mike when they walked into the garage, and they shook hands.

"You get that car all fixed up, Jack?"

"Sure did, Mike. It was a job, but she'll run smoothly now. Tell your friend to take good care of her—she deserves it. Even though she looks like a mess on the outside, she's still got a lot of pep."

"Thanks so much. Good job."

Janelle stood in the background and looked around as they talked about money. She'd always liked mechanic shops—they smelled like oil and gasoline and metal, and they fascinated her. On the rare occasions that her father wasn't drunk, he worked on his car. She'd watch from a safe distance, perched on the top of a stepladder in the garage.

Mike finished paying for the car, then came over to Janelle and handed her the keys.

"Jack says she's all fixed and running fine. Shall I follow you to Tom's apartment?"

Janelle liked the feel of Tom's car—even though her car was newer than his, her seats were leather upholstered, which she'd never really cared for. His were covered in an odd velvety material. The drive to his house was short, and when they arrived, she parked in the driveway then went back over to Mike.

"Are you sure you don't mind bringing me back?"

"Not at all! Hop in. I can always use an excuse to drink more coffee."

Maybe constant coffee consumption was what made him rock back and forth all the time.

"Thank you so much."

"No problem."

Mike looked at his watch.

"We'd better hurry. I have a meeting at one. I don't want to be too late for it."

Driving back to The Cup, he said,

"We have no idea when Tom is coming back, right?"

Janelle nodded, recalling the previous conversation. Mike continued,

"I know he'll need a ride home from the airport, unless he's planning on walking—which, all things considered, he might be. Maybe I should call him. He's an odd one. Nice, though. I wonder how he got to be this way?"

"You don't know much about him, then."

Janelle let her statement hang in the air. Mike looked at her oddly, as if he'd just realized it for the first time.

"Not much. He talked more about himself on the way to the airport than I've ever heard him talk at all. Talked about his family and his sister."

Janelle nodded, and said,

"I realized this week that I didn't actually know anything about him. I wondered if I was the only one, or if he keeps his life a secret from everyone. Has he ever said anything to you about a girl named Brittany?"

Mike shook his head, and replied

"I don't think so. Not that I can remember. We had our first real conversation ever on the way to the airport. Why?"

"She came to town this week. She was looking for him. She met me in Francie's and asked about coffee shops, then when I told her about The Cup, it sounded like she'd never heard of it. But then she asked about Tom, and didn't he work at a coffee shop, and how was he doing. It was odd. Then she came to The Cup and I happened to be there and she asked me where Tom was and why he wasn't here. She said they grew up together."

Mike raised his eyebrows, saying,

"Probably a girl from college who has too much time and money on her hands."

"I don't know—she seemed to know him better than that. She knew that he doesn't like going home. That's more than a normal acquaintance knows. Mike didn't reply, and the rest of the ride was silent. When they got back to The Cup, she thanked him for driving her, and went inside, back to her overstuffed chair and her book. She didn't read it. She just stared at the pages, thinking.

CHAPTER ELEVEN

Tom sat in the airport, staring at the TV in front of him that flashed the news about all the problems in the world, and gave long, over-dramatized explanations of the weather. He'd forgotten how much he missed talking to Mary, how well she knew him. Most people didn't take the time to know his last name; Mary took the time to ask about everything. And she loved him.

Besides the catastrophe and worry about Mary, home was the same. Tom knew he was appreciated—he knew his family loved him, but he sometimes felt like they forgot. His family, who knew him the best and loved him the most, made him feel loneliest. It had always been that way.

As the bright colors continued to parade on the screen in front of him, he closed his eyes. When he opened them, he saw an elderly man leaning solidly on a cane, taking slow steps towards him. His cane wobbling slightly with every step, and when he reached the seat next to Tom, he sighed and sat down heavily. He wore brown corduroy pants, a plaid flannel shirt, and a gray tweed vest. On his head was a checkered tweed cap, and resting on the bridge of his nose was a pair of enormous glasses. Tom didn't look up; he shifted in his seat as the man sat down, so they wouldn't be touching, and subconsciously wondered why he would choose to sit right next to Tom when the waiting area was almost empty. The man cleared his throat, and Tom looked over.

He had an entire newspaper rolled up and stuffed in his coat pocket, which was sagging with the weight. He reached for the paper with his hand, his knuckles swollen from arthritis, his wrinkled skin bagging in some places and stretching tight in others. For some reason, he reminded Tom of Mrs. Donahue, which reminded him of work. Suddenly, he remembered he needed a ride from the airport. Mike had said he would come get him; but Tom didn't want to inconvenience him. He tried to think of any other friends who would want to come get him. The list was short. Finally, he reached for his phone. Mike answered on the second ring, saying,

"Tom! The coffee's not the same without you! When are you coming home??!"

Tom paused before responding, adjusting to the unexpected enthusiasm.

"Hey, Mike. I'm actually coming home today. I forgot to call you earlier and tell you. If it's too much for—"

"What time should I be there?"

"Are you sure? It's short notice, and I know you're busy. I can figure something out."

"Tom, don't be ridiculous. I can come. When does your flight get in?"

"Twelve thirty. Are you sure?"

"Absolutely. I'll see you then. Gotta run."

The phone clicked before Tom could finish his thanks and goodbye. He liked Mike—Mike didn't seem to notice that Tom wanted to defend himself from care, instead penetrating Tom's insecurity without seeming to try.

"Excuse me, Son?"

The man interrupted Tom's thoughts.

"Yes?"

"Can I use your phone to call my granddaughter?"

His voice was even but raspy, and Tom couldn't figure out if it was a head cold, the normal timbre of his voice, or choked back tears. Tom handed him the phone, and the man's hands shook as he took it. Tom wouldn't have described him as frail, but as he watched, the man's age struck him. He pulled a scrap of paper from his vest pocket, and peered at it.

"I'm sorry, young man. Would you mind punching the numbers for me?"

Tom gently took the phone back, and the piece of paper. Scrawled on it in a shaky hand was a phone number and the name Virginia. He dialed and handed it back.

"Thank you, son."

He held the phone to his ear, and tilted his head sideways like an inquisitive puppy. Tom could hear the phone ringing on the other end of the line, and heard the answer. Immediately, the old man began to beam.

"Hello, Ginny?"

He tapped his fingers on his knee and bounced his toe along. The girl in her excitement rambled on and on, bringing delight to the man's features.

"Yes, I'm just here in the airport waiting to fly home. I'm using some nice boy's telephone. Did you find a boyfriend yet?"

Everything the girl said took much longer than everything the old man said.

"Oh. Well. This boy is really nice. In case that other one doesn't work out."

She must have scolded him at this point, because he listened for a moment then laughed. Tom liked his laugh—it sounded like he'd done a lot of laughing in his life, but there was the mellow note of understanding under his laughter, that he'd been through enough pain to enjoy happiness deeply.

"That's right, little girl. Tell your ma I'm about to get on a plane, and I'll be there soon."

He listened and laughed again, then said,

"Bye, honey. See you soon!"

He held the phone after he hung up, and stared at it. Handing it back to Tom, He said,

"Thank you, young man."

Tom said,

"You're welcome sir."

The man looked at him, narrowing his eyes behind his large glasses.

"Did you ever have anyone you loved more than anything else?"

Taken aback, Tom stared at the man, who continued,

"A girl, or a best friend. Maybe even a dog, if you're that kind of person."

The man sniffed and looked at him,

"I guess so."

Tom thought through the people he loved. His family, of course. A few of his closest friends. Brittany. He sighed.

"Who?"

Tom was wary. Although the man was old, Tom didn't know anyone else who struck up conversations with random strangers.

"My family, I suppose. I have a friend Tim. I did have a dog growing up that I really liked."

The man looked over his glasses at Tom, and asked,

"No one person in particular?"

Tom replied,

"Not anymore."

"Ahh. So there used to be?"

Tom sighed. He wasn't in the mood to tell his story to this mismatched stranger.

"Yes."

He turned his body away. The clue wasn't effective.

"What happened?"

The man was leaning forward slightly, squinting over his glasses at Tom.

"Well. Things just didn't work."

He remembered how much he'd shared with Brittany, all of the serious talks and times of delight.

"That's a shame. I'm sorry, son."

Tom nodded, and stared at his hands. The man cleared his throat, then said,

"My daughter loved her husband more than she loved anything in the world. But he left her for another woman. She's falling apart. There are a lot of things I'd like to do to that man, if there weren't laws."

He paused, his wrinkled, knobby hand curled into a fist. Tom didn't know what to say, but the man continued,

"My son's son got hit by a car and killed when he was almost five. My son almost went crazy, started drinking and hasn't ever stopped. Love will do mad things to you."

He took his glasses off and cleaned them meticulously with a cloth, slowly, carefully, as if waiting for dramatic effect before he said,

"It will make you go mad."

Tom said,

"I'm so sorry."

The man looked at him.

"My name's Reuben. My wife—her name was Mae. Reuben and Mae. I loved her more than anything else. She died of cancer, seven years ago. I think about her every day."

He twisted a scuffed and scratched gold ring around his finger. "I loved her so much. 54 years, we were married. 54 years. That's a long time."

He stopped, looking at the ring.

"I'm so sorry."

Nothing else Tom could think of seemed adequate. He'd learned, when you're hurting, you don't want people to try to fix the pain. You just want them to listen.

The man grunted, saying,

"It will never stop hurting."

Tom reached his hand over and patted him gently on the shoulder. He hadn't wanted to be part of this conversation—but he hated it when people were sad. Reuben sighed and looked at his shoes, forest green suede loafers. Tom wondered distractedly if he could have picked a worse shoe for his wardrobe selection. The old man broke his reverie, asking,

"What happened?"

Reuben stopped staring at his shoes and turned his head to look at Tom.

Tom didn't tell strangers about Brittany. But Reuben looked at him, expectantly.

"There was a girl. We grew up together. Everyone expected us to get married. I expected it too. I loved her. Then when I proposed, she said no. And ended it. Just like that. I didn't understand. I still don't. She just ended everything."

Reuben reached over and patted him, as Tom stared down at his own shoes now. They were brown leather wingtip oxfords, scuffed and battered from years of wear. Tom had gotten them from his roommate in college.

"Love never goes how we think it will."

Reuben pulled his newspaper from his pocket and opened it, seeming to forget Tom altogether. Tom didn't have the same ease moving back into casual thought. He tried not to think about Brittany, but it wasn't easy. They could have had a wonderful life together—instead she'd abandoned him. But now, she wrote him. And maybe she wanted to see him. And maybe she would love him again. Things could be like they were—they could be happy again. Things could be good. A small corner of his brain nagged with concern, but he silenced it. It wasn't wrong to hope.

The whole flight back, Tom reminisced over Brittany. Everyone called them the dream team. It had been hard sometimes—they'd had misunderstandings; but everyone has misunderstandings. He let himself dream, thinking about what could happen if they started talking.

Mike was waiting for him at the airport when he arrived, and Tom thought of the irony that his own family forgot him, but Mike was right on time.

"Tom! Welcome back!"

Mike's exuberance woke him from his Brittany daydreams, and Tom smiled.

"Hey, Mike! Good to see you."

It always took him a little bit to remember himself after being with his family. Their influence was so overwhelming that he had to readjust as his own person.

"How was your trip? How's Mary? We've been so worried about her."

Tom was shocked that Mike remembered her name.

"She's doing great! She has a broken leg and arm, and some other internal damage, and a concussion, but the doctors are impressed by how quickly she's healing. They say she should be able to leave the hospital sometime this week. Her brain didn't sustain any lasting injury, which surprised everyone."

"That's great, Tom! And how are your parents doing?"

"My mom was pretty upset. I don't think she slept for the whole first week. But, now that Mary is doing better, so is everyone else."

"Good. I know that's so hard."

Tom nodded, then said,

"How are things around here? Did anything happen while I was gone?"

"Not really. I worked. Ha! Nothing new."

Mike laughed at his own joke, as Tom replied,

"Working is good. How's Janelle?"

Tom paused, then asked,

"You know Janelle, right?"

Mike nodded, and said,

"Yes, I do. She's doing just fine. I actually saw her yesterday. We talked about you, we were wondering when you were coming home."

"Oh! Well. I'm home."

Tom smiled, and Mike tapped his thumb on the steering wheel excitedly.

"You are indeed, and we are exceedingly fortunate to have you back. The coffee really hasn't been as good."

"I'm sure it has."

Tom laughed.

"Well, it's not the same."

"I'm back now, so there's nothing to worry about."

Tom smiled, then said,

"Oh! Do you mind stopping by the graveyard to see if my car starts? I'm hoping it just needed a rest and will be miraculously healed."

"Actually, your car is at your house."

Tom looked quickly at Mike, and said,

"What? How?"

"Well, the thought of your car all lonely by that graveyard just made me really sad, so I got it home for you."

"How? Did it start?"

Mike smiled.

"In a manner of speaking."

"Don't tell me you towed my car for me. Mike! You didn't have to do that!"

"It's okay. I didn't tow it to your house."

Mike's eyes sparkled, and Tom sat silent, then said,

"Thank you."

"Oh, it was a pleasure. You're always helping other people and listening to them. Sometimes no one remembers to help you out. Don't worry about it. I loved to do it."

"Wow. Thanks."

"You're welcome. Did you say you wanted to swing by The Cup on your way home? I think they've missed you."

"I'd love to. I also have to figure out my hours and tell my boss I'm back. I don't think he wanted me to stay away forever."

Mike laughed as Tom called Phil.

"Hey, Phil?"

"Tom! Are you back?"

"Yes, today. When do you want me to come back to work?"

Phil laughed.

"As soon as you can. Maybe even sooner than you can."

"Absolutely. Tomorrow morning?"

"Yes, today if you wanted."

"Tomorrow is fine. Normal hours?"

"Yes sir. And don't be late."

Tom could hear the smile in Phil's voice. After he hung up, Tom didn't say anything for some time. Mike broke the silence.

"Do you know a Brittany?"

Tom cast his eyes sideways, searching for some indicator. Mike's face was straight.

"I knew a girl back home named Brittany."

Tom fingered the strap of his backpack.

"Why?"

"Oh, Janelle just mentioned a Brittany when we talked yesterday. You'll have to ask her."

Tom pulled his eyebrows together in a look his mother always said made him look like a wet cat.

"Okay."

"She didn't say much to me."

They talked of other things then, from the weather to Tom's home in Idaho. Mike had never lived in a small town, and he had most certainly never lived on a farm, so he had dozens of questions. Tom patiently answered each one, not laughing at even the absurd ones. Mike told him he'd always wanted animals when he was a kid, but his parents had never let him have any, so he'd gotten a dog as soon as he got married, but his wife didn't like animals, so it'd always been a source of contention. When his wife had left him, she'd also left the dog, but the dog had died shortly after. Mike was silent for a moment, then added,

"So then I didn't have a wife or a dog."

When Tom finally spoke, it was to say,

"I'm sorry."

Mike sighed.

"It's alright. It's not your fault, after all."

Mike pulled into The Cup parking lot, and Tom hesitated as he reached for the handle.

"Thanks for coming to pick me up. I appreciate it."

"No problem. Anything I can do for you. How are you going to get home from here?"

Tom said,

"I can get a ride with John. He works on Wednesdays."

"Are you sure? That won't be waiting for too long?"

"Nope. I might make a few drinks before I go home. I miss it."

"I get that. I like my job too. Oh. Here are your car keys. Your car's at your apartment."

"Thank you so much, Mike. I appreciate all you've done. Really. Thank you."

"Anytime. It was a pleasure. I'm glad to be your friend."

Chapter Twelve

Early that morning, Janelle woke up shivering, all her blankets on the floor. She'd dreamt that she was home in New York, and her father had been banging on her bedroom door. She'd locked it, as her mother had taught her to do whenever she was home alone, but as he knocked, the door started to shake. She looked for somewhere to hide from his fists, but suddenly all the furniture vanished, and it was just her, alone, in her empty room. She'd woken cold and whimpering as the door had splintered.

After that, she couldn't get back to sleep, so she got up and made bread. Her mother made bread when her father wasn't home and she had time to bake. She said it helped her think. As she kneaded the dough, Janelle thought about Brittany and Tom. There had been some connection between them. She just wasn't sure what.

She remembered her nightmare and sighed. She wondered when they would stop. They'd happened for as long as she could remember, but they were much less frequent since she had left home. She didn't wake up really afraid any more, just sad. The dreams made her miss her mother, because she'd loved Janelle. And even though she was essentially powerless, she'd tried very hard to protect Janelle from her father.

After the bread finished baking, Janelle went to The Cup to read. She'd spent a lot of time there while Tom was gone, but she didn't like it as much without him. He reminded her of everyone's big brother. The atmosphere was missing the family feel that she'd grown used to. She wanted him to come back.

As she read Dracula, the small bell over the door dinged merrily. She'd become used to tuning it out, but when the barista yelled,

"Hey! You're back!!!"

And Sherry Donahue, sitting by the window, shrieked,

"Tommy!"

And an older man waiting at the counter for his coffee turned, saying,

"Well it's about time! We were wondering if you'd ever come back. Welcome home, Thomas boy."

Janelle looked up. Mrs. Donahue was hugging him, and staring at him as if he was something she'd lost and had been searching for. The man who had greeted him was attempting to thump Tom's chest, which wasn't working because of Sherry's arms draped around him.

"Hi Mrs. Donahue, Mr. Peterson, hey John! It's good to see you all. I've missed it here."

The woman scoffed.

"It's practically a disaster here without you, Tommy."

She lifted an apologetic hand to the young man standing behind the counter. He nodded and smiled.

"It's just wrong to have you gone."

The man had gotten tired of waiting, and said,

"Now, Sherry, I want to give the boy a hug too."

She rolled her eyes at him, as he continued, saying,

"It really wasn't the same without you."

"Thanks, Mr. Peterson. It's great to be back."

Mr. Peterson and Mrs. Donahue were beaming at Tom. Janelle stood behind them, smiling, and Tom said quietly,

"Hey Janelle. It's good to see you."

"It's good to see you too, Tom! Welcome back."

After everyone had finished hugging him, Tom looked over to John, still making drinks behind the counter.

"You're doing a great job."

"Thanks, Tom. We missed you."

Tom moved over to the counter and asked,

"Need help?"

John shrugged, and added,

"If you'd like."

Tom grinned and reached for an apron. Mrs. Donahue went back to her seat, and as John handed Mr. Peterson his coffee, Mr. Peterson started telling him how difficult he expected the winter to be. Janelle moved back to her chair and picked up her book, but only stared at the pages. Tom was back. Cheer was back in the air. And she had so many questions.

* * *

Whit sat in Tom's driveway, faithful, rusted, and stationary, as usual.

"Thanks for the ride, John. I appreciate it."

"No problem, man. You let me know if you need anything else. I'm glad Mary's doing okay."

When he got upstairs, Tom looked around his small apartment. It was just as he'd left it. In his fridge, there was an old apple, some odds and ends, and a half gallon of milk that had expired while he was gone. He sighed, went to the cabinet, and got a can of beans. Beans seemed like the perfect food to keep around, and he was always eating them when he ran out of everything else.

After dinner, he went to bed. There was nothing else for him to do tonight, and suddenly he grew sad that no one had been waiting for him at his apartment. He missed family—he missed belonging, even at the cost of partial identity loss. His body was worn out from travel and sleep deprivation, but as he lay still, his mind kicked into gear. Mike had mentioned Brittany. She'd come. She hadn't stayed, but she'd come. She wanted to see him. He didn't know why, which bothered him. He'd moved on with his life, but in the quiet corners of his heart, he still missed her. His head told him to have nothing to do with her, that what ended in pain once would end in pain again. He stared at the ceiling, watching the shadows and listening to the steady fan in the refrigerator.

After his mind went in circles for a long time, he fell into a restless sleep. He had too many dreams. He was standing next to a pool, and someone he didn't recognize began taunting him. He stood there bearing it, trying not to fight back, when the person pushed him in. He climbed out. And got pushed in again. Climbed out. Pushed in. The last time he got pushed in, he couldn't swim, and started to sink.

The sheets were tangled around his legs when he woke up. It was 4 am. He got some water, and looked out the window into the street. No one was out, and the full moon gave the shadows personality. He didn't want to be awake, but he didn't want to sleep. He stood there for a long time, until the sun started lighting the treetops and he could go to work. He didn't give a second thought to Whit until he was half way to work and realized that nothing was wrong. Which was odd. Then he remembered Mike. And his suspiciously secretive delight. Tom grinned. No one had been waiting at his apartment for him—but Mike had fixed his car. He cared.

During the night, someone had taped flyers to the front of the shop for a college fair. Tom read the posters, then took them all down, but saved one to put on the bulletin board inside. Because he was at work so early, he didn't have to rush. He slowly got ready, and when Nicole came in, he'd already done everything.

"Hey Tom. How you doing?"

They didn't work together much, because Tom worked mostly mornings and she worked mostly nights.

"I'm pretty good. How are you?"

"Good. I hear you were in… Iowa?"

"Idaho."

"Oh yeah, sorry."

She was too tired to care.

"No, it's fine. People do that a lot."

She didn't say anything for a minute, then,

"Your... Sister? Something happened to your sister?"

"Yeah, she got hit by a car. She's fine now, the doctors think."

"Oh dear. I'm sorry. Poor thing."

She furrowed her brows in compassion like most girls do when they are expressing their heartfelt sympathy, and spun a small paper coffee cup on the counter with her fingers.

Opening time came, and with it no customers. Twenty minutes later, Mike was among the first to stop in. As soon as he was in the door, he yelled,

"Hey, Tom!"

Then he seemed to remember that it was early, and brought his voice down to a socially appropriate volume.

"I mean, hey Tom."

He bounced up to the counter.

"How are you today?"

He scrutinized Tom's face.

"Mike! Did you fix my car?"

Mike flashed an impish grin.

"Maybe."

"It drives smoother than it did when I first got it! It's great! Thank you so much."

Mike shrugged as if it was nothing, still grinning.

"I didn't want you to get stranded somewhere."

"Well, thank you so much. If there's ever anything I can do for you, please tell me."

Mike nodded, then asked,

"How are you today? You look a little glum."

"I'm fine, really."

"You look like you didn't sleep at all last night."

Mike looked skeptically at his eyes, then said,

"Hmmm. Okay." Tom didn't want to say anything else. "Well. I will have coffee. A large cup. Lots of caffeine." Tom poured the cup, and handed it over the counter. Mike watched him, thanked him, turned, and walked out. The rest of the morning was busy but uneventful, and

Tom had just finished wiping the counter for the third time in five minutes when Janelle came in around 11.

She walked through the door, and as soon as she saw him her face lit up.

"Hey, Tom! It's so good to have you back."

He smiled.

"Janelle! Hi. How are you?"

She put her hands on the counter and leaned against it.

"I'm doing well. Nothing important happened while you were gone. It's been boring. Winter is coming slowly, though, which means Christmas. I like Christmas. But how was your trip? Tell me more about it?"

Tom smiled. It was nice to be missed.

"It was alright. Mary's doing better. I'm glad to be back."

"Oh, I'm so glad! Was it really bad? What happened?"

"It was pretty bad. We were worried. She got hit by a car while she was crossing the street. She's doing much better now, and hopefully she'll be up and around in a few weeks."

"Oh good! Good. Did you do anything else while you were there?"

He looked at her fingers as she drummed them on the counter.

"Not really. Spent a lot of time in the hospital talking to my family. It was good."

He wanted to ask her about Brittany, but he didn't want to force it.

"That's nice."

Silence. She looked up at the menu, not really reading it.

"I'll have a large chai latte."

"That's right, I remember."

She watched him steam the milk.

"So..."

Her voice faded off. He looked at her with interest, and she continued.

"Well, while you were gone this girl came to Francie's Diner and sat there all afternoon."

This didn't seem to be special information.

"Oh, really? Doing what?"

"I think she was taking notes or something. She would write a lot of things, and occasionally sketch pictures. After she'd been there for a few hours she stopped me and asked me about good coffee shops. I told her to come here."

"I'm flattered,"

Tom replied teasingly.

"After I told her about this place, she asked me if I knew a Tom Bailey."

He raised his eyebrows.

"I told her I did, that you worked here, and that you were a friend of mine."

"What did she say?"

"Asked if you worked a lot, and asked how you were. I told her you did, and you were fine."

Tom finished making the latte, and set it on the counter gently.

"Girls coming to look for me. That's a new twist. Did she say her name?"

Janelle hesitated. She remembered the look on Tom's face when she had given him the letter, and thought of the mornings after when he looked like he hadn't slept at all.

"She didn't say it at first, but I asked her before she left the restaurant. Brittany... I don't think I ever asked her last name." But he seemed to stop hearing her as soon as she said Brittany. He looked down at the latte that he hadn't let go of and was now rotating slowly on the counter. Brittany had come to Denver looking for him. And she'd found him.

"Oh."

He couldn't think of anything else to say. As Janelle watched him, an intrigued look slowly crept over his face. Janelle said,

"I saw her again."

Jerked back to his spot behind the counter from wherever his mind had been, he said,

"Really?"

"Yeah. She came here the next morning looking for you. Asked Jennifer if you were here."

Janelle shifted her weight and leaned harder onto the counter.

"When she found out you weren't she bought a drink and sat down, and when she noticed me she started talking to me. Asked me where you were. I told her you were visiting home. She asked why, said it was hard for you to go home. I told her your sister had an accident and that you went to see her."

Tom's hands rested on the counter, the mug forgotten.

"She said you didn't like to go home very much, so I said you must have been close to him to know that. She said you were. We talked a little more about small stuff, then she left."

Tom stared at the mug.

"Wow."

He let his word fall into silence. Brittany knew where he was. She had entered back into his life, entered his town, his job. It was no longer his safe hideaway from his past. She knew. Janelle said,

"She seemed really nice. I liked her. Who is she?"

She asked. Tom stepped back from the counter and moved around behind the bar, like he was looking for something. After he wandered about the small space for several minutes, he stopped in front of her and stared at her face.

"I proposed to her once."

His restless hands betrayed the emotions hidden under his still face.

"Oh."

"Yeah. I wanted to marry her for a long time."

"Oh."

Janelle had known Tom for a little more than a month. She waited for him to say more, and after pushing her latte across the counter to her, he said,

"We grew up together. Everybody wanted it. We started dating in high school, and dated through most of college. Then I proposed. And she said no. That ended it."

It was almost becoming routine for Tom to tell the story—twice in two days.

"I'm so sorry."

It didn't seem like enough, but she didn't know what else to say.

"I wanted to die for a while."

It felt dangerous, but some small corner of his heart was crying with delight. She was listening, like she cared. He began to believe that she did.

"Oh, Tom."

He shrugged.

"I left school after that. I didn't have much left, but I didn't want to go back and be by her. Eventually I ended up here."

She knew there was more to the story than that, but if he wasn't going to tell her, she wouldn't pry. He'd already said more than she expected him to. She reached across the counter and put her small hand on his large one, and squeezed it. Tom, her friend.

"I'm glad you ended up here. Without you I'd probably still be sitting by the side of the road wondering why my car wouldn't start."

She giggled, and he smiled faintly.

"Good thing."

The mood shifted, and Janelle remembered the letter.

"Wait—she wrote you that letter that you dropped. What was it? And what was she doing here?"

Tom sighed.

"The letter apologized. I don't know why she came. I guess to see me. And talk to me."

Janelle scrunched her nose, and said,

"Huh."

"Yeah. Did she say she would come back?"

Janelle shook her head.

"We didn't talk very much besides when she was asking me where you were. I didn't know who she was and I didn't want to ask questions like that to a stranger."

"That's probably just as well."

Janelle hadn't had much time to for boys in high school, she'd always been busy trying to hide her bruised arms or working. She'd wanted someone to want her, but it didn't seem like anyone ever had. The little girl in her hadn't gotten a chance to be young—she'd grown out of childhood before she was ready. They stood, each in his and her own world, imagining what Brittany would do next. Their silence was broken as the bells over the door clinked. In marched Mrs. Donahue.

"Good morning, Tommy-boy! And… Michelle?"

Tom laughed.

"Good morning, Mrs. Donahue! It's Janelle."

She snapped her finger.

"Right. Janelle. Hi honey. I'm horrible with names. Took me almost half a year to get Tommy's straight."

She laughed at her own joke, with the self-satisfied look of someone who feels she has said something truly amusing. Janelle and Tom smiled at her and waited for her next statement.

"It's a beautiful fall, kids. The trees are about to change, and when they do they will be so orange and red and yellow! I won't be able to blink, ever."

Janelle thought to herself that the only thing that was old lady about this woman was her wrinkled face, and Tom laughed at the prospect of a wide, watery eyed Mrs. Donahue, wandering the public parks, mouth agape, looking skyward in delight and awe.

"Maybe you'd want to blink sometimes, Mrs. Donahue."

"Yes, yes, obviously sometimes, Tommy. You know what I mean."

She rolled her eyes at him.

"I want a drink."

"Yes?"

She ordered like this often, drawing out her request, sometimes making Tom guess what she wanted. Once she had made him guess through the entire menu, then ordered plain coffee. She had said she wanted to make sure he knew his product.

"I think I want something caffeinated."

"This is the right place to be, then."

"Maybe an espresso shot."

"That's a little stronger than usual."

She raised her eyebrows.

"I'm feeling risqué today, Tommy-boy. It is fall, and nobody can tell me what to do. Mr. D is at home painting a picture of last night's sunset, and I'm bored and out looking for adventure. Make me an espresso shot."

To finish her rant, she slapped her hand down on the counter and nodded emphatically. Janelle laughed and stepped aside, pulling her latte with her.

"Ma'am yes ma'am,"

Tom chimed, saluting her and reaching for his porta filter.

"Good boy, good boy. I knew you would help me."

She smiled at him.

"Now, where were you? You were gone. I didn't want to get coffee from anyone else while you were gone. None of them are as good as you are."

This wasn't true, Tom knew, but he smiled at her exuberance and dedication.

"I went home, Mrs. Donahue. You know that."

"Home to where, sweetie?"

She pushed her glasses up on her nose and peered through them at him.

"Idaho, Ma'am. My parents and most of my brothers and sisters live there."

She nodded.

"Ah. What were you doing there?"

He shook his head.

"We talked about this. You saw me when I got back yesterday. Remember? My big sister Mary? The car accident? I had to go make sure the doctors were taking care of her."

"Oh my! You just can't trust cars these days. I may vaguely remember. Is she better now?"

"Yes, she's doing well. The doctors think she can go back to work in the next few weeks, as long as she's feeling normal."

Mrs. Donahue nodded, and reached for the shot which Tom had finished. She examined it carefully, tilting the cup this way and that, then tasted the espresso with the tips of her lips.

"Good, good. I'm glad to hear she's going to be fine."

Then, referring to the espresso,

"This is pretty good today, hon. I see that even though you were gone you haven't lost your knack for the beans. Good job."

She then drank it and plunked the small mug on the counter.

"I think I want something else too."

"Are you going to pay for the first one?"

He looked down his nose at her and she laughed.

"Yes, yes, I'll pay for it. But make me something else first."

"What would you like?"

She eyed the menu up and down like she was looking over her daughter before a first date.

"I want..."

Much hesitation.

"I think I want a—well, I'm not sure. What do I want?"

Janelle motioned to the small blackboard next to the big menu board. Recently, The Cup had started making smoothies.

"You could get a smoothie."

Mrs. Donahue scrutinized the menu.

"Maybe, well, maybe."

Tom stood patiently. Just then, the bell over the door clinked and Mr. Peterson ambled in.

"Ah, Tom! How are you? I was just telling Murphy that it seemed like you would never come home. Would you believe it, fall is coming late this year! It looks like the leaves will never change colors. Just this morning I was walking Murphy down the street for our daily walk and I saw the first colored leaf on the big maple at the end of our lane. The first colored leaf! And it's already October! Does the late fall mean a cold winter? Or is it a warm winter? I think it's the cold winter. When

I was a boy we always looked in the almanac for these things—but then I grew up on a farm and that was just the way people did things back then. Now you young people just look at your phones or something. Good morning, Mrs. Donahue! How are you this fine day? Have you noticed that it's almost fall? It's going to be a beautiful one, I'm sure. Maybe that's what a late fall means."

He would have kept talking, but Tom interjected,

"Good morning, Mr. Peterson. It's good to see you today."

Mr. Peterson's eyebrows shot up.

"Oh yes, Tom! You've been gone! You look awful, son! You look like you haven't slept a wink. Did you go on a trip and forget how to take care of yourself? Look at him, Sherry. Doesn't he look like he was up all night?"

Tom shifted uncomfortably as Mrs. Donahue pulled him into focus and stared at him.

"Oh, Tommy boy, you do look a little gray. Have you been sleeping well? Is it your mattress? I know I wasn't sleeping well at all for a while and I got a new mattress and it made a world of difference. I feel young again, all the time. I feel like I haven't gotten a day older since I turned 70."

Janelle stood to the side, watching the two interact.

"You're right, maybe it is your mattress, Tom!"

Mr. Peterson proclaimed this as if it was a new insight onto one of the deeper mysteries of life.

"You know what you should get? A water bed. I've heard those work wonders for if you have back problems from sleeping. I'm not sure if it's true, but it's what I've heard. Before I moved houses in my neighborhood, my neighbor's son had one. Used to let us sit on it when we came over. I don't think I'd like one—always be getting seasick from all that rocking back and forth and unsteady waters and watching the ceiling move every time I turned over. But maybe you should get one, they might be better for young people."

Tom raised his eyebrows, saying,

"Wow, thanks for all the advice."

Mr. Peterson looked at him seriously.

"If need be, son, we can go to the store and order you one later today. I can drive my truck and we can pick everything up and set it up in your house."

He smiled smugly.

"Never underestimate the power of a generous offer to a young person," he added, to Mrs. Donahue.

"They always need help in some way or another. Why, just last week my neighbor-boy was outside trying to move his play set by himself. Pulling at the thing and shoving it and it wouldn't budge. I was out with Murphy, so we came over to see what he was doing. He said he wanted to see if it would float so he was taking it to the ocean. I told him he wasn't going to get very far if this was how he was going. Kids these days, I tell you. Anyways, Thomas, the mattress?"

Tom laughed.

"You know, actually, I think my mattress is fine. It's not very old, and it's never given me problems before. It's probably something else. But if it starts feeling lumpy, you know you'll be the first person I call."

Mr. Peterson reached over the counter and thumped him on the shoulder.

"Good, I like to see a man of action. You give me a call first thing. Now, Sherry, have you ordered? I want my coffee. I've barely even woken up yet."

Mrs. Donahue rolled her eyes at him.

"The way you talk, you've been practicing in your sleep. No, I haven't ordered yet. I'm still trying to decide what I want."

"Oh, for pete's sake, Sherry. They're all the same. Just order one. She'll have a cappuccino."

"No, Mr. P, no. I don't want a cappuccino. I want a smoothie, Tommy. A 'Perfect Peach Mango' smoothie. And I'll even pay for it now so you know I won't change my mind."

Tom rang her up, poured Mr. Peterson a cup of coffee, and started making the smoothie.

"How's your sister, Tom my man?"

Mr. Peterson got into lingo ruts, and tried to talk like a twenty-year-old whenever he wanted to feel hip. He didn't sound like a twenty-year-old, though. He sounded like an old man trying to be hip.

"She's doing much better, thanks for asking."

Tom smiled, asking,

"How's Murphy?"

Murphy was the large docile golden retriever that Mr. Peterson had bought when his wife died to keep him company. He took the dog almost everywhere, and talked about him with the frequency that comes from a mixture of habit and great affection.

"Oh, he's doing just fine. He's the best trained dog I ever had. Of course, he's the only dog I've ever had because first my parents, then Mrs. P wouldn't let me get one. Ha. Ha. But I did a good job training him, if I do say so myself. He chased a squirrel up a tree the other day and sat there staring at it for four hours before I called him in for dinner and to watch a movie with me. He's good company. A good dog. A good dog."

Tom handed Mrs. Donahue her smoothie, and rang Mr. Peterson's coffee up. The two of them struck up conversation about something that had happened in politics fifty years ago, and Tom looked at Janelle and shrugged. They both laughed, as the pair of old people wandered to the middle of the shop and sat in opposing chairs discussing presidents and plebeians and prose.

"Well, your life really isn't ever boring."

Janelle loved the small town feel that the little shop had, even though it was on the outskirts of a bustling impersonal city.

"No, it's really not."

For the rest of her day, Janelle rolled the morning over in her mind. Brittany had turned Tom down. Caring, kind, compassionate Tom. Janelle didn't want his romantic interest—but she did care about Tom, and she wanted well for him.

That night at work, Francie asked her,

"Well, it's been two months since you moved here. How are you liking it so far?"

Janelle gave the normal comments, mentioning how she loved The Cup, and the small town feel, and how much people cared about her. She even said something about Mike, and the big tip he had given her, and how he had fixed Tom's car. Francie looked amazed.

"Mike did that? Wow. I always knew he was incredibly kind. Did you hear about his wife?"

Janelle didn't know anything about Mike, besides that he seemed to have an inexhaustible well of energy, and that he must have a good job.

"No, I don't know anything about his wife. What happened?"

Francie leaned over.

"Well, she left him a few years ago because he was a workaholic. Worked all the time, like crazy. Must have come from a poor background. But anyways, she left him, lock stock and barrel. Completely. Well, he thought she left the city, but she didn't. Just moved to a different part of it and changed her stores and everything, so she knew she'd never see him.

Well. I get my hair cut at Sal's, you know, and last week when I went in for a trim, she was there! And she was prattling on and on about how she was about to get married, to such a wonderful man, and how she was so excited she could barely stand it. I could barely stand it myself, and I don't know how Nancy did, cutting her hair so peacefully. I guess the wedding is next week."

"Oh, really? Wow. Does Mike know?"

"I doubt it. He comes in here for meetings pretty often, and he seems to be the same. I don't think he knows. If he did, though, he would be pretty upset. He loved her so much. When she said she was going to leave him he tried and tried and tried to get her to stay but she wouldn't. He almost completely stopped working, and even went to counseling for her. I guess she didn't love him as much as he loved her—" she 'humphed,' and continued, "Maybe not at all."

"Poor man. How long has it been?"

Francie tapped her toe and put her finger to her nose to think. It was a nice nose, a little pudgy, but it fit well with her pleasantly wrinkled face and her wispy gray-brown hair.

"Let's see. It was the year we had rain all summer long. That must have been five—no, six years ago. Six years. He was a wreck for about a year and a half after, but then gradually he started getting better. We were all pretty worried about him for a while. He almost lost his job, but I guess he's really good at what he does so his boss wanted to keep him. Makes sense, I guess. Now he's really high in his company. Maybe a CEO or something. I'm not sure what exactly he does—but he makes a lot of money and he always leaves an extra big tip. And I always have him over for holidays now, because I don't want him to be alone. He's wonderful company, and very generous."

Janelle thought about the tray of cups she'd dropped and the tip Mike left that night. He didn't seem to be the kind of person who had experienced much pain—but when she thought back to her ride with him when they were fixing Tom's car, she remembered his steady gentle attitude; that didn't come from an easy life. Janelle moved off to check tables, and Francie went back to mixing the cake she would serve for the late dessert that night.

The next morning, Janelle got ready for work earlier than usual, and went to The Cup before work. She noted the leaves as she parked her car, and wondered if Mrs. Donahue had noticed them in all their color. They seemed to have changed overnight. The bells over the door clinked as she walked in. A couple sat in the front corner having an involved discussion, and Mrs. Donahue sat in her usual solitary spot by the front window, drinking something (could've been anything with her habits) from a mug and looking out the window with wide eyes, like it was the first time she'd ever seen the world. Tom was sweeping the floor up by the counter.

"Hey, good morning Janelle! You're later than usual today. On your way to work?"

"Yeah, I decided to get ready for work before I came so I wouldn't have to drive back and forth. Felt like a good idea."

She realized she was saying it apologetically, but she wasn't apologizing for anything. He nodded.

"That was a good idea. How's your car?"

Something about him this morning seemed different. He was happier. His eyes sparkled a little when he looked at her.

"She's doing just fine."

"That's great. I'm glad to hear it."

She waited for him to finish sweeping and looked up at the menu. She didn't feel like chai today—something stronger sounded good.

"The usual?"

He started to punch the codes into the cash register.

"No, wait. I want something else today."

"Oh, branching out! Good, good. What can I make for you?"

She still hadn't decided. Besides the normal flavors of everything, The Cup also had different fascinating lattes that they made. There was blueberry dill, and basil lavender, and pepper fig. She wasn't much one for different drinks, but maybe it was time to start branching out. She was free from anyone telling her how to live life, and she had an extra 65 cents for a fancier drink.

"I think I'll have a pepper fig latte. That sounds good. I've never had one."

He smiled.

"Those are good. The first time I had one I couldn't figure it out, but all the ones I've had since I've enjoyed."

"Do you actually put table pepper into it?"

Pepper didn't sound good in coffee.

"We get the unground black pepper and grind it finer, so it's like dust that we put in. The flavor is there, but you're not chewing on chunks of pepper and getting black things stuck in your teeth. Then the fig flavor comes from fig juice concentrate, just a squirt or two. It's pretty good."

"Okay. I'll do it. Sounds interesting."

He rang her up, and she handed him a five.

"Keep the change." He smiled, and said,

"Thanks."

He started grinding the beans to pull her shot, and she leaned over the counter and said,

"What do you know about Mike?"

"What do I know about him? Well, his wife left him. He used to have a dog but he doesn't anymore. He works a lot. He has more energy than any middle aged man I've ever known. Uh… I don't know much else, actually."

He looked at her oddly.

"Why?"

"Well, Francie told me something yesterday that I didn't know. Mike's wife left him 5 or 6 years ago, and he went off the deep end. Almost lost his job, was a mess for a pretty long time, she said. He thought she left the state, but she actually still lives in Denver, just the opposite side, working a different job and shopping in different stores. Francie told me she's getting remarried. She said they go to the same salon and they were both there at the same time last week and his wife—I don't actually know her name, come to think of it—was there, and she talked all about how she was getting married and how she couldn't wait and all that." Tom looked at her in disbelief.

"Really?"

She nodded.

"That's what Francie told me, and I'm sure she knows."

"Did she say if Mike knew?"

"She doesn't think so. She said he would be a wreck if he did. She said he loved her so much, he just had a blind spot about work, and didn't realize he was hurting their relationship by working so much. Everyone has a blind spot, I guess."

"Do you think he'll find out?"

Janelle shook her head.

"I don't think so. Not unless there's a strange series of coincidences."

Tom paused, then said,

"I'd be interested to know more about him. He seems like a fascinating person, someone worth knowing."

"Most people are."

Janelle surprised herself as she said this—usually she thought things like this but didn't voice them for fear of sounding cliché. Her brother used to tease her about her 'nuggets' as he called them. 'A nugget of wisdom, Janelle! A nugget!' he used to say, laughing. Tom looked at her, squinting his eyes as if he were trying to focus.

"Anyways," she went on, "we'd better keep a close eye on him. If he finds out, Francie says he'll be a mess. You probably see him more than I do—if he starts to look unwell, ask him why and see if we can help him."

Tom nodded, still lost in thought.

"By the way," Janelle added, "you look different today. What happened?"

He snapped out of his reverie, and looked at her.

"I called Brittany last night."

Not what she expected to hear.

"You did?"

"I did."

He smiled.

"Well?"

She did like Brittany, and she wanted Tom to be happy. He said, "She said you were nice."

Janelle smiled.

"I doubt that's all she said."

"She said she missed seeing me when she was here."

Pause.

"And…?"

"She's going to come back. This weekend."

Suddenly, Janelle understood more than she knew she could. Brittany had been scared the first time, scared of doing something that wouldn't be good for them both. But she still wanted Tom. She didn't know if it would work this time, but she wanted to try, because she wanted him.

"That's quick."

He was obviously excited, and Janelle tried to match her tone of voice to his excitement.

"I know! She wants to spend the whole weekend with me, just getting to know me again."

Janelle noted the hint of distress underneath his excitement.

"What about everything she did to you?"

He had prepared her drink, and was playing with the mug on the counter, which was becoming a habit.

"Well, sometimes it's not so hard to forgive and forget. And maybe she'll tell me the reason now."

It sounded like he'd rehearsed it in the mirror.

"Maybe."

Her words fell feebly on the counter, and she looked at him. He didn't realize how much people loved him. He thought his was the only life he influenced. She thought about all the ways she could tell him he mattered to everyone, but nothing seemed suitable for the moment. Time passed, as each stood there thinking. Finally, he gently pushed her drink across the counter and she asked,

"When is she coming?"

"Friday night."

"Where is she going to stay?"

"She said she booked a hotel."

Janelle thought about offering her house, but she didn't have any extra sleeping space, and she didn't have an extra key.

"Well, let me know if you need anything from me. You know, like if you run out of food and need to feed her peanut butter and jelly. I do that. I'm good at that."

They both laughed, and she picked up her latte and tasted it.

"Hmm. It's good."

He nodded.

"It is. I'm glad you like it."

She smiled and said,

"Thanks." She walked over to her special chair and her book.

Janelle spent a considerable amount of time during the next few days thinking about Brittany. She would be a good fit for Tom— confident, kind, classy. But if they worked out, he would probably move to Texas to be with her. He would leave. Her first real friend here, and he would be gone. Janelle sighed often as she read, while she brought orders out at Francie's, and while she sat at home in her one stuffed chair, playing with Mike the hedgehog. Everything in life she ever cared about or wanted, she either lost or wasn't allowed to have.

CHAPTER THIRTEEN

Tom whistled the week away. Brittany was coming to see him. He cleaned his apartment feverishly, preparing for her, making it nice. He thought of his favorite places that he could take her. He had, in his excitement, forgotten that he didn't know why she was coming, and forgotten that she had thrown a wrench into his life plans. All he could think about was a pile of clouds with a castle atop.

Friday came, and Friday morning at work, Janelle didn't come in. He didn't think of it till he was wiping his hands on the towel as he got ready to leave.

"Hey, Jennifer, if you think of it, text me if Janelle doesn't come in today."

"Janelle."

Pause.

"She's the little blonde one, right?"

He nodded.

"Yes, that's her."

"Alright. I'll let you know."

She saluted him, and he grabbed his bag off the hook in the back and swung it over his shoulder as he whistled his way out. Brittany's flight came in at 6. He was planning a casual dinner out, then he would drop her off at her hotel for the night. He had time to go home, shower and shave, and do some last minute tidying before leaving to pick Brittany up.

He got to the airport early, parked, and went inside to wait. At 6, he started getting nervous, and by 6:15 he was working hard not to pace back and forth. A few minutes later, she appeared, carrying a leather tote. A girl would have noticed her perfect appearance: every hair in place, impossibly unwrinkled clothes and dauntingly pointed high heels, and masterfully applied makeup. Tom just noticed that she was there, and she was smiling at him like she was glad to see him. The last time he'd seen her, she was laughing with her friends as he walked past with his belongings that he had been picking up from school when he didn't return for the spring semester. Now he walked hurriedly up to her, as if she would change her mind and turn to leave. When he got close enough for contact, he reached out a hand, but she opened her arms for a hug. He hugged her quickly, then stepped back. She smelled the same as she used to. She looked him up and down and noted his plaid flannel, worn jeans, and scuffed leather loafers.

"Brittany! It's so good to see you again!"

"Hello, Tom! It's nice to see you too. Some things never change, I see."

Motioning toward his clothes.

"What? Oh."

Laughed nervously.

"I guess not. I like my clothes."

She smiled, then said,

"Well, I checked a bag. You know me, I had to bring my whole closet for a weekend."

Her turn to laugh nervously, and he laughed along with her, trying to help her feel comfortable.

"You never know when you might need a change of clothes."

He pushed his hands into his pockets.

"Did they tell you which baggage claim?"

"Six, I think."

They got her bag, a full-sized piece of luggage. Tom wondered what it was like to be a woman, so dependent on so many items. There weren't too many awkward lulls, as she caught Tom up on her life, and chattered about the flight and the food and the lady sitting next to her who fell asleep with her mouth open and drooled on her book. Brittany had a way of posing things with a certain amount of irony that always struck Tom as funny. Sometimes it had bothered her, because when she was upset about something he would laugh. When they were dating, he'd learned to keep his thoughts to himself until later. He wheeled her bag into the parking lot, and when she saw Whit, parked faithfully at the far end of the lot, Brittany exclaimed,

"Wow, you still have this old thing!?"

"Yes, I do. He's working quite faithfully for me. Most of the time, at least."

"How nice."

He put her suitcase in the back, and opened the door for her.

"I was thinking we could stop somewhere and eat some dinner, then if you wanted to see my apartment we could swing by, or if you're tired I could bring you to straight to your hotel."

"Dinner sounds great."

"Alright. There's this cute little place called Francie's—oh, you've been there! Does that sound good, or do you want something quicker?"

"That's great."

She was just like he remembered her, but older. Kind and unassuming, and pleasant. They didn't talk about anything serious at dinner, just work and other light things. Because she'd grown up with his family, Brittany knew them all and liked them, and took an interest in them. Dinner over, he asked her what she wanted to do.

"It's getting a little late for me. Bring me to my hotel? I'll see your apartment tomorrow."

He obliged, then carried her luggage up to her room for her. As he set her bags down on the floor near the wall, she sat on the bed and slipped her heels off.

"Thanks, Tom. It's nice to be here."

"It's nice to have you. Thanks for coming."

She stood to give him a hug, and as she did he remembered how she was always the perfect height to fit right under his chin. Just like she was made for it. The steady hurt that had started pressing on his heart as soon as he'd seen her became heavier. He sighed, but she didn't notice, instead saying,

"I'll call you tomorrow morning when I wake up."

She had always slept later than he had.

"That's fine, I'll come get you whenever you're ready."

"Have a good night."

"Thanks—you too."

Tom's heart was a fumbled mixture of sadness and delight as he left the hotel. He was delighted that she was here with him, but felt strongly the reminder that she hadn't wanted him. When he'd called, she had seemed eager to see him, but she hadn't really referenced their past. He wondered how long he should leave it that way.

He didn't check his phone till he got home, and when he did there was a text from Jennifer. Janelle hadn't come to The Cup all day. Tom frowned when he read it, and looked at his watch. It was 9:30, and she was probably still working. He could go check on her and make sure she was fine. He hushed his conscience. She was probably fine. He crawled into bed grinning, and fell asleep promptly, sleeping well for the first time in quite a while.

When Brittany called him for a ride the next morning, Tom had been awake for two hours already, pacing about his apartment waiting for her. He hung up the phone and was at his car seconds later. She looked fresh and classy, but he didn't notice. He just noticed that she was beautiful, waiting for him outside the hotel, and she smiled when he pulled up.

"Good morning! Your chariot awaits!"

He didn't hear her sigh. She had always told him Whit was going to die one day when they were in dire straits of need, and leave them in the lurch. He'd always laughed it off.

"Thanks for coming to pick me up."

"Always, ma'am."

They drove back to his house, and he parked in the driveway and led her inside.

"It's small, but at least it's neat. I cleaned it a lot for you. Welcome!"

She walked around, stopped in the middle of the living room, and turned about looking at everything. Tom noticed the imperfections, that there was dust on his bookshelf and that the rug on the floor was crooked. She smiled.

"It's quaint. I love it."

She looked at the small kitchen, raising her eyebrows at the bare counters and running her finger along the refrigerator handle. She had stopped cleaning her own house when she got a good job, and now a woman came and cleaned it for her once a week. She liked things to be clean, and for a man, this was impressive. Tom began apologetically,

"I know it's not much, but it is home. I like it. I don't spend much time here, because I'm always at work."

She looked at the framed picture on his kitchen counter. Mary had sent it to him for his birthday the year before. It was the two of them at her college graduation. Tom had been a freshman in high school, and he had braces and a chubby face.

"It's cute. I remember you like that. You've certainly grown up quite a bit."

She paused, frowning slightly, then said,

"Now, I'm starving. What's for breakfast?"

"Well, I can make eggs and bacon and toast."

She didn't make breakfast for herself very often; her life was too busy.

"That sounds delicious."

"Perfect. And orange juice?"

She nodded. She'd always liked it, and he'd bought it special for her coming. Opening all the appropriate packages and pulling out the frying pans, he stood, spatula in hand, scrutinizing his bacon and eggs. The words came unbidden to his mouth.

"What are you really doing here?"

He said it before he realized he was saying it. It sounded more abrupt than he had intended.

"Visiting you, of course!"

She grinned, passing off the question as a joke. Now that he'd voiced his thoughts, he wasn't quick to let them go.

"The last time we were together I didn't expect that you would ever want to see me again."

She shrugged, still treating it like nothing had happened.

"Well, turns out, I did."

She fidgeted at the counter and started playing with the silver ring on her right hand. He served the eggs and toast and poured juice for them, then motioned to one of two chairs at his tiny table.

"You can sit here."

"Thanks."

He moved to pick up his fork, and she said,

"Shall we pray?"

He had stopped praying for his food a long time ago. There didn't seem to be a point—it's not like it came dropping out of heaven. But he nodded, saying,

"Sure."

He bowed his head and, hands folded in his lap, thanked God for their food and Brittany's safe trip. Finished, he looked up at her.

"I'm glad you're here."

She smiled gently, with the air of a woman who has just been complimented on her most subtle finery.

"Thanks. Me too."

She took a bite of eggs and put her fork down.

"I missed you. I've been talking to a lot of people, and thinking about my life, and the best times were with you. You brought me life and excitement, and full color. I want that again."

She paused, and reached her hand across the table.

"I want you back in my life."

Her brown eyes were sincere. She added,

"But I don't want to spoil breakfast. So let's talk about it later." She set in on her eggs, neatly piling each bite on her fork before lifting it to her mouth.

He couldn't think of anything to say, so he took a contemplative bite of his bacon. It all sounded good. She was everything that he'd always wanted and more. But in the back of his mind an insistent whisper reminded him that she had broken his heart. Flipped his life over and ruined it. Dramatically, but not permanently. He wanted to know why she hadn't wanted him the first time, but the pain, the sleepless nights, the tears, all fell by the wayside as he thought about what it would feel like for someone to want him again. She watched him closely, waiting for his answer. He took another bite of bacon, and said,

"Well."

Was he supposed to tell her how much she'd hurt him? He didn't know if it would make a difference. He could try.

"You hurt me a lot."

She nodded.

"I know."

She looked down, saying,

"I'm sorry."

She sighed, and he said,

"Why? Why did you do it?"

Two questions he'd wanted to ask her for years.

"I don't know, really. I was scared. Scared that I was going to marry you because everyone expected it. Scared that we would grow old together and never actually know each other. Scared that we didn't belong together. I knew how much I was going to hurt you by ending it, but I was more terrified of ruining your life by marrying you."

It came out in a torrent of words, like she'd rehearsed it dozens of times in her mind.

"But I've done a lot of thinking, and maybe I was all wrong. No assurances, but I thought maybe we could give it a second try."

She looked at him, hopefully, adding,

"Give us a second chance."

"Oh."

He nodded slowly. It was renewing all the hurt he'd felt, but he perceived, as she clutched her fork nervously, that she had also been hurt.

"I've missed you, Tom. You always treated me better than anyone else."

He didn't say anything, and she eventually reached for the butter and jam, and spread them on her toast, took a few bites, shifted in her chair, cleared her throat, and said,

"What do you think?"

Her eyes were eager, her face turned toward him intently. She gripped her fork in one hand, and toast in the other. She wanted him. It drummed through his brain again and again. Wanted. Important. Wanted. He didn't think long about what it would mean for his life to date her. Gone was the pain she'd caused him. Absent from his mind were the warning tones of his family, the look on Janelle's face, or Mike's raised eyebrows if he knew the whole story. He thought about being wanted.

"Well."

He paused, and she waited on edge. Although it sounded perfect, he couldn't instantly re-attach himself to her. He needed to think about it.

"Let me think about it?"

She nodded, then said,

"That's fair."

Pause.

"How long?"

He laughed.

"We'll see."

Silence. She took another bite of toast. He changed the subject, and asked her more about her job. Her face lit up. Fashion had always been her passion—now, working for a small clothing boutique she was always in the middle of it.

The rest of the day, they wandered the city, Tom showing her all his favorite places, and even exploring parts of town he'd never been before. They got hot dogs from a street vendor, and went to Tom's favorite park. The more he talked to her, the more he realized how lonely she was. She lived alone in Texas, far away from her family and friends. She was a successful businesswoman, but she worked a lot and didn't have time to invest in people. And she'd always been more of an introvert. She worked and went to the gym, and spent her spare time at home. Without realizing it, he began to pity her. Her life was sad, and though she worked to make the best of it with an optimistic attitude, she was unhappy. When she said that the last time she could remember being truly delighted was when she had been with him years before, he stopped mid-step and looked at her.

"No, don't look at me like that. It's true. My life isn't bad. I just don't have a lot in it to make me happy. Sometimes it's a little lonely."

He sighed. They ate dinner together at his apartment, ravioli and creamed corn and rolls. When they finished, he said,

"Do you want ice cream?"

He loved ice cream, but in the past he'd had to convince her it was worth eating. She counted her calories.

"I suppose being here with you is a good reason."

She was stacking his plate on hers, standing to carry them over to the sink. Without thinking, he moved away from the freezer next to her at the table, and said,

"Well, let me give you an even better reason."

He placed the ice cream scoop on the table, put his hands on her waist, and kissed her, slowly, gently, kindly. Stunned at first, she didn't react, but when she realized what was happening, she kissed him back. Then he straightened, and said,

"I think I'd like you to be part of my life again."

She nodded, grinning, and said,

"I think I'd like that."

He gathered her into his arms, and they stood, mutual delight surrounding them. He couldn't grasp the delight that someone wanted him. He was wanted. She saw an end to her loneliness, and couldn't imagine a better reason. Nothing noteworthy for the reader happened the rest of the evening, and as he drove back from dropping her off at his hotel, Tom felt like he might actually be luminescent. She wanted him again. He bounced into his house, and flopped face up on his bed, and stared at the ceiling for a long time before going to sleep. He wasn't alone anymore. Someone cared again. He fell asleep grinning, shoes on and phone unheeded.

CHAPTER FOURTEEN

Janelle didn't go into The Cup on Friday, because even though Brittany was nice, she was afraid that everything would change, and she didn't want to see Tom. She knew it was petty, but in her denial she thought maybe if she ignored him, nothing would happen between Brittany and him. Friday night at work, she was distracted, and more than once, Francie said,

"What is it, girl? You have your head somewhere besides my diner."

Every time, Janelle sighed and replied,

"Oh, Francie. It's nothing, really."

She worked late, and went home and straight to bed. She slept fitfully, dreaming. She dreamt she had gone into The Cup to read, as usual, but even though she went in the morning when it was usually so peaceful, every seat was full. As she looked around, she realized that every chair was occupied by the same person, someone she didn't recognize. She walked to the counter and Tom was there, but it seemed like he couldn't hear her. Every time she spoke he ignored her, instead motioning at the shop full of people. Janelle turned to look, and realized that every person was Brittany. When she turned around, Tom was gone. She woke up groaning.

On Saturday Janelle wandered around her tiny apartment, stir crazy. After making herself take a walk to kill time, she went to work. On the way to Francie's, her car started making a scraping noise. She sighed, thought about scheduling an appointment for it at a shop, and then completely forgot about it. Saturday nights were always busy. Mike was having another business meeting, and there were two separate birthday celebrations going on, cake and balloons and many people at each. Janelle wondered why Mike always scheduled his big meetings on the weekends, but it didn't matter much to her. He always tipped her well. And he was kind. His was the usually last group in the restaurant, and tonight when they left she hurried to clean their table and wash their dishes, so she could leave.

Less than half-way home, Janelle's car started shaking. It was dark, but it looked like maybe smoke was coming from under the hood. She pulled over, got out, and opened the hood. It was smoking. The chill of late fall penetrated her light jacket, and she stood there staring at her engine wondering what to do. She knew nothing about cars. A car drove past, but it was going fast and she didn't know if she wanted help from a stranger in the middle of the night. She left the hood open to let the car cool off, and sat down inside to keep warm. Thinking through her options, she decided to call Tom. He would willingly help her. He could be sleeping, but he might wake up to his phone. She called him, but he didn't answer, and after letting it ring through, she left a message.

"Hey, Tom, it's Janelle. My car died. I'm not sure what's wrong with it. But can you come help me if you wake up and get this? I'm not sure what I'm going to do. Okay, uh, well, thanks. Bye."

Resting her head on the steering wheel, she thought of her only other option. Mike would definitely still be awake. She didn't debate long. It was late, and it wasn't safe for her to sit in her broken car on the side of the road, so she called Mike. He picked up on the second ring.

"Hey, Janelle. Is everything okay?"

"Hi Mike, I'm really sorry to bother you. I'm on my way home, but my car started shaking and smoking. I'm on the side of the road now, and I don't know what to do."

He didn't hesitate.

"Where are you?"

"I'm on the long stretch on Harvest, past the grocery store but before the big memory tree."

"I'll be there in fifteen minutes. Stay in your car and lock the doors."

Janelle hung up. Mike hadn't paused. He was coming to help her. Her dad had never gone out of his way to do anything for her. If her car had died in New York, she wouldn't even have called him. Mike was there in less than fifteen minutes. He looked in her hood for a while, said,

"Hmmmm."

Looking at her, he said,

"I'll call a tow truck in the morning. Do you have anything valuable in it?"

She laughed.

"Not unless you call cracked leather seats and broken windshield wipers valuable."

"Hop in my car and I'll give you a ride home."

"Thank you so much, Mike."

"Not a problem at all. I'm glad to help."

They were silent in the car, Janelle tired from her day, and Mike preoccupied about his meeting. Eventually, Mike broke the silence.

"Tom didn't work this morning. He usually works Saturdays."

"Brittany came back to see him."

"Oh. Who is she, anyway?"

Janelle sighed.

"They grew up together. Dated for a long time, years, I think. He proposed, and she said no and broke up with him. So he dropped out of college, and eventually came here."

Mike nodded.

"That's rough."

"He told me he was a mess for a while."

"I would have been."

Mike paused.

"What does she want with him now?"

147

Janelle rubbed her hand on her pants.

"I don't know. She was here last weekend and didn't tell me anything. I don't want to jump to wild conclusions—"

She paused. Was it a wild conclusion to assume Brittany would want Tom back? It was crazy to think he would want her back, but he had seemed so excited that she was coming to see him. She continued,

"—but, maybe she wants him back."

"Do you think he'd take her?"

"I don't know."

"She looked at him, then added, "You're a man. You might be able to answer that better than I would."

"I guess it depends. On how much time he spent fantasizing about the relationship. And how lonely he is. And how badly she wants him, if she does. He might take her back. He probably shouldn't—she sounds risky."

"I agree."

They sat in silence, then Janelle added,

"We'll just have to wait and see."

They had pulled into her driveway.

"Thank you so much, Mike. I appreciate you."

"Anytime, Janelle. I'll get your car to a shop tomorrow."

She knew even if she protested, he wouldn't listen.

"Thank you. You're a blessing."

"It's a pleasure to help you."

She closed her door and was walking to her house when he yelled out of his window.

"Wait! Do you work tomorrow? Will you need a ride?"

"Sunday is my day off this week—I'll lay low. If it's still not better by Monday I'll figure something out."

He eyed her.

"I'll be calling you. Take care."

"Thanks, Mike."

* * *

Brittany's flight left late Sunday night, so Tom and Brittany spent the morning relaxing. She had important meetings and shows the next few weekends, so she wouldn't be able to come see him, and he didn't have the money to fly to visit her. They were just beginning to talk about their relationship when he got several texts, all in a row. His phone was on the counter by his keys where he'd left it the night before, but he got up to check all the buzzing. The texts were from his coworker Jennifer, asking him to cover her shift on Monday. He saw then that he had a voicemail from the night before. It was from Janelle. Janelle had never called him before.

"Who was that text from?"

Brittany didn't like phones very much. More accurately, she didn't like it when he spent time on his phone around her. He said,

"Hold on. I got a voicemail that I should probably listen to."

He put the phone to his ear without waiting for her consent, and she sighed and examined her nails closely. His face fell as he listened to the message.

"What, what is it? What happened?"

She wasn't very patient.

"I have to call Janelle real quick."

"Janelle? Why?"

"Her car broke down last night and she called me for help and I didn't get it or help her."

Her tone completely changing, Brittany said,

"Oh! Is she okay?"

He shook his head, phone to his ear. Janelle answered on the second ring.

"Hey, Tom."

"Janelle, I'm so sorry I missed your call last night. Are you okay?"

"Yeah, Mike came and helped me."

She sounded sad.

"Oh. Good. Is your car alright?"

"It's at the shop now."

If Brittany hadn't come, he would probably be fixing it for her right now.

"Do you work today?"

Brittany tapped her foot behind him.

"No, it's my day off. I work tomorrow though."

"Okay. If your car isn't fixed, you can call me and I'll give you a ride."

"Thanks, Tom. Is Brittany still there?"

There was a note of silence in her voice.

"Yes, she is. She's leaving tonight."

"Okay good. Well, I'll see you tomorrow. I guess I won't be coming to The Cup if my car is broken."

"Call me if you need anything."

"Okay. Thanks, Tom."

As soon as he hung up, Brittany said,

"Is she okay?"

He nodded. She said,

"Okay, good. I want you all to myself."

He raised his eyebrows and she grinned.

When he dropped her off at the airport, she kissed him, then said,

"I'm glad you're going to be part of my life. You're very special to me."

Then she turned and walked off. He smiled as he waved at her back. His smile would have faded if he'd seen her wink at the security guard as she walked past.

He went home in a trance. Brittany wanted him again. Nothing else mattered. He didn't think about Janelle, or Mike, just Brittany. That night he dreamt that he was at work, and every customer looked like Brittany. Soon the cafe was full of Brittany, drinking coffee and chatting away or looking at papers. Janelle came in after a long time, but when she tried to talk he couldn't hear her. When every version of Brittany saw Janelle, they all stood and started coming towards her. She ran out. Tom woke up with his hands clenched into fists, powerless behind the bar to do anything but stand and watch.

Monday morning at The Cup was moving slowly, until Mike came in holding a newspaper. That was unusual, but Tom didn't think anything of it till he got a good look at Mike's face. It was gray. And frozen, not with cold, but with shocked emotion.

"Mike, what's the matter?"

John had turned to look as well. The friendships between Tom and his customers fascinated John and most of the time he observed like he was watching zoo animals. Mike opened his mouth to speak but no noise came out. He cleared his throat, then forced out two words.

"My wife."

His wife. Mike's wife. Dread filled the pit of Tom's stomach.

"Your wife?"

Tom hoped against hope Mike hadn't found out.

"She got remarried."

"Oh, Mike."

Mike stood there like a child in trouble, looking down at his toes and letting his shoulders slump. The tears came gradually, first a faint hiccup, then a few more gasps, then a full progression of heaving sobs. Tom walked out from behind the counter, and led Mike to a chair. Tom had never seen a grown man cry so hard. Mike clutched the newspaper in his sweaty palms, working it back and forth as he cried. Before long the paper was damped and wrinkled, and Mike's hands were blackened with ink.

"Mike."

Mike's sobs subsided and he cried in silence, between gasps for air. Tom sat next to him. Mike didn't need anyone to pat his back or rub his shoulders. He didn't want it, really. If he wanted to, Mike could talk later. Tom guessed, based on the 'Marriages' headline in the newspaper, that someone had either pointed it out to him, or he'd found it on his own. Tom got a box of tissues, put them in front of Mike, then went back behind the counter and helped John do drinks. The morning rush was beginning. None of the customers seemed distressed by the crying man, although they cast looks of pity at him. It was The Cup—something different was always happening at The Cup. Eventually his tears slowed, and he wiped his face with a tissue. The tears streaming down his face had made a wet spot on the front of his white shirt, and stained his striped pink tie a shade darker. He threw the newspaper down, saying,

"It was all my fault. If I had worked less, if I had paid more attention to her, and listened to her when she asked me to spend time with her, it wouldn't have happened."

Tom moved from behind the counter and came over to him as Mike continued.

"This new guy is probably way better than me. He never works late, never has meetings on the weekend, and never takes business trips. I'm a failure as a person. I'll never succeed at anything in life."

I'm a failure as a person. The words rang through Tom's mind. Mike was always confident. He was always well dressed, always sure of himself, and had a better job than most of the people Tom knew. He was competent and capable, socially suave (besides his perpetual rocking) and comfortable in every situation. And he thought he was a failure as a person. Tom said,

"No, Mike, you're not."

Paused.

"You're not a failure."

"I am. Michaela left me. She was my life. She didn't think I was worth staying with. I'm not. I'm not worth anything. She loved better than anyone else, and she wasn't able to love me. I don't matter. I'll never matter. I'm worthless."

"No one is worthless, Mike. You are not worthless."

Mike squared his shoulders.

"She was all I ever wanted in my life, and I didn't get to keep her."

This brought on a stream of fresh tears, but now they were silent. The string of customers had slowed down, and Tom asked John to make some apple cinnamon tea. Phil Kohle said it was a comfort drink, and kept it stocked for the occasional disconsolate. John brewed a cup and brought it out to Mike. Drinking it calmed him down, and his face became less gray. The tears, the expression of his broken heart, had a calming influence on him, and he sighed.

"Thanks, Tom."

Tom nodded. Countless times Tim had just sat with him while he cried. Eventually, when he'd stopped crying all the time, Tim told him he'd gone through 21 boxes of tissues. They had a good laugh over it, tempered by Tom's pain.

"You're welcome. Are you going to work?"

Mike nodded.

"It'll preoccupy me. I think I'll sit here for a while though."

Tom nodded.

"I'll give you some coffee when you're ready to go, and you can start your day off just like normal, but a little later."

It was Mike's turn to nod. It was already 8.

* * *

Mike had called the shop about her car Sunday afternoon, and told Janelle it would be fixed by Tuesday. She decided to wait till Monday morning to call Tom, because when she'd been talking to him she thought she'd heard Brittany in the background. On Monday morning she called The Cup. Tom answered.

"Hello, this is The Cup, Tom speaking. How can I help you?"

"Hey, Tom. It's Janelle."

"Oh, hi Janelle! How are you? How's your car?"

He always sounded excited to hear from her.

"I'm doing well. My car is still in the shop, Mike said it would be done tomorrow morning before work."

"Oh, good, I'm glad to hear that."

She paused, then gathered her courage and said,

"Can I have a ride to work this afternoon?"

"What time do you need to be there?"

"Three. If it's too much trouble you really don't need to, I'll find another way."

She could almost hear him shaking his head.

"No, that's fine. I get off at 2, so I can come right over."

"Are you sure it's not too much?"

"Not at all. I look forward to it."

"Okay. Thank you so much, Tom!"

"No problem. I'll see you around 2:20."

At 2:15, Janelle put on her coat and went out to wait on the front steps. Fall was almost over, the serious chill of winter was swiftly approaching. When Tom arrived, he got out of the car to open her door, saying,

"I'm sorry I didn't come help you on Saturday night."

"It's okay. Mike came."

Tom nodded, and said,

"I brought this for you, since you couldn't get it this morning."

He handed her a drink. She took it gratefully, saying,

"Thank you! I appreciate that."

"Anything for a friend. Hey, have you heard from Mike today?"

"No, I haven't. Why?"

Tom recounted in full detail everything that had happened that morning. She said,

"Wow. Francie said that if he found out he would be a mess, but somehow I guess I hoped she was wrong."

Tom replied,

"Nope. She was right. Very right. He was a mess. I think he cried for at least an hour."

"Poor Mike. Always doing the nice thing for everyone else, but he has all kinds of sadness himself. And you would never know, looking at him."

"He's devastated, even so many years later." Janelle nodded, and said,

"It must never really get all the way better, does it?"

"I don't think so."

Each was lost in his own world for some time, until Janelle broke the silence.

"How was it to have Brittany here?"

He smiled.

"It was really good. We hung out and walked around and saw all the sights."

Silence. She looked out of her window at the cheery blue sky and the red and orange and yellow leaves shaking happily in the wind. Everything outside the car was happy. She should be happy too, but she was leery of the note of delight in Tom's voice. She liked Brittany, but she didn't want Tom's heart to be broken again. He said,

"Maybe next time she comes back the three of us can hang out!"

Janelle involuntarily raised her eyebrows, but he was paying attention to a cat on the side of the road and didn't see her face. Instead of voicing her thoughts, she said,

"Sounds nice."

He added,

"She's just as wonderful as I always remember her being."

Janelle wanted to tell him to be careful.

"Tom..."

"What?"

She carefully chose her next words, but couldn't finish.

"I think... Never mind. That's fun. I'm glad you had such a good time."

"Thanks, Janelle! She's great."

Conversation wandered for the last few minutes of the drive, and when they got to Francie's, Tom asked,

"When do you usually get off?"

"I'm not sure, it's always a little different. It's usually between 11 and 12 on weeknights."

"Alright. Well, call me when you think quitting time is twenty minutes away, and I'll come get you."

"Thanks, Tom. I appreciate you a lot."

"Anytime. I'm here for you."

She walked into the restaurant, happy to have such a friend, but sad that now his focus would be on someone else.

CHAPTER FIFTEEN

Tom called Mary while he was driving home from Francie's. She picked up on the third ring, but didn't say anything.

"Hey, Mary?"

"Shhhh."

Tom waited. Sometimes she did things like this when he called her. She was usually in a meeting. After a minute or two, she spoke.

"Hey Tom! I'm watching birds on my back porch because I'm not allowed to go to work yet. There was a beautiful cardinal eating from the feeder. He just flew away."

She paused, and he imagined her straining her neck to watch the bird depart. Then she added,

"How are you?"

"No, me first. How are you? How's your head? And your arms and legs?"

It had been a week since he left.

"You've taken up birdwatching?"

"I know, I know. It's a little bit crazy. I just get so bored. I want to be doing something. All I did last week was lay in bed. After two days I was so tired of doing nothing I could barely see straight."

He laughed.

"That's true, the stationary lifestyle was never really for you."

"No. Not really. But how are you?"

He grinned even though she couldn't see him, and said,

"I'm good. Just brought Janelle to work—her car broke down this weekend."

"Aww, good job buddy. How is she?"

"Oh, she's fine, very good. Actually…"

He paused. He always remembered her distaste for Brittany after she had ended their relationship.

"Actually, Brittany came to see me this weekend."

She took a while to respond, finally saying,

"Oh, really?"

"Yes, she did. And we had a great time."

He didn't want to have to defend this to Mary—he wanted her to be excited for him.

"Wow, Tom! That's great."

She sounded half excited. He tried to make it better.

"She came to see me while I was in Idaho, but obviously I wasn't here. When I got back we talked, and she asked if she could come back. So she came for the weekend and we did all kinds of things together and had some good conversations and a wonderful time."

She was still silent.

"I think she cares about me, Mary."

Mary sighed. She knew Brittany. She'd known her for years, most of Brittany's life, and she'd always scrutinized her closely because everyone made a fuss about Brittany and Tom. She knew Brittany was a good girl, but she didn't always know what she wanted, which had gotten her into trouble frequently.

"I hope so, Tom. Thanks for calling to let me know!"

She tried to say more but it didn't come out. Tom said,

"I wanted to tell you because I knew you would want to know. I knew you would be excited. I'm so excited."

"Thanks, Tom."

Her voice quivered, so faintly it was barely noticeable.

"Be careful, okay? Don't wear too much of your heart on your sleeve."

"Thanks, Mary. I'll call again soon. You take care of yourself, okay? Happy bird watching."

He could hear the grin in her voice as she said,

"Bye, Little T. Love you."

"Love you too."

That night, Tom called Brittany after dinner. She didn't pick up, but texted him and told him she was exercising and she'd call him later. She did call him later, several hours later. He had gotten tired of sitting up waiting, and was in bed, drifting off to sleep, when his phone rang.

"Hi Brittany."

He tried not to sound like he had just woken up.

"Hi Tom, sorry it took me so long to call you back. I was working out, then I had to take a shower, then one of my girlfriends called me, then I needed to do some stuff around the apartment. How are you?"

"Fine, fine. How are you?"

They talked of their respective days for a while, then Brittany asked if anything else interesting happened. Tom thought of Mike.

"Mike came in this morning. He was a mess. You didn't meet him, right?"

Brittany replied that she had not, and Tom continued, telling her the whole story, from his wife leaving him, to Francie's haircut and Mike's tears. Brittany listened quietly, and when he finished, said,

"Sounds like an emotional morning."

Tom nodded, realized she couldn't see him, then said,

"Yes. It was sad."

Brittany was silent for a moment, then said,

"It doesn't make sense, though."

"What?"

It all made sense to Tom.

"Why does he still like her so much? He should have moved on. She was done with him, he could have at least repaid the favor."

"I don't think that's exactly how it works, Brittany."

He paused, then continued,

"It's not very easy to just turn off your heart to someone, especially when you've loved them so much."

For the second time that day he thought about the 21 boxes of tissues. She said,

"Maybe, but it seems a little overdone. I'm sure you weren't that upset when I broke up with you, were you?"

She said it with very little feeling, but he wondered if it was a play, or mere curiosity. He nodded vigorously, realized she couldn't see him, and said softly,

"Actually, I was quite upset."

He paused, less for dramatic effect than to push down the lump in his throat, then said,

"I cried a lot."

She didn't say anything. He added,

"I cried through 21 boxes of tissues. I loved you."

Her silence continued, and he sat there, his heart twisting from the pain. When she spoke, all she said was,

"Oh."

Then a pause, then,

"I didn't realize. I'm sorry."

It didn't make up for the months of sadness that he'd lived through, but it was nice to hear her apologize. He listened to her breathe. Eventually she spoke again, saying,

"I guess it was kind of cruel."

He didn't respond, and she fumbled about for more to say. He tried to tell her it was alright, but even rehearsing it in his head sounded insincere. After a moment more of silence, Brittany said,

"Well, thanks for talking. I should go to bed."

Tom wanted her to keep talking to him, to keep her on the phone so he could hear what she'd been thinking, but he couldn't muster the words to stop her. Instead, he said,

"Yeah, thanks for talking. Miss you. Bye."

He sighed, and closed his eyes again. In his mind he saw Brittany, standing, shrugging, unable to believe that he'd formed such a deep attachment to her in so short a time. He sighed and rolled over, resigned being awake and sad late into the night.

* * *

As the weeks passed at The Cup, Tom grew more and more distant. Though he worked the same hours, he talked to Brittany most nights and she came to visit him most weekends. It was wonderful, almost. There seemed to be some disconnect between them, but Tom couldn't figure out what it was. Their relationship drained him, until even the prospect of her visits seemed like less of a pleasure and more of a responsibility. He was less rested, and became impatient at everything. She took his time, his attention, and what little money he was working hard to save. Although she was always happy to see him and be with him, he always sensed some undercurrent of motive, that she wasn't telling him the truth. She never seemed quite settled in their relationship, like she was just testing it out.

Work continued predictably for Janelle, except that her car didn't break down on the way home in the middle of the night anymore. Mike's mechanic had fixed it beautifully, and Mike told her to call him if anything ever happened again. Mike was still sad, but he didn't seem as miserable as he had been when he first learned about Michaela's marriage. He just didn't bounce around as much when he came into The Cup to get his morning coffee. He worked all the time, even more than he had before the news, and helped Tom and Janelle every time they needed anything. Sherry Donahue still came into The Cup every morning and pestered Tom, and Mr. Peterson still talked just as much. Tom was more distracted, and everyone around him noticed, but no one said anything. They figured it was the new excitement of dating. No one thought the dark circles under his eyes indicated pain.

Two months passed. Thanksgiving was over, and Christmas was a week away. There was frost on the ground in the mornings. A few times it snowed, but nothing accumulated. Tom rode his bike to work some days, but in the beginning of December, after a few weeks of his toes taking most of the day to warm up, he started driving.

Everything had been static for a while. Brittany was keeping track of him (as Mike put it), Janelle was planning on staying for the holidays (she didn't want to go home, as she told everyone who asked) and Mike had settled back into bachelor life, content, if sad and lonely. Thursday morning of the week before Christmas, Tom was cleaning the counters when Janelle came in. She didn't come in as often as she'd used to, but Tom was always glad to see her when she did.

"Hi, Janelle! How are you? It's been a few days since you've been here!"

She smiled faintly.

"I've been busy. I took up knitting so I could make presents because I thought it would be cheap but then yarn was expensive so I stopped, and now I've been painting presents instead."

"Wow. That's talent."

"Don't say that, you haven't seen them."

They both laughed. After the joke, they both stood awkwardly. It had been weeks since they really talked. Tom broke the silence first.

"How are you doing? We don't talk much anymore."

"I'm fine. Christmas is a good season to be a waitress because everyone is busy so they eat out, and everyone is feeling generous so they leave big tips."

"Perfect. Is your car still working?"

"Yep. Ever since Mike had her fixed for me. No more midnight breakdowns."

"I'm glad to hear that."

She grinned.

"Me too."

She traced the wood grains across the counter with her fingers.

"How are you? How's Brittany?"

She sighed imperceptibly after the second question, but he was too busy being happy to notice.

"I'm doing great! We're doing pretty well. She's coming for almost a week for Christmas."

Janelle watched as the smallest flicker of weariness crossed his face.

"Wow, neat. That will be fun."

She said it without much conviction.

"It will be. Hey, what are you doing for Christmas? Are you going home?"

He hadn't talked to her much after he'd realized that home probably wasn't a happy place, because Brittany had reentered the scene and taken his attention.

"No, I'm not going home. That would be bad."

She didn't offer more information. It would have been his habit in the past to ask why, but he was too distracted now.

"Well, maybe the three of us can all get together and hang out! That would be fun!"

She wasn't sure she wanted that, but she said,

"That's an idea."

It was the best thing she had to say.

"Hey, do you see Mike often?"

Tom saw him in the mornings, but he didn't talk to him very much because he was always there during the early morning rush.

"I see him at Francie's. He seems to be doing alright. Still sad, but not as bad as he was when he first got the news. I think he'll be okay."

"I'm glad. I haven't talked to him recently."

"It's okay. I'm reading A Christmas Carol, and if I start right now I'll probably be able to finish it before work. It's been good to see you, Tom. Take care of yourself."

The emotional distance that had been there when they first met had slowly returned. He realized it, but didn't know why, and before he could spend time figuring it out, Mrs. Donahue came in.

"Hello, Tommy! Christmas is coming so soon! I love all the colors everywhere, the greens and reds and lights and ribbons. It's good for my soul."

He grinned.

162

"Good morning, Mrs. Donahue. You are right. Christmas is just around the corner. How are you today?"

"Quite well, quite well. I don't have time to stay and chat today, I'm on my way to the store to do some special Christmas shopping. I just want a drink. Something Christmas-y. Maybe Gingerbread, or peppermint or something."

"How about our Plum Pudding latte? It's a new favorite."

She squealed like a little girl.

"My great aunt used to make us plum pudding! I could never eat more than a few bites of it because it was so rich, but I loved it and I always wished it would last longer. How delicious! I want a large. The biggest cup you have."

He made it for her, and just as he finished pouring the steamed milk into the large cup, Mr. Peterson came walking through the doors. Tom had noticed that they always came in at the same time every day, usually within minutes of each other. He wondered if it was intentional.

"Well good morning, Tom son! How are you this fine day? It's beginning to look a lot like Christmas out! Ha Ha!! Did you see the snow on the ground this morning? There wasn't much, but there was a little! I love Christmas. I was just telling the neighbor boy today that if he wants to he can start shoveling my driveway. Which is funny, because there's never any snow on my driveway because it's heated. Ha Ha! Did that for the missus years ago so she wouldn't slip and fall down and break her hip or something. And now it's just wonderful because I never have to shovel it! So I'll let the neighbor boys do something else for me. Like clean the snow off of my roof. That will be a good use for their exuberance."

He was in rare form this morning, delighted and full of glee about something, Tom wondered what.

"Oh, Mr. P! You are a hoot. Those poor neighbor boys are probably heartbroken that their largest source of income is a farce. You are a case."

Mrs. Donahue cast a mock glare upon him.

"Oh, Sherry, please. It's good for them. Gives a little excitement to their lives. Makes them wonder what life really means."

Mrs. Donahue 'humphed'.

"I doubt that, Mr. P. I doubt that."

Tom held his coffee out over the counter and said,

"Here's your coffee, Mr. Peterson. You know how much it costs."

Mr. Peterson laughed as if it was the funniest thing he'd ever heard in his life.

"Oh, Mr. P. What is your problem? You are crazy."

"Oh, please, Sherry. I'm completely normal."

Tom smiled. The two of them together could never get along, but there were still friends. Mrs. Donahue rolled her eyes, as they walked from the counter together, her to her usual seat in the window where she could look at all the colors, and him to his large chair in the middle of the cafe. Tom watched them and wondered how long they'd known each other, and how many years they'd been coming to The Cup at the exact same time every morning. It could have been forever, the way they treated each other.

Soon his mind drifted to other things. It was Thursday. Christmas was next Thursday. Brittany was coming in on Monday, and staying till Sunday. It would be their first Christmas just the two of them. It used to be complicated because they had to split things between their families, and someone always ended up being disappointed. But this year, it would be different. Brittany would come just to be with him, and it would be the two of them together, and it would be a wonderful time. He had saved and saved and scraped together and was planning to buy her diamond earrings—3/4 carat studs. He was going to wrap a lot of big boxes up for her, but not put the diamonds inside, and instead put a set of the plastic dress up earrings his sisters had worn as little girls. Then when she was confused, he would give her the real diamonds and she would be delighted. It was all mapped out in his mind.

On his way home, he stopped at a local jewelers. There was a tall slim woman behind the counter, and several people wandered about looking in different cases. The woman nodded and smiled as he walked in, and came over to him. She spoke.

"Good afternoon sir, how may I help you?"

Tom cleared his throat. He'd never bought jewelry from a jeweler before.

"Hi."

He grinned noncommittally, then continued,

"I'm here to buy some earrings for my girlfriend."

She nodded, and said,

"Did you have something in particular in mind?"

He said,

"Yes, I was thinking I'd like to do diamond studs."

She motioned, saying,

"Just step over here and you'll see what we have to offer."

She led him to a case full of sparkle, and he looked down at the jewels, somewhat overwhelmed. As he looked down, she said,

"Is this for Christmas?"

He nodded, and she said,

"Ah. These are some of our most popular ones."

As she spoke, she pointed to a fancy pair of princess cut ¾ studs, and looked at him expectantly. They were perfect, very expensive, but perfect.

"May I look at them, please?"

She reached for them and pulled them out, putting the card on the counter for him to see. He bent over and looked at them closely. Light caught all the different facets, and they sparkled as if they were alive. After a moment's deliberation, he nodded, and said,

"I'll take these."

She looked at him, surprised.

"Do you want to look at anything else?"

He shook his head.

"No, these are perfect."

She smiled at his excitement, and said,

"Alright, come over here and I'll ring you up."

He walked out of the store with the diamonds nestled neatly in a black velvet box, feeling like the richest man in the world, although he had spent close to his last cent on the earrings. Brittany would think they were beautiful. He couldn't wait to see the look on her face.

CHAPTER SIXTEEN

Janelle had avoided Tom for several weeks, and even when she had seen him, he'd seemed distracted and didn't try to engage her in conversation. He seemed more tired, and less caring. The familiar warm light in his eyes that she had grown so used to was gone. He was no longer carefree and caring, now he seemed worn and unhappy. She thought maybe she was just imagining it, but when Mike had come in to Francie's early for a meeting last week and talked to her, he had agreed. Brittany was taking away Tom's delight. Talking to him at The Cup that morning had confirmed her suspicion. The next day, Friday, Janelle didn't feel quite right. Her throat was scratchy, and she hadn't eaten lunch because she felt nauseous. She kept needing to sit down, winded, and Francie commented several times about how she looked like she didn't feel well.

Mike came in alone a little later, and looked towards the back. He saw Janelle and grinned, and motioned for her to come out.

"Hey, Mike. Welcome to Francie's. Can I get you started with something to drink?"

He grinned.

"Hi Janelle. Water's fine for now. Maybe something more with my meal. How are you?"

She looked down at him wearily.

"You're looking not so great."

"Thanks Mike. That's a real confidence booster for a girl."

"Yeah, anytime. You look a little sick. Are you feeling okay?"

"Not really. But I'll be alright."

He scrutinized her face closely.

"Mhmm. Well, I didn't come to talk to you about your health. I came to ask you if you were going to be all alone on Christmas."

Janelle was already lonely thinking about her Christmas by herself. Even though her home life had been less than ideal, she'd always been surrounded by siblings who loved her and coworkers who took care of her.

"Well…"

She paused, uncomfortably, then decided to admit the truth.

"Well, yeah, I think so." His face lit up.

"Perfect! I mean, uh, not perfect. I'm sorry that you have no family here. Oh, dear. Sorry. Shouldn't have said that. Well, anyways. You know Sherry Donahue? Little old lady who's always excited about something? I think she goes to The Cup every day, you might have seen her there a time or two."

"Oh, yes, I've met her! She's wonderful."

Just then someone motioned for her, and she said,

"I'll be right back."

After filling more drink orders and bringing out a few plates of dessert, Janelle went back to Mike.

"Can I get you some dinner?"

"Yeah, I'll have the meatloaf and whatever. Lots of it. And a big dish of barbecue sauce. Maybe just bring out the whole bottle."

He grinned, delighted because, like most people, he thought his own jokes were the funniest.

"Right. I'll make sure we bring you enough."

"Anyways, Sherry Donahue. Every year when I've been alone, she's invited me over to her house for Christmas Eve and Christmas day. Most of her kids come home, and a bunch of her grandchildren. It's a wonderful time. She saw me and invited me yesterday, and told me if I saw you I need to invite you too. So, please come. I'd hate for you to be alone on Christmas. She even said you could stay at her house. She lives in a big old house right near Capitol Hill. She could probably fit an army into it. She'll let you stay for as long as you want."

Belonging. Janelle had always longed for a safe place to belong.

"Really? That's so nice of her! I would love to. That would be wonderful. You can tell her I will absolutely come."

"Perfect. I'll tell her you're coming and give her your phone number so she can call you."

"Thanks, Mike. Incidentally, how do you know her?"

"Church. She's always super nice to all of the new people, and when I first started going a year or two after Michaela left, she welcomed me like I was an old friend and still hasn't stopped reaching out. The Lord is good to make people like Sherry Donahue."

The owners of Janelle's restaurant in New York had been Christians. She'd gone to church with them a few times, but it had always irritated her father when he was sober, and made him irate when he was drunk. She'd liked the church—people had been kind to her. She didn't understand it. Mike watched her in silence as all these thoughts played across her mind. All she said was,

"Oh."

"So that's the deal. Come for Christmas. I don't want to keep you here if you should be serving. Francie will get on my case."

He laughed. Francie loved the small town feel her diner had, but she also valued efficiency, as she'd told Janelle when she hired her.

"I should get back to work. Thanks, Mike. I appreciate it."

"You're welcome. And take care, Janelle. Go home and sleep."

By the time she got home, Janelle felt awful. The insides of her eyelids were scratchy, and all she wanted to do was close them. She crawled into bed without changing out of her work clothes.

* * *

The weekend was a whirlwind, as Tom prepared for Brittany, and worked extra hours to make up for the time the shop would be closed.

Phil Kohle liked to give his employees enough time off, so The Cup would be closed Tuesday-Friday, so everyone was free for Christmas.

Tom cleaned his apartment from top to bottom, scrubbing most things twice. Then he decorated, putting up a tree and stringing Christmas lights. He put a wreath on the front door, and dug the old nativity set his mother had given him out of the back of the closet where'd he'd forgotten it. He bought a little Christmas welcome mat for in front of the door, and a cinnamon spice air freshener. Even when he cleaned thoroughly, Brittany told him his house smelled like man. He didn't want to take any chances. He didn't bake much, but Sunday night he made Christmas cookies and bought eggnog to serve with them. When he went to bed that night, he was convinced everything was perfect. He would work all day Monday, then pick Brittany up at the airport late that night.

His parents had been sad that he wasn't coming home for Christmas, but he told them he would come home for a weekend soon. When they found out he was dating Brittany again, they characteristically reminded him to go slow and make good choices. He still remembered the silence on the other end of the phone line when he had called to tell them. He didn't tell them she was coming for Christmas, instead making an excuse about needing to stay and work and not having much money. They would have been sad to know why he was actually staying. He crawled into bed Sunday night tired, but excited.

Mike came in earlier than usual Monday morning, bouncing through the door proclaiming Christmas cheer and greetings.

"Good morning, good morning, Tom! Christmas is so soon!"

"Hey, Mike. Yes, Christmas is coming!"

Mike smiled and bounced up to the counter.

"How are you, Tom? How's that girl? I haven't really talked to you much. You look a little tired."

Tom laughed. He'd missed Mike's direct confrontations.

"I'm doing well. Brittany is coming to see me tomorrow. She's staying for a week. I'm so glad. I haven't seen her for two weeks. I am tired. I've been busier lately. Girls keep you busy, I guess."

He paused as if to add something else, but seemed to think better of it, and didn't.

"They sure do. That's good that she gets to come visit you. You must be excited."

"I'm so excited. It'll be so good."

After a brief silence, Mike asked,

"Have you seen Janelle in the past few days?"

Tom thought for a moment.

"I haven't. I saw her on Thursday, but that was the last time."

"Oh. Huh. I went to Francie's on Friday night and she served me, but she looked pretty bad. I think she was getting sick. She was pale, and her voice sounded raspy."

Tom raised his eyebrows.

"That's a bummer! I hope she's okay."

"I think I'll call and check on her. Just to make sure. She doesn't have anyone watching out for her."

He ended as if he was finished, then added,

"That falls to us, Tom."

Tom nodded. Realization was beginning to melt into his consciousness. He hadn't thought of anyone or anything besides Brittany since she'd come back to him, and it had hurt his relationships with the friends he was beginning to make.

"It does, doesn't it? I haven't talked to her for a while. When I saw her on Thursday we talked a little but not very long."

"She misses you, I think."

Tom didn't think anyone would notice his mental absence.

"That's nice."

"No, Tom, she actually misses you. She told me she doesn't talk to you much and it makes her sad."

At that moment, Mike's phone rang.

171

"Sorry man, I gotta get this, and I gotta get to work. Have a great Christmas. Maybe I'll see you around."

He picked up his phone as he ran out, answering questions. Apparently Mike wasn't the only one in his company who went to work at an ungodly hour in the morning.

Janelle missed him. It was a warm feeling. It felt like belonging, and it felt like being loved for who he was. The rest of the day flew past with very little event. Mrs. Donahue came in exclaiming about how she hoped there would be snow because holly bushes looked so pretty in the snow,

"The white just dresses up the green like a bride with spring accents!"

Mr. Peterson came in scheming about the neighbor boys and their habits, then reminiscing on and on about how Christmas had been when Mrs. Peterson was still alive. Tom listening to him and wondered how it must feel to do something with a person every day of most of your life, then lose her suddenly. When tears came to Mr. Peterson's eyes, Toms were also moist.

Quitting time, and there was a slow gentle snow falling. It wasn't enough to delay Brittany's flight, but it did have a peaceful effect on Tom's soul. Christmas. Almost a week of vacation. With Brittany. The woman he loved. It was going to be wonderful.

He called his parents on the way to the airport. His mom answered.

"Oh, Tommy! Hello!"

She was always so happy to hear from him.

"Hi ma, Merry almost Christmas! How are you?"

"I'm doing well, Tommy, really well. Jake and Michelle are coming in tomorrow morning, and Elizabeth and John are coming in tomorrow night. Matt and Maggie are having Christmas at her family's house, and you of course are staying there, but it will still be a full house. I'll miss you though."

"Thanks, momma."

Besides the years he'd spent with Brittany, it would be the first time he hadn't gone home for Christmas when he easily could have. The very bottom of his heart hurt. He realized, suddenly, that he wanted to be home. They would do all the Christmas traditions. His mother would make dozens of cookies, which they would eat after every meal. Elizabeth would play the piano and they would sing Christmas carols every night, and Bach (the ancient golden retriever) would howl in the background, making his own special music. They would build gingerbread houses, and make eggnog, and sit around the glowing tree in the dark. All of the nostalgia welled up within him, and Tom sighed.

"What are your plans for Christmas, Son? I hope you're not going to be alone."

She was so glad to be talking to him—she loved him so much. Casting reason aside, he told her about Brittany.

"Actually, Brittany wanted to come, so she's coming tonight and leaving on Sunday."

His mother was silent.

"Oh."

He kept trying.

"She's different, mom, she really is. She loves me, I think. She cares about me."

In the farthest corner of his heart, he doubted it, but whenever those thoughts sprung up he quickly laid them to rest. Of course it was true. She had done so much to find him again, and come to him.

"Does she?"

His mother maintained a pleasant noncommittal interest. Like Mary, she was suspicious of Brittany.

"I think so, momma. I think so."

"Well, son, if you think she loves you, then I'll love her. All I want is for you to be loved, really truly loved."

"I know, ma, I know."

She contemplated for a while, then said,

"What did you get her for Christmas?"

He smiled in spite of himself.

"I got her diamond earrings, pretty big ones. She's going to love them."

"She's always been a diamond earrings kind of girl, hasn't she?"

Tom's mother paused.

"I've always been more of a pearl lady, myself."

That's when Tom realized that he hadn't sent his parents presents. Presents in the Bailey family were a big deal. Everyone always got presents for everyone else, and sat around opening them Christmas morning after a big breakfast of sweet rolls and sausage and eggs. Tom's parents loved to give presents that were useful but not dull, so that each person could get better at something they wanted to do, or gain a new talent. The kids always tried to get their parents something big, worthwhile, that adults would want. The best part of Christmas, though, everyone always agreed, was watching Mr. and Mrs. Bailey exchange presents. He always bought her something more big and elaborate than he could afford. She spent weeks and weeks beforehand trying to think of the perfect gift for him, and when she finally did she executed the completion of the idea like an army sergeant, methodically, carefully, and full of excitement. So finally, when Christmas day came, each would be erupting with excitement, like so many anxious volcanos. One year she bought him a new laptop to replace his old one (it was more like an abacus, in truth), and he couldn't speak for almost an hour. He sat there in shock, staring at the box in his lap, then looking back at her and smiling. The year he bought her a new bike was also memorable. He hid it in the car and made her look for it, and when she finally found it she couldn't stop gushing over it. It was a low point in her life when, eight months later, it got stolen right off of the bike rack where it was locked in a public park.

All these thoughts swirled through Tom's head as he tried to hurriedly think of what he could send home for Christmas. He didn't have much time, and he didn't have many resources. He clicked back to the present when he realized his mother was still talking.

"… Said to her that was a good idea, and I didn't mind if she did it. Do you think that was the right thing to do?"

"I'm sure it was, Ma. I trust your judgment."

"Okay, that's good. What are you doing right now?"

"I'm on my way to the airport to pick up Brittany."

"Ah. Well, I hope her visit is good. Call when you can. I love you very much, and I'm going to miss you a lot."

"I love you too, momma."

Talking to his mother always made Tom homesick. As much as it had been a struggle for him to grow up feeling occasionally overlooked, he had begun to realize that sometimes that was just how it happened, that amidst all of the felt injustice, his family loved him very much. He took that love for granted, but as he began to realize it, he became more and more grateful. Not everyone had so much love, he realized. He was lucky.

He was almost to the airport, and started to turn his mind very seriously to what he was going to do for Christmas presents. He had to send them tomorrow if he wanted them to have any chance of getting there for Christmas, or even when everyone was still there. For the past few years his gifts had centered around coffee or mugs or something barista classic. This year he didn't have the time to do anything really creative, but he brainstormed as he sat in the car and waited to go into the airport. Maybe Brittany would have ideas. Not long after he went inside, she came walking down the security lane, looking perfect, as usual. Tom, too excited to see her, didn't notice the note of weariness in her smile.

"Hi Brittany! Merry Christmas!"

"Tom! Hi Tom! Merry Christmas!"

He hugged her, and she pulled away quickly. He noticed, but thought little of it.

"How was your flight?"

"It was good. Uneventful. Let's go get my bag."

Tom had grown used to the massive piece of luggage that she always brought with her, and how it always felt like she packed four cinderblocks.

"I'm so glad you're here. We're going to have such a good Christmas."

She smiled and linked her arm through his, and worked hard to be as excited as he was. She wanted comfort and security that Tom gave her, but she didn't know if she actually wanted him. She'd wanted to be part of his life again—but as she realized what that meant she became less certain. Was it worth spending the rest of her life with someone who she wasn't truly connected to, because he made her feel good about herself? It didn't seem fair to either of them. Time would tell, she supposed. His voice pulled her out of her reverie.

"I just realized it, so I was wondering if you had any ideas."

His words yanked her back to him and she looked over.

"I'm sorry honey, I wasn't paying attention. What do I have ideas about?"

"Christmas presents. I forgot to send my family Christmas presents and I need to so I was wondering if you had any ideas."

"It's a little late for that, dear."

"I know, I know, but I've been so busy getting ready for everything, for you to come and for Christmas and for The Cup being closed that I completely forgot. And now I have to come up with something for them and I don't know what to do. I need your help."

Brittany wasn't overly creative—she had never needed to be. Her family had always had money, so instead of making things for her own amusement, she bought them.

"Well…"

She paused, thinking. Presents weren't a very big deal in her family.

"You could give them a cheese basket. Or a membership to a wine club. Or monogrammed hand towels."

She was thinking of all of the presents she'd want to get.

"Hmmm. Those are some ideas. Any others?"

"Well, you could send them mugs. Coffee is your thing."

"I did that one year."

They were waiting at the baggage claim, and an old man was standing on their left side. It was apparent that he was listening in on their conversation, but neither of them realized it.

"Maybe coffee? Or have you done that too?"

"I did that too."

"Well, there's always just a nice card."

"I know, but my family loves presents. I need to send them something."

Right then the old man interrupted.

"Excuse me, I can't help but overhearing that you're in a bit of a pickle."

Both turned to him, surprised.

"It's just that I have a bit of a habit of giving presents. You might say I'm an expert. What are your parents like?"

Tom and Brittany looked at him. Brittany stepped back, as if trying to avoid him, but Tom, nothing to lose, said,

"Well, they're great. My dad loves to work with his hands, but he also likes to think hard about big things. He reads a lot, but also enjoys being active. My mom doesn't like to work with her hands as much, but she likes to make things too. She's good at learning, and teaching, and she can do whatever she decides to do. She also really likes to be active."

The old man rubbed one hand across his stubbly chin, and with the other smoothed the front of his red and green flannel shirt.

"That does seem to be a bit of a pickle. Do you want to get them one present, or each separate presents?"

"I'm not sure. At this point I just need an idea. I figured when I came up with the perfect thing, I would know."

Brittany turned away and looked down at her phone. The man looked at her briefly, then back at Tom.

"Do you make things?"

Tom nodded, saying,

"When I have time."

"Well, I always loved it when my kids made me things, no matter if they were great or not. You know, like crafts? Except when you're an adult, I guess you don't call them crafts. Art, would it be? Make them some art."

Tom had always liked art, but he had never felt very good at it. That had always been Elizabeth's thing (his sister next to Mary), and so even when he was in school his teachers would just talk about how good she was, and ask him if he was as good as she was, and tell him that she had always been excellent and that there were so many things he could learn from her. It had grown old.

"I'll think about it. Do you think that's a good idea, honey?"

He put his arm on Brittany's elbow, trying to draw her back into the conversation. She had a habit of mentally disconnecting when she didn't want to be talking to someone about something.

"Oh, yes, sure, dear. That'll be fine. Just let me know what I need to do."

The man raised his eyebrows at Brittany, and Tom looked over at her, as she stood absorbed in the bright screen of her phone, not paying attention to him at all.

"Well, anyways, give it a thought."

"I will, I will."

At that moment, luggage started coming around the belt, and both men turned their attention to the bags circling in front of them. Brittany's bag was near the front, so Tom pulled it off the belt and tried to set it down gently, and they quickly made their way out. She stopped looking at her phone once they got to the car, and turned her brain back to conversation.

"What was that guy saying to you?"

She turned her innocent eyes to Tom.

"He was trying to help me figure out what to give my parents for Christmas."

Like I wanted you to. He didn't voice his thought.

"Oh. I thought I was getting a phone call, then when I pulled it out I realized I had a few important emails to catch up on."

"That's fine, honey."

He could always ask Janelle to paint them pictures quickly. He remembered at some point she said she like to paint.

178

"Hey, do you remember Janelle? What if I asked her to paint me some pictures to send my parents?"

Brittany frowned. She remembered Janelle. She remembered Janelle was pretty and small and had big soft eyes and wispy blonde hair. All she said was,

"Janelle... Hmmm, maybe. I can't quite seem to put a face to a name. Is she that waitress girl?"

Tom rarely thought of her in the capacity of being a waitress—to him she was the occupant of the plush purple wingback chair, feet curled up next to her, large book in hand, and chai on the table.

"Oh, yes. She is a waitress. And she paints. I think she's good."

Brittany made the noise people make when they're not sure.

"Mmmm, babe, I don't know. I don't really think that's a good idea. What if she's busy with her own Christmas plans?"

Clearly, she was opposed to it.

"Okay, it's alright. I don't need to ask her. Should we stop at the store so I can look for ideas?"

Brittany yawned.

"I'm really tired tonight. I just want to go home. Can we just do that? I don't feel like shopping."

Tom stopped listening after 'go home.' He wished he had a home with her.

"I'll take you to your hotel."

They drove the rest of the way in relative silence, him thinking of his family and presents, her dwelling on work, and what had happened that day. The snow was steadily falling when they arrived, and when Tom opened her door for her, she said,

"Help me up the walk, Tom? I don't want to break an ankle in my shoes."

Her laugh was tight as she held her hand out for his arm. He helped her to the hotel lobby, and stood behind her patiently, carrying her bag up to her room after she checked in.

"Aw, thanks, Tom. I appreciate it. That's nice of you."

He smiled, and after slipping her heels off, she moved across the room, let him take her in his arms, and kissed him. After moments, she breathed in deeply, and he said,

"It's going to be a good week. I'm so glad you're here."

CHAPTER SEVENTEEN

When Janelle woke up on Saturday morning, she couldn't get out of bed. She called Francie and asked off work, planning on sleeping the whole day to get better. Sunday morning she woke and instead of feeling better, felt worse. She had developed a cough deep in her chest, and went between being intensely cold and shivering, or intensely hot and sweating. Monday morning she felt no better, so she called Francie for another day off.

"Hi, Janelle, how are you?"

"Hi Francie, I'm okay. I can't seem to lick this cold. Can I have today off too? Hopefully I'll be better by tomorrow."

"Absolutely honey, that's fine. Take as much time as you need."

"Thanks, Francie."

"Sure, sure. Let me know if you want anything. I'll be right over as soon as you say you do."

"Thanks."

It hurt to talk. Janelle couldn't remember the last time she'd felt so sick—although she was used to pain, she wasn't used to her head feeling like it might explode. Now she felt awful on the inside, not the outside. She lay in bed all day, sleeping some and mostly feeling miserable. The next morning, Tuesday, she had taken a turn for the worse, and though she didn't know it herself, her fever had gone up and she'd become delirious. She forgot to call Francie to ask off work, in her half-conscious state. Around dinnertime, when she would usually be at work, her phone rang. She realized it and reached for it, answering it. Her voice had become raspy from thirst and sickness.

"Hello?"

It came out as more of a whisper.

"Janelle? Are you okay?"

"Uh, yeah, I'm okay."

Still a whisper. She tried to clear her throat but it hurt too much.

"Janelle, Mike here. I'm just calling to see if you've called Sherry Donahue."

"Oh, no, I forgot to ca—"

The whisper broke and she started to cough violently.

"Janelle, you're sick. How long have you been sick?"

"I think Friday, maybe."

He was silent.

"Don't go anywhere. I'm going to come get you."

"No, I'm okay."

She tried to speak loud enough for him to hear.

"No, I'm coming. Hold tight."

He hung up before she could protest, and she lay there in silence, wheezing and coughing and sweating everywhere. A while later, there was a knock on her door, and she weakly made her way across her small room. She had to stop and rest a few times. She hadn't eaten since she'd gotten sick, and she'd done nothing but lay in bed. She hoped Mike wouldn't leave before she finally got there. He didn't. When she slowly unlocked the door and pulled it open, he pushed it from the outside and walked in. As he did so, she slipped and began to fall back, and he caught her by the shoulders.

"Janelle, you look terrible. Get your things, it's all arranged."

"What? Where are you taking me?"

She slumped down and sat on the ground, leaning against the wall with her eyes closed.

"I'm taking you to Sherry Donahue. I called her on the way over, she wants you to come immediately."

"Ohh."

She groaned.

"I'm sick. I don't want to make her family sick."

Her raspy whisper gave the situation a humorously pitiable attitude.

"You won't. You just sit here, I'll get your things."

He walked off, and came back fifteen minutes later with a bag full of whatever he had deemed necessary for her to have. Janelle foggily hoped he had remembered her glasses, that she'd left sitting on the nightstand.

"Where's your house key?"

"A hook in the kitchen."

She kept her eyes closed, shivering and hugging herself. He came back and, slinging her bag across his shoulder, stooped down and picked her up. He didn't appear very muscular, but he picked her up easily, as if she weighed nothing at all. She rested her head against his shoulder, shivering in her sweats and hoodie, and closed her eyes. The next thing she knew, she was waking up in the dark in a house she didn't recognize, muffled laughter and voices in the background. She was still feverish, and thrashed about, hot under the covers and her clothes. Delirious, she called out, and Sherry Donahue came in a moment later. The light from the doorway hit Janelle's face, and she drew back in fear.

"Oh, sweetheart. How are you feeling?"

Janelle moaned and tried to answer, but her throat didn't seem to work and all that came out was a raspy,

"Unngh."

"It's alright, you're here now. We're going to take good care of you."

She put a cool hand on Janelle's forehead, and stroked her hair back. Janelle sighed and laid her head back on the pillow. Even when she was little her mother hadn't been able to baby her—having a drunk father changed a lot of things.

"Mike is staying here too now. If you need anything, just give a yell. If you can't yell, ring this bell till one of us comes. Let me take your temperature. Open your mouth."

Janelle complied, and when Mrs. Donahue saw her tongue, she said,

"Oh, honey. You need water. Keep that in your mouth till it beeps, then spit it out if I'm not back."

She hurried out and Janelle, hot and sweaty, tried not to move the thermometer around with her tongue. Mrs. Donahue came back before it was done with a glass of ice water and a spoon. As the thermometer beeped, she swooped down and plucked it from Janelle's mouth.

"Wow, honey. You're at 104.1. If you don't start getting better we're going to need to take you to the hospital."

Sherry started spooning ice water into her mouth, spoonful by spoonful, till she had given her a quarter of the glass.

"Get some rest. We'll keep checking on you."

Janelle tossed back and forth, restless. Her warm was too hot and her cool was freezing. Sherry or Mike came in often, to check on her and take her temperature. It didn't go up, but it didn't go down either. Janelle fell into a restless sleep, and when she woke up she heard voices outside her door. It was cracked, and she strained to listen.

"… pretty hot."

It sounded like Mike.

"I know, but I don't know any of her information and it worries me to bring her to the hospital."

That was Sherry.

"Is she going to get better if we don't?"

Janelle didn't recognize the third voice, and assumed it belonged to Sherry's husband, Bob. She'd never met him, but Tom had told her about him. He'd said he was a nice man, calm and steady to combat Sherry's ebullience.

"I'm not sure. I think so, but you can never quite tell. We should have enough time to get her to the hospital if it does take a turn for the worse, we just have to monitor her constantly. Someone should stay up with her all the time—we can take turns."

"I'll go first."

This was Mike, solid and determined.

"Good. Here's the deal—we'll keep it hot in there, with steamy air. Take the covers off her and give her just a sheet. I'll change her and put her in shorts and a tank top so she's not hot from her clothes. You stay up with her for three hours, then wake me, and when it's been three hours I'll wake Mr. D. up."

The whispers moved away, and Janelle sighed. She wanted to call out for them to come back, to tell them they didn't have to do all this for her, but she wasn't strong enough. She just lay, quietly, wishing she weren't sick. Brittany must be here with Tom now. If Brittany wasn't here, Tom would be at the Donahue's with them, relaxing and enjoying Christmas. But she would be sick still, sweating in bed, struggling to string one coherent thought to the next.

* * *

On Tuesday morning Brittany called Tom later than usual for a ride, and he was surprised to see her wearing sweatpants and no make-up. When he hugged her, she said,

"I just felt like being comfortable."

Back at his house, he returned to the table to continue his project. She wandered around his small apartment looking at his Christmas decorations. Her parents always hired companies to come put up decorations at their house. There were lights everywhere, greenery and bows, and every year the 18 foot Christmas tree that stood in their great room had a different theme of decorations. His family put the same decorations on the tree every year, the same lights on the front of the house, and the same little nativity scenes on different bookshelves and tables. His was a homey Christmas, hers was a production. She said,

"Honey, your Christmas is so cute."

She kissed his head, and looked down at what he was doing. He was painting. Four small pictures lay before him—one of the mountains, one of a city, one of an ocean, and one of a Ferris wheel. He was biting his bottom lip, and would paint one for a while, then move to the next, then the next. Brittany didn't study them, and instead leaned down and kissed him. He was distracted for a while. When he finally looked back to his work, she looked too, and said,

"Wow, honey! These are good! You're an artist!"

She was being completely honest. Each of his paintings seemed to tell a story. There was detail, and whimsy, and the colors blended well.

"When did you become an artist?"

He shrugged, looking self-satisfied and smugly delighted.

"I guess I just started and it was easier than I thought it would be."

"These are great. What are they for?"

She had completely forgotten.

"They're for my family, remember? I have to finish them and mail them. I want them to know I love them for Christmas."

She said,

"Oh, yeah,"

but he didn't hear her, as he turned his face completely back to his work. She made herself coffee, then wandered back and lowered herself into the chair across the table from him, and distractedly picked at the knee of her sweat pants.

"Honey?"

"Hmm?"

He wasn't really listening, she could tell. It was the perfect time.

"I'm thinking about moving in with you."

He still wasn't listening, and responded, nonplussed,

"Okay dear."

This was exactly the reaction she was hoping for, so later when she told him again, she could say he'd already said yes. He kept painting, almost feverishly.

After some time, he finished, and wrote names and notes on the back of each one, then put them all into a large manila envelope and said,

"Come to the post office with me?"

She nodded and stood, reaching for her jacket and boots. It had snowed several inches the night before, bringing them the white Christmas Mrs. Donahue had so desperately been hoping for. Tom pulled his coat on, slid his feet into his boots, and didn't reach for his keys.

"What, are we walking?"

He looked over at her and nodded.

"It's not very far, and I figured the exercise would do us good. We're going to be eating a lot in the next few days. Wouldn't want to get fat."

He laughed at his own joke, and she rolled her eyes at him. They walked to the post office hand in hand, and on the way back, when he turned a different way, she didn't notice. They walked slowly. He was enjoying the winter and her company, while she was enjoying the winter and her coat. Half way back from the post office, he stopped abruptly in front of a small house and looked intently at the top windows. Brittany looked at him.

"What, what are you looking at?"

It was Janelle's house, and the lights were off. She should be home. It wasn't late in the morning, The Cup was closed, and she never worked this early. Tom furrowed his brow in concern, then answered Brittany's question indirectly.

"Oh, just looking up at that attic. This is a cute house, don't you think?"

Thinking he was referring to a future home for them, she wrinkled her nose and said,

"It's okay, I guess. I was thinking somewhere bigger, personally."

She lived in a four bedroom apartment in Texas. She knew she didn't need such a large apartment, people seldom came to visit her, but she liked the space. She had an exercise room and an activity room and a TV room, and her bedroom, of course. They walked on in silence. Tom knew he shouldn't be worried about the lights in Janelle's house, he guessed she was probably fine. He also knew that if he said anything about Janelle to Brittany, she would be upset. He instead listened when she began to chatter about her job, and the people who she met, including the different men she'd been with after college. When she asked him about girls he was quiet. So she probed.

"What about them, Tom Bailey? Girls?"

He looked at her, slowly. This was a game to her. He loved who she had been, but he was slowly realizing that she wasn't with him for the long road; she was with him for the entertainment. Maybe she'd started dating him again, and realized it wouldn't work, but didn't want the hassle of separation. It was a game to her; a painstaking, heart-breaking, costly game.

"No, Brittany. There were none. I was heart-broken after you left me. I dropped out of school. I didn't think about anyone but you for months after. You were all I wanted. You knew that, and you still didn't want me. All I wanted was to marry you, to make my life with you. I loved you, Brittany, and you broke my heart. Almost broke my life. I didn't graduate. I don't even have a college degree. I didn't want to keep living when you left me—I hoped my life would end. But it didn't, and here I am, and now you're back."

He paused, shocked by the words that were coming from his mouth. He barely knew he'd felt this deeply.

"Do you understand what you did to me, Brittany? Do you understand?"

He had stopped walking somewhere in the paragraph, and stood, trembling, tears slowly leaking from his eyes. She stared at him. He went on.

"People aren't objects, Brittany. You can't use them, walk all over them, then put them back in a closet and expect them to be fine. You can hurt people. People have hearts, and emotions, and feelings. We live. We breath. We cry. We bleed. I'm not a toy."

He took a deep breath, then said,

"It isn't your fault—everyone chooses how they react to things, and I reacted badly. But I was so hurt. And I didn't know what to do. Or how to continue life normally. So I left."

He was almost out of steam, but he launched into his last words with everything he had left.

"You don't love me anymore. You did once. I know. I know what it feels like. Now you don't. I'm not stupid."

Hands shoved in her pockets, Brittany stared at the toes of her new boots. They had cost her a fortune. Calf skin and sheep wool, they were warm and waterproof. She'd bought them for this trip. She didn't need boots in Texas, and she didn't often travel to cold places.

"I don't know, Brittany. I don't know if you really want me, or if you're just playing pretend, but you need to decide, because it's not fair for me to love you if you're not going to love me back. I care about you, Brittany. You are an amazing valuable woman, and if you make the right choices, life stretches out in front of you rich and happy. But make the right choices, because if you don't, the rest of your life will be as lonely and unhappy as the past four years have been."

He hadn't expected to say any of this—he had barely even realized it was in his heart, but once he started talking, he couldn't stop. The catharsis, once it began, was too strong to stop until it all ran out. Everything he'd wanted to say years ago was coming out now. A tear trickled down her face, and she looked up at him. It wasn't fair. She shouldn't be dating him. She wanted his love, but she didn't want the attachment. She wanted his goodness. She wanted the comfort she'd thought he would give her, but she was wrong. He worked in a coffee shop, scraping up just enough to pay rent and buy food every month, saving pennies on the side.

"Oh, Tom."

They stood in the snow, slate gray sky above, the occasional bird drifting past. It was cold, but not unbearable. He looked at her, the real her. The facade was down, makeup off, sweats tucked into her boots. He cared about her. He had never stopped caring about her. But if it was going to be this way, her distant and distracted while he poured everything into loving her, he couldn't do it. It was a one way street, and that one way street was not the recipe for a relationship. He felt more to say, and let it come.

"I could love you, Brittany. I could spend the rest of my life loving you, and maybe you could learn to love me, but I don't think that's what you want. I think you came to me because you wanted to see if you liked me again, but now you're bored. I wish it wasn't true, but I think it is."

His hands were fists, not because he wanted to fight, but because it was taking all his effort to continue, now that the initial burden was released. He had loved feeling like someone wanted to pay attention to him, but he realized as he dated her that the attention she paid was not the attention he wanted. It was his need paired with her desire, and it was a broken system.

"I try Tom, I do."

Her words were feeble. Breathing in deeply, she sighed.

"I'm sorry for all of it. This wasn't the way I wanted it to be. I wanted it to work. I wanted you back. I wanted us to do well together."

He shook his head.

"But we couldn't. We're too different. We would never work. I knew in college but I wasn't mature enough to say it right so I just rejected you with no explanation. Then I thought maybe growing up would help us both—but it didn't."

She paced to the right and the left, then stepped in front of him and looked him full in the face.

"It didn't."

He put his hands on her waist. She let them stay there for a moment, then gently removed them.

"Tom, you're an incredible man. You have value that you don't understand, that the people around you have never told you about. You are talented, you are smart, and you are kind. Your family should have told you that from the moment you were able to understand words strung together, but they didn't. They accidentally overlooked you sometimes. That wasn't evidence of their lack of love for you, they were just too busy trying to do their own thing well. Tom, you were overlooked sometimes, but it is no reflection of your value as a person. You are important. You are worth knowing. You are a caliber all of your own. I have never known anyone like you."

Her bottom lip was quivering, and a steady stream of tears fell to her coat, but she was determined to finish.

"You are too good for me. I never wanted to hurt you so much, but I did. And I'm sorry. Let me go in your heart, Tom, and let other people in. Please let people in, people who will love you in the right way."

Pause.

"Please." He stood amazed. He had never heard this much honesty from Brittany, not before when they were dating, and never in the past three months.

"And what's more, Tom, you need to go back to school. Stop living this mediocre life here. You're too good for this. You should be doing something that requires more talent, anything. You could be an artist, you could be a doctor, just stop living a stalemate life and do something. You have the talent, you're simply lacking the drive."

She motioned to herself.

"Well, here I am. The drive. Make something of yourself."

She stepped in close to him, stood on her tiptoes, and kissed him, simply and gently, upon his tear-wet lips.

"I loved you, Tom, but not in the way you needed. Your love is deeper than mine. I hope you find a woman who loves you like you deserve."

Snow began to fall around them in the most cliché way, as they stood there crying. He knew it was the end. The end of everything he'd held onto for years, first investing in and hoping for, then mourning over. But this was a whole end, this was the end it should have been the first time, if either of them would have had the courage or the wisdom. This was the end that they both deserved. It was the end that strong good people can bring to something when they care about someone.

In silence, they walked back. He drove her to her hotel where she packed her bags, then to the airport. He stayed with her as she changed her flight, and booked it to New England where her family now lived, instead of Texas. He walked her to security, and as she turned to hug him goodbye, he pulled the earrings out of his coat.

"I bought these for you. I thought your face might make them look pretty."

She opened the box and started to cry again.

"Tom, they're beautiful. But I can't. Save them for someone else."

He shook his head.

"No. I want to give them to you. Remember, when you wear them, that you're a person of value, a woman of worth, and that you may not settle for anything less than the best."

She fingered them, looking at him.

"Thank you."

"You're welcome. Merry Christmas."

He kissed her gently, and squeezed her arm.

"Goodbye, Tom."

"Goodbye, Brittany."

He turned and walked away. She watched him walk out of her life, and she cried. He was the best man she'd ever known, and the most valuable man she'd ever loved, and she didn't want him to leave. But she knew, deep down, he was not hers. He never had been. She'd always known, but she'd always hoped the feeling was wrong. Maybe now, she could move on with her life, become the woman she was meant to be, without always hoping for something that she was not to have. Maybe he could too.

CHAPTER EIGHTEEN

Wednesday morning brought winter sunshine, and no decrease in Janelle's fever. Sherry Donahue decided that if it hadn't broken by midday Wednesday, they would take her to the hospital. She was weak, less delirious now, and didn't cry out as often. When Mike came in her room in the morning, he took one look at her and marched out.

"Sherry!"

She was in the kitchen making breakfast.

"Sherry, I'm taking her to the hospital."

Sherry held a spatula in one hand and a block of cheese in the other. She held them both still as he spoke.

"She isn't going to die, dear, her fever will come down."

"Sherry, you are an amazing wonderful god-fearing woman, but Janelle is my friend, and I watch out for my friends, and if they're close to death, I want them in the hospital where they can get official medical attention. I'm taking her to the hospital."

Sherry sighed. She was well meaning—she wanted Janelle to get better, she just didn't want to let the girl out of her sight. She was fond of her, even though she hadn't known her for long.

"Alright, Mike. Drive safely in the snow, and keep me updated."

With no further words, he walked into Janelle's bedroom, lifted her light frame from the bed, and took her to the emergency room. When he walked in the doors and the nurses saw them, they admitted her quickly, one checking her pulse as another carried paperwork and directed him through the double doors and down the hall. He laid her gently on a clean white bed, and one nurse showed him out as the doctor walked in.

"You're going to have to sit in the waiting room, sir. Please fill out this paperwork. We'll be with you as soon as we can."

He filled out Janelle's paperwork as well as he could, which wasn't very well at all. He guessed on her birthday and a lot of other things. He figured he could clear it up later. Or not hand it in at all, as it turned out. He was just finishing when the nurse came back out to him.

"Excuse me, sir? The girl…"

"Her name is Janelle."

"Yes, well, Janelle is very sick. She has a bad case of bacterial pneumonia. It's not beyond help, but she's probably going to need to be in the hospital for a night or two. May I ask, how are you related?"

"I'm her brother."

Didn't miss a beat, didn't bat an eye.

"Ah yes. Well…"

"Mike."

"Mike, yes. After we give her drugs and her condition stabilizes, you're free to sit with her as long as you wear a mask."

She said a lot more things to him as well, about treatments, and time and her temperature and had it been high for a long time, and he answered as well as he could. She told him he might want to get what he needed now if he was going to stay with her, because he wouldn't be allowed to see her for a few hours.

"Oh, and Mike?"

"Yes?"

"It's a good thing you brought her when you did. If you had waited any longer, there might have been long-term effects."

He nodded. His mother always told him he was a person of action.

As he sat in the waiting room, he wondered what her story was. She'd never talked to him about them, and he'd never asked. Granted, they didn't know each other very well, but it was a common mistake to care about someone and not try to learn more about them, simply for forgetfulness or lack of time. Then the longer the relationship continued, the more awkward it became to ask. Mike decided then to ask regardless. It was always more important to know people than bear the awkwardness of asking late. He wondered where her family was, and if he should tell them she was sick, and if they would even care. She seemed so much happier than she had when she first come. He wondered what she would have done for Christmas at her house, and if it would have been a good time or a sad time, and if she had brothers and sisters. She seemed like an older sister. He was the youngest in his family, and his oldest sister had always watched out for him like a ferocious lion. After he sat there for quite some time, the nurse came back out and told him he could see her.

She lay in the bed, still and pale. She wasn't thrashing about as she had before, but her breathing was still faint and raspy. Mike turned to the nurse.

"Is she okay?"

"She's going to be fine. How long has she been sick?"

"When I saw her on Friday she wasn't looking too good, but she wasn't really sick yet. So probably Saturday."

"Does she live alone?"

"Yes, she does."

"When this is over, she's going to need to live with someone, at least for a few weeks. She's going to be weak for a while. Does she have a job?"

"Yes, she's a waitress at Francie's."

"Oh, my husband loves Francie's. Goes there all the time for business."

"It's a great place for meetings."

The nurse continued.

"Anyways, she's probably going to want to tell Francie that she can't work for a few weeks. Usually we recommend waiting a week or two after you've been this sick. "

Mike nodded.

"How long will she need to be here?"

It was the day before Christmas. Mike didn't want her in the hospital for what might be the first Christmas she had ever had away from home.

"Well, if her condition gets stabilized completely and her fever breaks, as long as she stays on drugs we would probably send her home tomorrow, under close supervision."

He nodded again.

"Okay. Can I stay here for the night?"

She smiled,

"That's fine. A lonely Christmas Eve doesn't sound good at all."

"That's what I was thinking."

He left to get a few things from his house, and on his way back to the hospital swung by Sherry Donahue's house. All the family was gathered in the kitchen, working on three gingerbread houses. It was an annual competition, undertaken with fervor and gusto. When Mike walked in, Sherry was in the middle of icing a roof, and there was sugar everywhere. No one noticed Mike till Sherry finished and looked up.

"Oh, Mike! Hello! You're quiet as a mouse! How is our sweet girl?"

"She's going to be fine. She's sleeping right now, and they told me as long as we keep her on drugs and take good care of her, they'll let her come home tomorrow."

"Oh, praise the Lord!!!! What else did they say?"

"The nurse said she couldn't work for a few weeks, and that she shouldn't live alone for that time either."

"Oh, sweet girl. She can stay here, that will be fine. Mike, you'll have to bring her clothes and things over later.

"Good. I can do that."

Mike had expected her to offer, but he was still relieved that she did.

"And do you want me to call Francie, or do you want to? Is Francie's even open today?"

"I think it is, but only for lunch."

"You'd better hurry and call, if you want to catch her."

Mike nodded, and dialed. Francie answered on the second ring.

"Hello, Francie's Diner, Francie here."

The clatter of dishes and conversation hummed in the background.

"Hi Francie, this is Mike Reston."

"Hi Mike, how are you?"

"I'm doing well, thanks, Francie. I'm calling about Janelle."

"Yes, she didn't come in yesterday and she was sick all weekend. Is she okay?"

"Well, she's going to be okay. She's in the hospital with pneumonia. I'm calling to tell you she won't be coming in today, and probably not for a few weeks, is what the nurse told me. Is that going to be okay?"

"Absolutely! Poor sweet girl. It'll be fine if she doesn't come in. My niece is coming to visit me for a month, and she loves to work while she's here. She'll get more hours than she bargained for this time. Is Janelle going to be okay? What can we do for her?"

"Thanks, Francie. I think she'll be fine. If she's looking okay tomorrow, we get to bring her home. She's going to be staying with Sherry Donahue for a few weeks, so she's not alone. She'll probably be lonely and want company sometimes, and I also know that if she's not working she's going to need her rent covered. We can all pool in for that. That's all I can think of."

"Oh, Don and I would be glad to help with that."

"Thank you so much, Francie. Oh, one more thing. She doesn't have any family that I know of, so I don't think she'll be getting any Christmas presents from them. Sherry and I both got something for her, but I was thinking, well, you know. Don't feel any pressure, but if you see something you…"

His voice trailed off. Mike would shamelessly ask for things if they weren't for him, but this was a lot of shameless asking.

"I understand, Mike. We'll see what we can do."

"You're an angel, Francie. Thank you."

"Of course, honey. Have a Merry Christmas Eve now. Call me if you think of anything we can do for that sweet girl."

Sherry had been standing by listening, as the rest of her family slowly worked on their gingerbread houses.

"What'd she say? Francie is such a doll."

"She said they'll help, and the she doesn't have to come in to work for a few weeks. And if we can think of anything else she needs, we can let them know."

"Wonderful. We'll take such good care of her. Is there anyone else we should call?"

Mike stood there. Tom would want to know. He was probably busy with Brittany, but he would want to know. He called, but Tom didn't pick up and after the second ring, it went to the dial tone. Mike made a mental note to call him later, and went to get his things and go back to the hospital.

CHAPTER NINETEEN

Tom went home and packed a bag, then called Mary on his way back to the airport.

"Hey, Little T! What's up?"

"Brittany left and I'm coming home."

"Oh."

He started crying.

"Are you okay, little brother? What happened?"

"I'm okay. We broke up. I'm on my way to the airport."

After a moment's pause, she asked,

"Do you already have a flight?"

"Not yet. I was planning on getting the next one out."

She answered without hesitating,

"I can look it up here and buy it for you."

"Are you sure?"

"Absolutely. I have more money than I know what to do with anyways."

"Thanks, Mary."

"I'll call you back in a few minutes with your information. And I'll come get you from the airport when you get here."

"Thanks, Mary. Oh, and don't tell the family? I want it to be a surprise."

"Sure, Little T. I love you."

"I love you too."

Mary booked the next flight to Idaho for him and called back, and thirty minutes later Tom was waiting at the gate. In twenty minutes he'd be boarding a plane to go see his family. His family that loved him. Sitting in his chair looking down at his feet, Tom realized he hadn't talked to Janelle or Mike very much lately. Brittany had taken up all of his time. She'd consumed his thoughts and his actions, and he'd completely forgotten about everyone else. There was a sense of guilt, as he remembered what it felt like when his brothers started dating, and seemed to forget him. It felt like abandonment, like he was being ignored, like they didn't care about him. As much as he told himself it wasn't true, he couldn't help but feel it was. He wondered if Mike and Janelle felt the same way about him, not as siblings, but as friends.

Time to board, and Tom found himself walking to his seat at the back of the plane, the second to last row. He sat in the window seat, next to a mother with a baby and a toddler. The two children were keeping the young woman quite busy.

"Hey, I'm Tom."

"Tom, pleasure to meet you. I'm Grace, this is Michelle, and this is Mae."

"Mae."

The toddler repeated her name, enthusiastically pointing at herself.

The little girl was active, and before long, Tom found himself working hard to keep her entertained. She had coloring books and a few small toys, but it wasn't long till each one lost her attention and she squirmed and squirmed, till Tom started telling her a story. When he was little, Mary would tell him story after story, about knights and castles and normal boys living in cul-de-sacs. He told Mae a long story about a princess who lived in a far off land and could make magic curtains. By the time he finished telling the story, she was drowsy and drifted off to sleep. The baby was also sleeping, and Tom turned to their mother.

"Your girls are very well-behaved."

She smiled.

"Thank you, I like them."

He laughed.

"That's always good. How old is Mae?"

"Almost three."

"And that one?"

This motioning towards the sleeping baby.

"Six months last Friday."

"She's pretty."

"They get their good looks from their dad."

She sighed lightly.

"I bet they get some of their good looks from you too."

It wasn't creepy or smarmy, she decided, as she looked at him, and she turned up the corners of her lips in a faint smile.

"Thank you."

"No need to answer if you don't want to, but where is their dad?"

The question didn't faze her—at least, not at first.

"He's gone."

She paused.

"He died."

"Oh."

Tom hadn't dealt with death often. When he was little his great-grandpa died, but it hadn't meant anything to him. His main reference for death was among the sick elderly, not healthy young husbands.

"He was coming home from work one day last winter in his truck, and a garbage truck blew through a stop sign and t-boned him. He was in critical condition when the ambulance came, and he died the next day."

"I'm so sorry."

She wasn't crying, but he could feel her pain.

"Thank you."

"You must have loved him very much."

"I did. I miss him so much."

Tom sat silent. He was much better acquainted with joy, and making people happy, than with sorrow. He didn't want to do the wrong thing or say the wrong thing in his attempt to help her be happy. Quietly, he realized it would be better to let her mourn, even though it must have been some time past.

"Do you want to tell me about him?"

She looked at him, then bluntly said,

"I barely know you. I don't want to bore you."

"It's not a bore at all. I just broke up with my girlfriend this morning, and I could use something to get my mind off of it."

She wrinkled her eyebrows, saying,

"Oh."

Then, rubbing the arm of her seat with her free hand, she continued.

"We broke up a few times before we got married. Once he was jealous because he thought I was cheating on him. I wasn't, but it still took a while to clear up. Another time I dumped him because he didn't have his priorities straight and wasn't taking enough time out of his schedule for me. He almost quit his job so he could spend more time with me. The third time it was really short—we'd reached the part of the relationship where you're deciding if you're going to stay together or be done. He thought maybe he would have some clarity if we broke up. We had clarity."

She nodded, and grinned.

"I don't think either of us slept all week. He called me on Saturday morning crying and apologizing. Seemed like pretty good clarity to us."

Tom smiled too. She told the story like it was still happening around her, like she was still enjoying the feel of his hand in hers, his arms around her.

"So then a few months later he proposed, and a few months after that we were married. He was done with school, but I had to finish before we could have kids. He said as soon as I was done we could have a baby, so I finished in 6 months instead of 12, and got pregnant right away. That was Mae. He always loved May, the flowers blooming and the smells of summer. He named her. We were happy. He was so good to me, always taking care of me and loving me better than I deserved. A little less than two years later, when I was three months pregnant with Michelle, I got the phone call. I didn't know what to do. My neighbor took Mae, and I went to the emergency room, and stayed with him until the very end. He only barely woke up once, just enough to look at me and tell me he loved me."

She stopped, quietly. The plane was cruising smoothly, the girls were both sleeping, and there was another hour of flight before them. She looked at her baby, sleeping peacefully in her lap, little fists curled by her face. Tom said,

"It's a wonderful story to carry with you."

She nodded.

"The best. Just a premature ending."

She stroked Michelle's soft hair, and after a moment, Tom asked,

"So what do you do?"

"I'm a high school English teacher. My next door neighbor keeps the girls every day, she's the sweetest little old lady. They love her so much, Mae calls her Aunt Jo."

"That's good. I'm glad. Where are you going?"

"Home to my family. I'm the only girl in a six kid family, and my brothers are all coming home for Christmas, so I'm coming too. I might move back to Idaho eventually, after a few years. I'm not sure."

The pain of her husband's death seemed to have faded, as she got further from the subject.

"Home is a good place to go."

"I think so. They love me, even if sometimes they forget to act like it."

Tom slowly realized that it was a common trend in every family.

"That's true. I'm going home too. It's the same way. Sometimes I just have to tell myself that they love me, because they forget to."

She laughed.

"Oh, family."

Paused.

"So, if you don't mind me asking, what happened with your girlfriend?"

"Oh."

He'd forgotten about it in the few minutes he'd been distracted by Grace's story.

"Brittany. We dated in college for a few years, then when I proposed she said no and broke up with me. I always wanted her back, so when she came to Denver to see me in October, we started dating again. But, it wasn't right. I didn't realize it at first, it was more gradual. I finally understood that we weren't going to work this weekend. We broke up this morning."

He sighed. He had cried all of his tears, but his heart still hurt.

"That's hard. I'm sorry. I only dated James, but I know every time we broke up it felt like my heart was going to stop working. It was awful."

Tom nodded.

"It is."

Tom didn't look at her for several minutes, giving her time to think, and when he did look back, she had fallen asleep, her head resting on the side of her seat, her breathing steady and gentle. The three sleeping girls, a small family, left accidentally stranded without anyone to take care of them. It saddened Tom. All three of them woke up right before the plane touched down, and when she began gathering her things, he had the paper ready.

"Here, Grace. When you get back to Denver, if you ever need anything, call me. I'd be happy to help with whatever I can."

She smiled at him, grateful.

"Thank you, Tom. It was good to meet you. Enjoy your Christmas with your family. It's going to be okay."

"Thanks, Grace. It is. You have a wonderful Christmas too."

They parted ways friends.

Mary was waiting for him outside of security, beaming.

"Merry Christmas, Little Brother! Welcome home!"

"Last time I saw you, you were wrapped up in a hospital bed, pale and broken. You're doing so much better!"

She grinned.

"That's right. An old broken leg can't keep me down. I got my cast off two weeks ago."

"How are you feeling?"

"I still get headaches, but I'm usually fine. Did you check a bag?"

"Nope. This is all."

He motioned at his small carry on.

"Great. Let's go! All the celebrating awaits! I didn't tell anyone you were coming, they think I'm out buying last minute gifts. Mom was giving a big stink because she thought that you weren't coming and she couldn't stand that her baby wasn't going to be here for Christmas, skipping it for Brittany."

She paused, looking closely at him as they walked.

"Are you okay?"

"Not now. But I will be. It was the right thing. For the first time in my life, I had enough backbone not to let myself get walked all over. It was good. Not easy, but good."

"You're all grown up, Little T."

He shrugged.

"Maybe. Something like that."

The drive home was happy, as they talked. Besides Brittany, Tom had very little news. Mary was still at the library, and had just been asked out by one of her new co-workers.

"Do you like him?"

"He's nice. We'll see. I think I could, but I'm not sure. We're going out on Friday night. The parents don't know though. I'm too grown up for telling them about every little thing I do. You'll have to figure out how to get me out of the house without them knowing where I'm going."

Tom and Mary had always been conspiracy partners.

Tom told her more about Janelle, and Mike, and how he hadn't seen either of them much since he'd started dating Brittany, and how he'd just realized how much he missed them. When they pulled into the driveway, Mary turned her lights off. It was dusk, and the house was all lit up. They could see the family in the living room through the windows.

"You stay in the car. I'll have the boys come out to carry things, and they can come back in with you. I'll get everyone into the kitchen."

He climbed into the back seat and watched Mary go into the house. She called the boys over and motioned with great animation and large gestures about the size of the box she wanted carried in. She led everyone else into the kitchen, digging around in her large purse to show them something.

Jake and John came traipsing out through the snow in their big boots, and when they opened the door and saw Tom sitting there, instead of a big box, they both yelled with delight. Bear hugs and back thumps later, they picked Tom up and brought him inside.

"Everyone will be so happy to see you! And on Christmas Eve! The best present!!!"

He laughed, and they brought him in, banging the front door closed and carrying him into the kitchen.

"Hey, look what we found!"

His mother screamed, and Elizabeth and Michelle both ran to hug him. His father just beamed down at him, smiling, and all the little kids jumped around making noise and adding to the mayhem.

"Tom! You're home!!"

He laughed.

"I'm home!"

They continued their exuberant welcoming, his mother hugging him like she'd never seen him before. His cell phone rang, but he didn't even look at it. It felt even better than he expected to be back with his family, to be loved.

* * *

Mike sat in Janelle's tiny room in the hospital. She was sleeping fitfully now, tossing and turning. It was never as bad as it had been the night before at Sherry's, but Mike was still worried. He didn't have much experience with sickness. When the nurse came in to check on her, he stopped her.

"Is it normal that she's tossing and turning so much? Is she okay?"

The nurse smiled down at him. He'd only been there for a few hours, and already everyone liked him. To them, he was the caring older brother who didn't know anything about hospitals or pneumonia, with a big heart and a cheerful, if worried, countenance.

"Yes, she'll be fine. It's good that she's a little bit active. We would actually be more worried if she were lethargic. I'm here to give her the drugs she'll need for the night, and she should just calm down and sleep."

"Oh, okay, good. I was worried. I don't know anything about pneumonia."

The nurse smiled at him.

"It's okay, sweetie. She's your sister. It's alright to worry."

She patted his shoulder, did what she needed to do for Janelle, and then walked out, humming a Christmas carol. It was Christmas Eve, and Mike was sitting in the hospital with a sick girl who he'd only known for a few months, because he didn't want her to have to spend it alone. And she wouldn't even know because she was sleeping. But he didn't mind. It was a good time to think, but also a bad time, because Mike's thoughts could run wild. He thought about Michaela, and wondered how her first Christmas with a new husband was. He started to cry, gently. He'd loved Christmas with her, and he'd always done all he could to make her feel special. When she left him, he'd already been planning what he was going to give her that year. She'd always wanted a cat, so he was going to buy her a kitten. She left him in November, right after he'd picked out and bought the kitten, ready to pick up right before Christmas. He gave it to his neighbors instead, and the three little girls named him Keys and took him everywhere. He smiled sadly. Even when he'd been miserable and missing Michaela, someone had benefitted. The girls had been delighted. As his thoughts wandered aimlessly, go and come as they may, he tried to call Tom again. He didn't answer. Mike guessed Brittany was keeping him fully occupied, so he wasn't surprised when Tom didn't answer. He left a message.

"Hey, Tom, it's Mike. Just calling to say Merry Christmas Eve. Also, call me when you get this—it's about Janelle. Alright, that's all. Bye."

He called his parents too. He knew they would be at the Christmas Eve service, but he wanted them to know he was thinking about them. Then he sat in silence waiting for the morning, waiting for her fever to break, waiting for anything good. There was a black clock in the corner, with a white face and red numbers. It was two minutes slow, compared to his watch. He stared at the hands, mindlessly. It was 9. Then 10. Then 11. Janelle was resting quietly, only calling out occasionally. This was new, she hadn't done it before. The first time, it had been only gentle, a slight cry,

"Alex, no! Stop!"

That was all she'd said. Then, later on, she swung her arm up and moaned,

"No, no, stop!"

Then a pause, then,

"No, not mom!"

She thrashed about, and whimpered, "Please, daddy, please."

And she started to moan, softly. As Mike watched her closely in amazement, he saw tears form and begin to stream down her face. Upset as she seemed to be, she was still sleeping soundly. He moved closer to the bed and took her hand, and she squeezed it, tight. The silence was still punctuated by her words, but they weren't always clear. After a while, Mike dozed off. It'd been a long day. Suddenly, his phone started to ring, he jumped, and holding Janelle's hand, jerked her arm. She jumped, and screamed a little in her sleep, crying out,

"Please don't! Tom! Help!"

Mike squeezed her hand tightly and struggled to get his phone from his pocket. Incidentally, it was Tom.

"Tom! Tom, hello!"

He cleared his throat, trying to clear his grogginess.

"Hey, Mike, did I wake you up? I'm sorry. I called as soon as I got your message. What's going on?"

Tom was sitting in the living room watching the fire crackling in the fireplace, petting Cumulo, his dad's dog. Mike cleared his throat again.

"You're fine. How's Brittany?"

Tom didn't cater to that, instead asking,

"You said something happened to Janelle. What happened to Janelle?"

"Yeah, so, uh,"

Mike collected his thoughts, slowly.

"She's in the hospital."

"What? Mike, is she okay?"

"Yes, yes, she's fine. She's got a pretty bad case of pneumonia, but I brought her in today and the doctors say she'll be fine, so now it's a waiting game."

Tom sighed.

"Oh, Mike. What happened?"

"I went to her house the day before yesterday because Sherry hadn't heard from her about Christmas, and she was so sick and weak she could barely make it to the door to let me in. I took her to Sherry's, then this morning took her to the emergency room when she wasn't any better. She's on drugs now and the doctors say if she's looking better tomorrow, which they expect her to, I can take her home."

"Oh, Mike. I wish I were there."

"Me too."

He paused, then asked again.

"How's Brittany?"

Tom was silent for a long time.

"Well, I guess she's good."

"You guess?"

"Yeah. She's home with her family. And I'm home. With my family."

Tom sighed, and Mike asked,

"What happened?"

"We broke up. This morning. On the sidewalk in front of Janelle's house."

"Oh."

Mike's turn to be silent.

"So I came home, and she went home."

"I'm sorry, Tom."

"It was for the best. I think it was going to happen eventually, so maybe it was better that it happened now."

"But it still hurts."

Tom sighed again.

"Yes, it does."

"When are you coming back?"

Mike realized how much he'd missed Tom's mental presence and kindness, though he'd been there physically.

"I haven't bought a return ticket yet, but maybe now that I know all this is happening I'll come home Saturday."

He paused, then said, "Mike?"

"Tom?"

"Is she going to be okay? I mean really? Is she actually going to be okay, like fine and back to normal?"

"I think so, Tom. The nurse told me it was good I brought her when I did, but she seems to be on the mend."

"Okay. Good. Good. Keep me informed, especially if she gets worse."

"Okay, Tom. Quick question."

"Yes?"

"What do you know about Janelle's past? Anything?"

"Not really. I know she's from New York and she doesn't want to go back, and when she first moved here she had fading bruises on her arms."

That answered Mike's question perfectly. He marveled that the one thing Tom knew was the one thing he'd wondered.

"That's all I need to know. Thanks, Tom."

"Sure. Like I said, call me if anything happens and I'll come back sooner."

"Will do. Oh, Tom?"

"Huh?"

"Merry Christmas."

"Thanks, Mike. You too."

Janelle was sleeping soundly, he guessed calmed by the noise of his voice, so he kept talking to her.

"You know, I always wanted a sister. It was me and a bunch of brothers. We had fun, but we all beat each other up. My dad always said we needed a woman to soften us. We all got married eventually, but he always said there's just something about a sister that nothing else quite touches. She gets deep down into your heart and holds on tight, and there's not really anything you can do about it. And you never really want to let her go. I never got to feel it, but I always wanted to. I guess that's why it's easy to pretend to be your brother."

She stirred, and he was silent. When she stayed asleep, he kept talking, about his life, about his family, about Michaela. Before long, it was early into the morning, and he had fallen asleep, his head on the side of the bed, holding her hand. The nurse came in to check on her, and smiled at the sight. She had a brother of her own, and he was one of her dearest friends. She loved him. As the nurse stood there and watched, Janelle twitched, stirred, thrashed about, and suddenly opened her eyes. Completely conscious. The nurse spoke.

"Hi honey. Your fever just broke. How do you feel?"

Janelle sighed, looking up at her, then over at Mike.

"Mike."

"Yes, honey, he's been here with you this whole time. Your brother loves you, sweetheart."

Janelle just looked at the nurse, gathering her eyebrows together. The nurse assumed it was a struggle to recall.

"Yes, he's even the one who brought you. Do you remember that?"

Janelle looked at Mike and looked at the nurse, then sighed and faintly smiled.

"No, but I'm sure it was nice."

The nurse, Hannah, laughed, checked what else she needed to, and left. Janelle looked at Mike and raised her eyebrows. He'd opened his eyes as the nurse walked out.

"My brother?"

He grinned sheepishly, squeezing her hand that he still held.

"I was worried that if I weren't related to you, they wouldn't let me stay with you."

Janelle nodded, and said,

"Ah."

She let her eyes close, and just breathed, her breath still raspy, but not as shallow. After some time, she opened her eyes and looked at Mike. He was still watching her.

"Thank you."

He nodded, and said,

"You're welcome. I wish I could do more."

She closed her eyes again. The last thing she remembered was crawling into bed Friday night after work with a scratchy throat and sore eyes. She didn't know what day it was, or how long it had been. She looked back at Mike. He'd fallen asleep with his head propped on her bed, facing her. His face looked exhausted. He was holding her hand tightly. She smiled. She was taken care of. She was loved. She turned over and went back to sleep, for suddenly she was exhausted.

CHAPTER TWENTY

Christmas morning, Tom opened his eyes to see his father, kneeling in front of the wood burning stove, building a fire. It was cold during the nights after the fire went out, and Tom stayed on the couch under the thick down comforter his mother had brought out for him. His father finished the fire, and sitting back to admire his work, noticed that Tom was awake.

"Good morning, Son."

"Hi, Dad. Merry Christmas."

"Ah, yes, Merry Christmas. You're the best present we got this year."

Tom smiled.

"But I thought you were staying home for Brittany?"

The family hadn't asked any questions last night—just swallowed Tom into their happenings and enjoyed his presence.

"I was."

His dad looked at him curiously.

"She came. I did everything to get ready for her. But yesterday morning, on the way back from the post office, we decided we weren't going to work."

His father's face was alive with pity.

"Oh, Tom."

"Except, this time, Dad, it was me. And it was right. And I knew it was right, so I didn't mind doing it."

Mr. Bailey nodded.

"And she cried, and I cried, and we both said a lot of nice things. Then I brought her to the airport, and gave her the diamond earrings I bought her for Christmas, and told her to remember she's valuable. Then she left, and I packed a bag and came home. Because I wanted to be here for Christmas."

He smiled, feebly. He'd fallen asleep crying the night before, sad from the loss. Sad because, no matter who, and no matter how, the end of a relationship is the death of something you brought to life yourself.

"Oh, Tom. I'm proud of you."

And his dad sat there beaming at him. The world stopped spinning around Tom. His dad was proud of him. He had done the right thing, and although it had been hard, it was worth it. At that moment, his two nieces came trampling down the stairs giggling and squealing, and running to their grandpa.

"Grandpa, Grandpa, Christmas!"

And from then on, all sobriety ceased, and one by one the members of the family came down, robed in warmth and garbed with joy, because on Christmas, everyone wanted to be happy all day long. They ate a big breakfast, then opened presents, then the family sat around well-fed and content. The little girls played with their toys, Grandpa talked to his sons, and Tom and Mary took Cumulo out for a long walk in the snow.

"Tom, what really happened? Tell me all about it. Unless, of course, you don't want to."

"I don't mind. I'll tell you."

He told her all of it, from the beginning, in as much detail as she asked for. They walked and walked under the bright sun (for it was a perfect Christmas day, the sky a cloudless blue, the snow crisp and deep, and the trees wearing their white winter coats), as he told her more about how it began, and how it had continued with his hope that maybe something would be different this time.

He told her how he realized his value, as Mike and Janelle had taken interest in him and done things for him and been kind to him just because they wanted to. It was a lesson that everyone must learn, but some learn it sooner than others, and it was only now dawning on him. He told her how peaceably they'd parted, and that Brittany had told him to go back to school, to leave his mediocre life and to make something of himself because he had potential and great capabilities, but he lacked motivation.

"That's what happened. And here I am."

They had come to a bench, woods behind, open field in front, and Tom unhooked Cumulo's collar to let him frolic in the wide snowy banks. Although they'd been walking slowly for a long time, the dog took off and began tossing up snow with his paws. After a long period of silence, listening to the sound of the quiet, Mary spoke.

"You did it, Tom."

"What, what did I do?"

"You grew up."

He sighed, then said,

"I guess so."

"What are you going to do now?"

She wasn't one to skirt the major issues.

"I don't know. I guess I haven't had much time to think about it."

He told her about the young mother on the plane, and how he'd never thought about anyone dying that young, and about the two beautiful little girls she had to raise all by herself. He also told her that Janelle was in the hospital, and might have died if Mike hadn't come when he did.

"So I haven't really even thought through it all yet."

"You certainly don't make your life easy."

"I mean, I didn't want it to be boring."

He laughed gently through the tears that were slowly sliding down his face.

"She was right, you know."

He turned to her, blinking, and said,

"About what?"

"You should go back to school. You have too much potential to be sitting around making coffee for the rest of your life. You can't do it. You wouldn't want to. You'll start to hate it soon, the same mundane things, day after day. Tom, you could be anything you set your mind to. You are excellent."

He sighed. He knew, deep down, she was right about his contentment. Even though he loved it now, the prospect of years and years of making coffee was dread in his mind.

"What do you have to lose? How many credits do you have till you get your degree?"

He thought for a while.

"I think I have 40 credits left, and I can probably take most of them from a local college and transfer the credits, while I'm still working. If I take them part time and work at the same time, I can probably do it in a year or two."

"Did you finish paying off all your debt from last time?"

He nodded.

"Just two or three months ago, finally."

"Good job, little T. Even a coffee shop job can do the trick. But no more debt for you. Do you have any money saved? Oh, that's right, no. Well, that's okay. Hard work was never bad. Go back to school, Tom. Finish your degree."

She nodded, then added,

"Get a real job, doing real things, making real money, so you can have a family."

She had become exercised—she wanted Tom to make something of himself. He had all the potential to be a thriving success, and it was exactly what she wanted for him. After her rampage, in a moment of calm, she asked,

"Actually, what do you want to do?"

He had never had a definitive passion, or so she thought.

"I think…"

His voice faded away. He could barely say it.

"I think I'd like…"

He paused again. Somehow saying it made it a reality, and also made it terrifying.

"Yes?"

She waited patiently. Mary was used to indecision—she worked in a library. There were two kinds of library people, she'd learned. It spilled over into life. People who knew what they wanted, and people who didn't. But sometimes the categories were mixed, and the people who knew what they wanted didn't want to say it, or the people who didn't know just said everything they thought of.

"Well, I think I could want to be an artist. But maybe I also want to be a teacher. I like high schoolers. I think it could be great."

She smiled. Tom, with a passion. Tom, with a dream. Tom, putting his foot down and claiming something.

"I think you would be great."

He was surprised.

"You do?"

"Absolutely. I think you should do both."

He leaned over and scooped up a handful of snow, watching as the corners of the handful melted in his bare hand. Both. He'd barely formulated the idea. It had dawned on him to be an artist when he painted his family the pictures and they were good. He'd enjoyed it. It had felt free. And he'd always loved working with people, although he hadn't enjoyed high school himself.

"I guess I'll think about it."

"Think about it."

"Thanks, Mary."

Cumulo was racing back and forth, rolling in the snow then licking it, shaking his coat and barking at the birds in the trees. They were both lost in thought when Tom broke the silence.

"What about this date tomorrow night?"

"Ah, yes. Perfect. At 7:30. I'm supposed to be meeting him at the restaurant—it's a new little local place, step up from fast food, but not too pretentious."

"How'd you meet this guy? What's his name?"

"Brian. I did his library orientation, and I think I made him really nervous. He kept dropping books."

They both laughed.

"Well, it shows he has good taste."

"Ha! Well thanks. I don't know why I told him I'd go tomorrow night. That was my worst planning. I hate leaving when the whole family is home. I just wasn't thinking. I suppose I could call and switch it…"

Her voice trailed off and she traced a line through the trampled snow slowly.

"You want to go."

It wasn't accusatory, just an observation. She looked away, then looked back.

"I do. I like him."

"You're blushing!"

She covered her face with her gloves, and said,

"No, no, it's the cold."

He laughed, scooped up a handful of snow, and tossed it at her.

"Okay sure, the cold."

She retaliated in kind, and they stood up and started back towards the house. When they reached home Christmas dinner was in the works. Tom's mother was charging about the steaming kitchen like a drill sergeant she could've been. She instead became a mother, a similar, but, more challenging job.

CHAPTER TWENTY-ONE

The Christmas mid-morning sun found Janelle sleeping peacefully in her white bed, Mike still resting his head on the corner of the mattress and holding her hand. He woke up first, and when he saw her pale still form, he was convinced she was dead. He leapt from his seat and ran into the hallway, looking left and right for a nurse. One had just rounded the corner at the end of the hall, and he went sprinting towards her.

"Nurse! Ma'am! Excuse me!"

She turned around quickly, clipboard in hand.

"Yes? What is it?"

"She's dead! I think she's dead!"

Her arm dropped to her side as she walked hastily towards the room with him, saying,

"What? Are you sure?"

"Uh. No. I just woke up and she looked dead."

The nurse looked at him.

"You woke up less than a minute ago."

"Uh, yeah."

They walked into the room, and where Janelle had lain still and quiet a moment before, she was now sitting up, eyes open, looking at them.

"Good morning, ma'am. It's good to see you looking so well!"

The nurse smiled at her, then looked at Mike. He apologized.

"I guess I'd be a bad doctor."

She smiled, and Janelle said,

"Good morning, can I have something to eat? I'm hungry."

"Absolutely, dear. Do you want anything in particular?"

"Can I order anything I want?"

The nurse paused.

"Well…"

"Can I have a donut?"

The nurse, Kelly, laughed.

"I can bring you a donut. Anything else?"

"Eggs? And sausage. And orange juice? And toast."

She paused, as if thinking if she wanted anything else, then added,

"Please."

"Gracious, by the sound of it you haven't eaten for a year!"

"I haven't eaten since Friday."

Kelly raised her eyebrows.

"You're a trooper. I'll see what we can do. You get some rest—if you keep improving, you'll get to go home soon. As long as you're going somewhere that they'll feed you."

Janelle beamed. Though she hadn't been cognizant for most of her sickness, she still wanted to be in a home for Christmas, feeling the love of family, eating holiday food. She said,

"Thank you."

Kelly walked out. Mike sat on the edge of her bed.

"How're you feeling?"

She looked around blearily for her glasses, found them, and slid them onto her face.

"Really much better."

Paused.

"How long have I been here?"

He shook his head, saying,

"Not very long. Just since yesterday morning."

She nodded, and said,

"I don't remember."

He replied,

"You were pretty sick."

After a moment of thought, she said,

"Thanks, Mike."

He nodded.

Eventually the nurse came back with her breakfast, much more food than Janelle had asked for, and Janelle beamed.

"Thank you so much. This looks so good."

Kelly smiled as Janelle started eating like her life depended on it— which, loosely of course, it did.

"Is pneumonia contagious?"

She didn't know anything about it.

"No, I don't think so. Just the bacteria you were sick with at first."

"Good. Are you hungry?"

She motioned towards her tray as she spoke, saying,

"I'm not going to be able eat all of this."

He smiled, and took a donut.

"Thanks."

Later that day the doctor came in and checked on her.

"You should be able to go home soon."

"Thank you, thank you so much."

"Absolutely. I'm sorry you have to be in the hospital on Christmas day. But we're glad you're doing so much better."

* * *

At 7, Tom and Mary snuck out of the house, although it looked less like sneaking and more like casually walking out while the grandparents were playing with the little girls and everyone else was watching a movie and eating popcorn.

"Remember, be engaging, have good manners, and don't tell corny jokes till you've decided he'll like them."

She laughed.

"Do you think I've never gone on a date?"

Eight years his senior, she hadn't talked to him about her romance life until recently, and he'd never thought to ask. He looked over at her, then back at the road.

"I don't know, I never thought about it. Have you?"

"Tom! Of course I have. There was Patrick. Then Brent. Lee was a trip. And Sam wasn't very fun. But, yes. I go out a lot. That happens when you get to be my age and still aren't married. Everyone assumes you've got some great character flaw, or that you're always on the hunt, but they're all a little curious. So you go out with a lot of men once, and sometimes it's good and sometimes it's not. And sometimes you go out twice. But usually not."

"Oh. Wow. Well then I'm sure you know what to do."

"I do my best. Don't sneeze too much, make good eye contact, find a subject of personal interest to you both and go from there, yeah. Dad gave me lots of first date lectures, so I have the technique down."

She shook her head, then pointed.

"Tom, that's him! In front of the doors! That's him! He's here first and he's waiting for me outside!"

Tom looked him over closely. He had all the engineering of a nice man, clean cut, neatly dressed, and an engaging smile that he flashed, as he looked over and saw Mary.

"Alright. You be good. Text or call me if you need anything. I love you."

He watched her walk up to him, a bounce in her step that he hadn't seen for a long time (maybe because of the broken leg). Mary deserved to be loved. It only made sense.

He hadn't bothered with an excuse for leaving, because no one had noticed when he took the keys from the hook in the kitchen and walked out. He drove to his favorite place to go at night—a wide open field. He'd always kept a blanket in the trunk of his car in high school, and whenever there was something particularly pressing he needed to think about, he would drive out to the field and lay on the hood of his car. He'd stay warm with a blanket and stare up at the stars for hours.

He hadn't just sat to think for weeks, probably at least since everything with Brittany started. He'd been too busy working, so he could afford to take time off when she was with him. As he lay on his back watching the blackness and the sparkles, and listening to the night, he wondered what his life would have been without her.

Janelle was sick, in the hospital. What if she had died? She was his friend. He wanted to see her succeed; to do well. He didn't want her to die. He let his mind wander around Denver, around The Cup, around all the places he went and the people he knew. It was a good life—but it wasn't the best life for him, and the slow nagging that had begun months ago was becoming more persistent, clicking in the back of his mind, reminding him that he ought to do something more. When he was little and he complained, his mother would just look at him, and say,

"Tom, is your life hard?"

He would groan and affirm that it was, indeed, harder than almost anyone else's.

"Why?"

He would invariably be working on some project, either homework or something fun he'd started just because he wanted to, and he would begin anew bemoaning the difficulties.

"Are you good at it?"

The first time she'd asked him this, he'd looked at what he was making. It was a modelling clay pot, and while it was obviously a first try, it wasn't awful. He had said maybe he wasn't the worst, and she'd nodded.

"You're good at a lot, Tom. You're talented. You'll have to do hard things."

He would sigh, accepting the challenge wrapped in a compliment.

Now his life was a different kind of hard, the hard of the daily grind, of waking up in the morning and feeling like a failure. College swirled around in his mind, the pressure, the responsibility, yet always the open gateway to living a life that would surpass the mediocre and mean he was worth commemorating. The minutes ticked on and on, and still he watched the stars and his breath mingle in the cold winter air. When several hours had passed after dropping Mary off, and he couldn't feel his toes or his fingers, he got a text from her. It was two thumbs up, and said Brian was dropping her off at home. He texted back two thumbs up, and started his car. Mary, and a man who wanted her. A foreign prospect till now, but one for which he hoped, fervently. Mary loved would be a delight. He reached home before they did, and was sitting in his car in the driveway when Brian pulled up, got out of his car quickly, and got a bouquet of flowers from his trunk, which he handed to Mary. Tom couldn't hear her from the car, but she giggled, and smiled up at him. As he walked her to the front door, Mary motioned to Tom's car, and Tom did the friendly, I'm-a-protective-brother-so-I'm-not-overly-thrilled-to-meet-you wave. Brian smiled and waved back, then hugged Mary gently around the bouquet of delicate flowers that he'd gotten for her. Flowers that fit her personality perfectly, because they were just like her. Tom knew he'd picked them out intentionally, and he began to like Brian. After he left, Tom went inside and found Mary in the kitchen, putting her flowers in a vase. They could hear the family playing games in the basement.

"Well? How was it?"

She didn't really seem to hear him. She was fingering the small winter flowers, and blushing, the corners of her lips creeping up onto her cheeks. Moments later, she answered.

"It was wonderful."

She giggled and sighed, and Tom eyed her suspiciously. Mary kept her head on straight and weighed all the pros and cons before getting swept away in something. Usually she was perfectly balanced. But then, he knew. He knew what the excitement of love could do.

* * *

The morning after Christmas, Mike took Janelle back to the Donahue's, who had waited for them to celebrate Christmas. Janelle cried a little, as Mike carried her into the house and set her on the rocker in the corner of the living room that would become her permanent seat during the vacation. Christmas at the Donahue's felt more like home than her home had ever felt. Janelle's mother had always tried, but fear always stole the joy away. At the Donahue's all was love, warmth, and delight, and she soaked it in like a too-dry sponge. Love has a way of expanding people, of bringing their goals and dreams and visions close and reachable, and making them comfortable with who they are.

Even in the short time the whole family was home, Janelle became part of it. They'd all gotten her Christmas presents, and all seemed to care wholeheartedly about her. One day, several days after Christmas, Janelle was in the living room with Sherry's oldest daughter Bethany. As a general rule, Janelle didn't tell people about her family. But she'd never been involved in a really functional family, and she blossomed under the love. Bethany was working on a puzzle on the coffee table, and Janelle was rocking the baby. Bethany suddenly broke the peaceful quiet, and said,

"What's your family like?"

There was the slightest moment of hesitation, as Janelle remembered that she didn't trust people. But Bethany was so calm, so kind, so listening. Without understanding how she was doing it, Janelle spoke.

"Well, I'm the oldest of four. There used to be five of us, but when I was little my big brother ran into the street and got hit by a car."

Janelle hadn't told very many people—she paused and sighed. Bethany said,

"I'm so sorry."

"It's okay. I have nightmares about it sometimes."

Bethany just looked at her. Janelle didn't know, but Bethany was a clinical counselor, and had already made a guess about Janelle's past.

"It must have been hard. How old were you?"

"I was four and he was five. We were playing with a ball in the yard, which was a hill, and he tripped over the curb and into the street right in front of the car. The doctors tried to save him…"

She was sitting in the rocking chair, rubbing her toes against the footrest. The rest of the family was out on a walk.

"… But it was too late, and he died. My mom was pregnant with my little brother."

"She must have been devastated."

"She was. A lot of things changed after that."

Janelle barely remembered life before she was four, but she did remember one thing: peace. And she had loved to sit in her daddy's lap.

"What happened?"

Without knowing why, Janelle wanted to tell Bethany everything: the drinking, the fear in her mother's eyes every day when her father came home, the pain when he didn't come home at all.

"My dad started drinking."

"Oh, dear."

"Yeah."

She paused. She didn't talk about it often, as people have the habit of judging the children for the sins of their parents. The only other people who she'd told were her bosses in New York, but it hadn't changed how they treated her.

"What happened?"

Janelle knew from her mother telling her, but she didn't remember the progression.

"At first it wasn't so bad. He drank some, I think to calm his nerves from the pain of losing his son. But then he started drinking more and more, and it became a habit, and my mom didn't have the time or attention to stop him, because she was taking care of my little brother."

It was numb there, the part of her heart where she thought about her family. She had turned off those feelings for so long she didn't know how to turn them back on.

"And he's been drinking ever since?"

Janelle nodded, looking at her hands folded on the knitted afghan that Mr. Donahue was constantly telling Mrs. Donahue was ugly, but Sherry insisted it reminded her of summer. It was yellow and green, and Janelle agreed with Mr. Donahue that it was atrocious, but it was also soft and warm, and Janelle was always cold.

"My mom bore the brunt of it. She finally told me to run away."

She looked sadly at the picture of the Donahue family, perched on the mantle, smiling down at the living room. They had no idea what this fear was.

"So you did."

It was a blank statement.

"When I moved here in September, it was because I got up one morning, and instead of going to work I went to the bus station and bought a ticket to Denver. I got here with enough to get a car and pay a month or two of rent, and found a job at Francie's."

"That's brave."

"I wanted to get away. It was less brave than staying at home with a broken mother and a drunken father."

"Does he work?"

"He's a car mechanic. Makes pretty good money, but he spends it all on liquor. My mom is a nurse. She spends all her time taking care of people and making them better, when she's the one who really needs it."

The irony had struck her for the first time in high school when her dad knocked her mom over onto the staircase, and she got a bruise the size of a paper plate on her abdomen.

"My dad would get rip roaring drunk and terrifyingly angry, then the next day he would apologize and be sweet as a kitten—but it would never last. That night, he would be drunk again, and the whole thing would repeat itself."

She sighed. It hurt, but it felt good to talk about it—almost like washing the sheets after you've been sick, or waking up with a new haircut; an invitation for a fresh beginning.

"Oh, honey."

Bethany had worked with abuse a lot. No daughter should fear her father. Janelle had been sitting so quietly that Bethany didn't notice when the tears started to roll down her cheeks. She sat in the chair in the corner, rocking back and forth slowly, crying silently. It was simply the overflow from a heart that had been damaged and broken so many times that it had stopped feeling. Bethany moved across the room and put her hand on Janelle's leg. She didn't say anything. After a long time, Janelle said,

"I always wanted my life to be normal, like my friends' lives—they seemed so happy. I always just pretended."

The pressure of performance had hit hard.

"Dear girl."

"And my mom told me to run away because she wanted something better for my life. So I did. I left them. And I haven't talked to them since, because my mom is scared my dad will try to find me."

"Would he?"

"I think so. I'm sure when he realized that I left he was angry."

Bethany nodded. It was common for these fathers to track down their children, so they could assert their control.

"You've had a hard life, sweet girl."

Janelle nodded, the silent tears still slipping down her cheeks. Just then, everyone came home from the walk, and all was chaos and cheer. Janelle cleaned her face, and Bethany squeezed her shoulder.

"Thank you for telling me."

"Thank you for caring."

Bethany nodded.

CHAPTER TWENTY-TWO

Tom left his parent's house on Saturday morning. As soon as he got home, he called Janelle. When she didn't answer, he called Mike, who also didn't answer. Leaning on the edge of his bed, he surveyed the room full of Christmas decorations. After he'd taken some down, his phone rang. It was Sherry Donahue.

"Hello?"

"Oh, hello, Tommy! So good to hear you. When are you coming back? We all missed you for Christmas."

"Actually, I'm back in town already."

"You are? Tommy, come over!"

He grinned. It was nice to be wanted.

"I'd love to. Do you have Janelle there?"

She said something to someone on the other end of the line, then there was a crash and a shriek, and she said,

"Hang on, Tommy,"

He heard the phone clunk down onto a hard surface. There were lots of voices in the background, the gentle pandemonium of family at home. He smiled. From one family to the next. She was gone for quite some time, and holding his phone on his shoulder, he packed up the last nativity scene. He finished before she returned.

"Sorry, Tommy dear. Lucas, my little grandson, was climbing on the back of the rocking chair which is usually okay because Janelle sits in it, but she was in the bathroom so it fell over backwards and I had to do my grandmotherly duty. Don't worry, he's fine. I'm a little out of breath from going down to the basement freezer for a Popsicle. Popsicles fix everything for kids, Tommy. Everything. You know what else works really well is—"

"Oh, dear, well I'm glad he's okay."

Sherry would've kept telling him about her grand parenting tricks if he hadn't interrupted.

"Hey, I was wondering, is Janelle still there?"

"She most certainly is, and looking better every day. Come by, Tommy!"

"I was going to ask you if that was alright."

"Most certainly. In fact, we're eating dinner soon, so if you hurry you'll make it in time for pork chops and mashed potatoes."

"That sounds delicious. I'd love to come. I'll be right over."

He was already walking out the door, his coat in one hand and his keys in the other.

"Perfect. See you soon, honey."

Dinner with Sherry Donahue was always an event. Tom had gone over a few times since he'd been living in Denver, and he always loved it. When the whole family was home, everyone talked at once and was so full of joy he couldn't help but be delighted. This dinner was no exception. Dishes were piled high, for besides pork chops and mashed potatoes, there were steamed vegetables and fruit salad and several different kinds of bread and rolls. He sat next to Janelle, who looked even paler and smaller than she had before. When dinner was over and the dishes were done, Sherry pulled Tom aside.

"I'm sure you want to catch up with Janelle."

"That'd be nice."

With no further ceremony, Sherry announced a family game time in the basement, with obligatory attendance. She winked at Tom, and herded the flock of grandchildren that had gathered around her to the basement steps. Janelle had moved back to her chair and was rocking slowly and Tom came over and sat down across from her. She was so small, her cough made her shake like a leaf in the wind. Still, she smiled, and said,

"Mike told me you went home?"

Mike wasn't there, but he was coming on Sunday.

"I did. He's right."

She looked at him.

"How was it?"

"It was great. Probably the best time I've ever had there."

She shifted and continued to stroke the sleeping kitten in her lap.

"Good, Tom. I'm glad."

"How are you? What happened?"

"Well, Friday morning I went to work feeling okay, but by the time I finished I felt awful, so I crawled into bed and didn't get out till Tuesday, when Mike came over to check on me, realized I was practically dying, and brought me here."

She said it with all of the gravitas of a senator, and he laughed. But underneath the mock seriousness he could tell she had been scared.

"At least, they tell me I was dying. I was asleep most of the time. Wednesday morning Mike brought me to the hospital, where I spent the night. They pumped me full of antibiotics and let me sleep for 24 hours straight, and the next day they let me come home, if I promised not to exert any energy. So here I am."

"Wow. I'm really glad you're okay."

Looking up at him, pushing her glasses up her nose, she smiled.

"Thanks. Mostly I don't remember any of it, but it's what Mike has assured me happened."

"Sounds awful. I was so worried about you—even though I didn't even know a lot of it till today."

She grinned.

"Thanks, Tom. I appreciate that."

She paused, then looked up at him, confused.

"But you went home? I thought Brittany was coming here?"

Mike hadn't told Janelle anything that had happened with Tom and Brittany. Mike knew it was Tom's news, and Janelle would rather hear it from Tom than from him.

"She was. She did."

He looked at his hands, which were busy fiddling with one of the many toys Sherry Donahue kept on her coffee table. Janelle waited for him to continue. He took his time, slowly gathering his mind. He felt like somehow he was letting her down. After a long silence, he said,

"We're done."

Janelle didn't seem fazed, but she was sad for Tom.

"Oh, Tom."

It felt like high school all over again, a heartbroken friend coming to Janelle, the strong one, asking her to pick up the pieces.

"We were walking home from the post office in the snow and I stopped to look at your windows because your lights weren't on and I was worried about you, and somehow, something clicked. I realized that she didn't want me, and that we would never really be happy."

"Tom, she wanted you. She knew you were a person of worth and she wanted to be a part of that."

He looked up from the toy he was fiddling with.

"She said she wanted to be with me so much but she didn't think it would work but she wanted to try because she thought I was amazing."

It was a compliment wrapped in a knife stab.

"I'm sorry. It hurts."

She didn't say anything else. He sighed.

"It does."

He told her everything else, how it ended, how he brought her to the airport and gave her the diamonds, how he went home and told Mary everything, how they had both told him to go back to school and he was thinking about it, and how no matter how hard he tried, he couldn't stop thinking about how he might have made it work.

"Tom, it's been four days. Of course you can't stop thinking about her. Everything reminds you of her, because she's part of your heart."

He wiped his nose on the sleeve of his flannel, and said,

"I guess."

"Also, Tom, you do need to go back to school. You need to make something out of your life. This sitting around and working a job anyone could do isn't for you. You need to make a difference in the world. You can, you're able to. Do something with your life—don't waste it."

She broke down in a fit of coughing, and the kitten stirred. They talked on, Janelle talking more, Tom talking some. After they'd talked through all of Tom's trouble, they were sat in peaceful silence, each distracted in thought. Tom's thoughts came around, and he looked up. Janelle was rocking slowly back and forth, humming a lullaby to the sleeping baby in her lap. Before he thought about it, Tom blurted his question.

"Were you abused?"

She stopped humming and looked at him. Intently. Eventually she looked back down at the furry animal in her arms.

"Yes. I was."

She'd spend most of her life hedging around the truth, trying to avoid telling it, working hard to conceal it so she didn't become a pity case, or so that the wrong person wouldn't find out and do something about it. Her mother told a few people, and all of them wanted her to leave her husband, but she hadn't. She loved her husband, even though he abused her. She loved him because she too clearly remembered how he had been before Alex died. She held onto a hope that maybe someday he would stop drinking. It was the last hope of a woman who had been loved, and been robbed of love, and wanted it back desperately.

Tom sat, in silence. He hadn't expected her to answer so easily.

"I'm sorry."

She nodded.

"What happened?"

For the second time in a week, she told what her life had been; the fear, the bruises, the heartache. For the second time that week, someone cared to hear just because of who she was. She told the story slowly, not leaving out any important parts, so that by the end Tom had reached both the depth of sorrow for her situation, and a righteous anger over a man who was irresponsible enough to drink away his sorrows and stop caring for his family the way a father should. Janelle's story ended in Denver, away from her brothers, sister, and mom, who she hadn't talked to in three months.

"She won't let you call her?"

"No. My dad, when he's not drunk, isn't too bad, but he's smart and gets angry easily. If he knew that my mom talked to me, I don't want to think about what would happen."

"Do you think he would look for you?"

She sighed. It was her worst recurring nightmare, her in a locked and empty room, him banging on the door in a drunken rage.

"I'm not sure. I think so. Not because he misses me, but because I'm sure he thinks I shouldn't have left. It doesn't make sense to me, but I can see it happening."

She paused, thinking about what she would do if he came for her, where she would run and hide, if she would even have time.

"You've had a hard life, haven't you?"

Not many people said it so bluntly.

"Yes. It has. I don't know how my mom does it. I used to cry myself to sleep just so I wouldn't have to hear her crying."

She paused, remembering the long nights, then added,

"We went to church for a while, but my dad made us stop. Some of the neighbors tried to help us, but that just made my dad upset."

He nodded. He knew the feeling. The misguided attempts of good people to express their concern often went amiss.

"I understand."

Each retreated into silence, considering her past. Tom now understood why it took so long for her to smile.

"Thanks, Tom. Thank you for asking."

The secret that she'd worked so hard to conceal for her entire life had suddenly become the thing she wanted to talk about more than anything else. She wanted to be known for who she really was, not for who she pretended to be, who she presented herself as.

"You're welcome. I care about you. You've taught me so much."

* * *

Weeks went by, and before Tom realized it, the middle of February had come with its gloom, gray skies and snow, and the occasional sunny day. Tom and Janelle talked often, and Tom and Mike talked often, and Mike and Janelle saw each other occasionally, and always there was the joy of belonging. Sherry Donahue had the three of them over for lunch after church every Sunday, and constantly asked Janelle and Tom to come to church with her. It didn't bother them—they liked her too much to be annoyed at her persistent care.

One day, like normal, Mike came bouncing into The Cup for his morning coffee, and Tom greeted him.

"Morning, Mike! How's your Wednesday?"

"Oh, you know. Cold, early, a little dreary, but half way through the week!"

Though he had calmed down slightly since Tom had known him, he still held on to his old habit of bouncing up and down as he waited in line.

"Good, good."

"Yes, yes it is."

Mike smiled, as Tom poured him coffee. Sometimes they had profound conversations—sometimes they didn't. Today, as Mike watched Tom's hands and bounced, he suddenly snapped his fingers.

"I've been meaning to ask you for a long time—remember when Janelle was sick and I thought she might be abused?"

Tom nodded. Somehow, they'd never finished up that conversation.

"Yeah, I remember."

Tom said.

"Did you ever find out?"

"She was."

He nodded as he said it.

"Oh, really?"

"Yeah."

Tom told him an abbreviated version of her story, and Mike nodded, saying,

"We need to watch out for her."

Tom thought the same thing.

"Yes. We do."

Mike nodded with determination, paid for his coffee and turned to leave.

"Have a good day, Tom!"

"Thanks, Mike! You too!"

For the rest of the day, Tom wondered how they could watch out for Janelle.

CHAPTER TWENTY-THREE

The night before Tom and Mike's brief conversation, Janelle was working. It was a busy evening; cold winter nights drove people to Francie's. Janelle was doing double service; one of the waitresses was sick, so Francie's was short staffed. They made more tip money, but it was stressful. Janelle was so busy she didn't pay attention to who came in or out, so when Francie, who acted as hostess and cook on these busy nights, called out that there was a man in the corner table facing out, she ran right over, not even looking at the back of his head.

"Hello, welcome to Francie's. My name's Janelle and I'll be..."

Her voice trailed off.

"Hi, sweetie."

She stared at him, frozen,

"What are you doing here?"

He cleared his throat.

"I came to bring you home."

Moving his knife and spoon on the tablecloth, he clanked them together.

"How did you find me? Why?"

"Because a girl belongs at home with her family, and we're your family."

He didn't seem drunk.

"Oh."

Just then she heard someone say, just loud enough to hear,

"I hope she comes by here soon."

She turned to check her tables and bring out orders. Francie was busy at the oven in the back, but when Janelle came in for plates Francie stopped her.

"What's the matter, dear? You look as if you've just seen a ghost."

"No, I'm fine, it's alright."

She picked up her plates and hurried out, two on each arm, balanced perfectly. It's a trick she'd picked up in New York during peak times when they ran out of trays for plates. Her father sat at his table in the corner watching her, picking his teeth with his fork. She tried to avoid his table, but she needed to serve him eventually, so she went back.

"How did you find me?"

He chuckled.

"My little girl, trying to run away, working hard to cover her tracks. It wasn't hard, once you gave your insurance card to the hospital. Hospitals send bills."

She sighed. She'd forgotten, and since she hadn't gotten any bills from the hospital, assumed it had all gone through. She hadn't even thought of that.

"It was easy after that. A few well-placed questions, a week or two of looking, and here I am."

"Oh."

It fell flat.

"Bring me dinner, whatever's best."

She sighed. On the outside, cool and collected, it was business as usual. But her head was running miles quicker. He was planning to kidnap her. Standing in the back, checking the clock and noticing it was half past 9, she pulled out her phone and prayed that Tom was awake. She didn't have time to call, so she texted:

Text me. Need you.

Then back to work. Bringing her father his meatloaf, he nodded.

"Just the way it should be, a young lady serving her father."

Then he took his fork and began shoveling the food into his mouth, without taking his eyes off her. She left him and served her other customers, and slowly they trickled out, yawning and looking at watches, strolling the slow walk of people who have eaten and been satisfied. Her father stayed and ordered coffee and pie when he'd finished his food. After almost everyone else had left and he was still there, Francie told Janelle she was free to go, because Carla was closing tonight. Janelle nodded. Francie was flustered and tired, but she looked at Janelle and asked,

"Are you sure you're okay?"

Janelle nodded mutely. She wanted to tell Francie—but now her father was a real threat again, and she was a prisoner to fear again.

Tom hadn't texted. She stood in the back to call him. His phone went straight to voicemail. She could leave from the back door, but her car was parked in front so she would have to walk past the windows, where he could see her. She took her purse and walked resolutely straight out the door without looking at him, but she heard the door open and close behind her and he yelled for her to stop. She didn't. He walked quickly up behind her and grabbed her arm.

"You're coming with me."

"No, please."

She struggled, but his grip only grew tighter.

"You need to come home. You don't belong here."

"No, I don't want to leave."

He was dragging her by the arm towards his familiar banged up pickup truck, casualty of at least a half-dozen drunken accidents.

"You're coming with me."

And he marched her to his truck, opened the door, and practically lifted her by the arm into the passenger seat, locking the door behind her. Seconds later he was in the driver seat, starting the engine. The truck was the same it'd always been. She'd only been in it a few times, usually to clean it out. There was garbage everywhere, full bottles of beer and hard liquor on the seat by her, and empty bottles littering the floor.

"Where are we going?"

He didn't respond, hands resolutely on the steering wheel. She asked again,

"Where are we going?"

He frowned at her. He pulled out into the road, stonily silent, and after several minutes passed she realized with terror that they were headed toward the interstate.

"I came to get you, and I'm bringing you home. Give me a beer."

"No."

He wasn't used to being refused, and the suddenness of it shocked him. He looked at her.

"What?"

"No. I don't want to go home with you and I won't give you a beer."

It took the last of her courage to say, but it didn't work. He looked at her tauntingly, and sneered. He'd used up his niceness.

"Well, I'm bringing you home and I'm going to have a beer. Give me one."

He smacked her shoulder with the flat of his palm, and the pain brought tears to her eyes. She reached down and handed him a can. He opened it with one hand, eying her suspiciously, then drank the whole can and crunched it, throwing it at her feet.

"Give me another one."

"You'll get drunk."

"Give me another one."

He struck her again, this time lower on the arm, twice. She winced, and leaned down toward the twelve pack. While she was bent over, he slammed his hand down on her back. She whimpered, and brought up another can. He took it, grinning maliciously. She looked out the window, tears in her eyes. They were on the freeway, heading east at seventy-five miles per hour, her father angry and determined, knuckles white as he grasped the steering wheel. No one knew where she was.

CHAPTER TWENTY-FOUR

As the morning passed quietly, Tom wondered where Janelle was. He looked at the clock for the forty-fifth time in ten minutes. She was late for her morning latte. Sherry Donahue and Mr. Peterson came and went, and still no Janelle. Maybe she hadn't had time to come in, or maybe she was working lunch today and hadn't told him. The possibilities rolled through his mind as he mechanically made drinks for customers, engaging them in polite but distant conversation. When three o'clock came, he clocked out quickly and pulled his phone from his bag where he'd left it all day. He rarely took it out at work—sometimes leaving it off till the end of his shift. Today was one of those days.

He walked through the snowy parking lot to his car, for the February flurries were consistent. He powered on his phone and turned on his car, letting them both warm up. Moments later his phone buzzed multiple times, and he looked down. Mike had texted him twice that morning. The first said,

Tell me if you see Janelle today.

And the second said,

I have a funny feeling about this. Hurry and text.

And he had a text from Janelle the night before, that said,

Text me. Need you.

He read them on autopilot, but suddenly his mind screeched to a halt. Need you. Janelle was in trouble. He called Mike, who answered on the first ring.

"Mike, Janelle's in trouble."

He heard Mike slam his fist on the desk.

"I knew it. I knew it. I knew something was wrong. How do you know? Where is she? What happened?"

Tom read him the text from the night before when his phone had been off. Almost before he was done, Mike said,

"We have to find her. Check her house and see if she's there."

"I'm on my way. I'll call and see if she answers."

She didn't. He tried twice more, and the third time it cut short before it finished ringing, and went straight to voicemail. He called Mike back and told him.

"At least we know she's alive. The third time I called someone cut the ringing short."

It wasn't much to go on, but it was hope. Tom sighed. He was close to her house by this point, and when he got there he didn't bother turning his car off—he ran up the walk, up the steps, and up to her small attic apartment door. He knocked vigorously then tried the handle—it was open, so he went in. It was neat and tidy, and there was a bowl full of milky water in the sink. Everything else looked normal. He thumbed through the mail on her counter before he walked out, dialing Mike.

"Not here. Everything looks normal clean, no sign of a struggle or rush."

Mike paused.

"What do you think happened?"

Tom hadn't wanted to verbalize it, even to himself, because he wanted so desperately for his assumption to be incorrect—but it began to seem like it must be true.

"Well, her dad…"

His voice trailed off. He could sense Mike nodding.

"Tom. We have to help her."

"Where are you?"

"I'm at work. I can leave."

Tom thought hard.

"I'm going to go to Francie's—maybe she'll know something."

Mike made an 'mhmm' sound, then said,

"I'll meet you there."

Tom drove there, speeding most of the way. He had a good reason to speed. Pulling into Francie's parking lot, he was immediately set at rest. Janelle's car was in its normal spot in the left corner of the lot. He parked and ran inside, expecting to see the blond hair pulled into a bun, but he didn't. Carla, one of her coworkers, was hosting, but before she could say anything, he said,

"Is Janelle here?"

Carla shook her head.

"I haven't seen her yet today. She was here last night, but she left before me."

"Did you notice anything unusual about when she left?"

Carla put a finger on her nose, concentrating very hard. She liked Tom—she thought he was cute and she didn't want to let him down.

"Well, as soon as she left some guy went running after her. But we were pretty busy last night and I was cleaning up tables by then and I didn't watch to see what happened."

Tom sighed. Some guy.

"Did you notice how old he was?"

Carla thought for a minute, then said,

"I think at least old enough to be her dad. I'm not sure who he was. She didn't seem happy to see him, I did notice that."

Tom nodded.

"Thanks, Carla. You're the best. Is Francie here?"

Carla nodded, pointing to the back with her thumb.

"Thanks."

"Anytime, really."

And she sighed as he walked away. Why he liked Janelle and not her gave her all the faint misery in the world—but then, such was life.

Tom walked into the back, where Francie stood at the island mashing raw ground beef in a bowl for meatloaf. He kissed her on the cheek—Francie reminded him of one of his aunts, and his aunt always loved that. Francie did too.

"Hey doll. How can I help you?"

He moved across the island from her.

"Is Janelle supposed to be working today?"

She looked up at the clock on the wall, and frowned.

"Yes, she is. She's supposed to be here by now. She's not."

He shook his head.

"No, she's not."

"Oh, dear."

Francie kept mashing her meat, but she looked worried.

"She was here yesterday, right?"

Francie nodded.

"Did you notice when she left, was she okay?"

Francie scrunched her eyebrows, hands busy, reaching for various ingredients, all the things that made her meatloaf famous.

"You know, it's funny you should ask. I looked out and saw her talking to some man sitting at the corner table, and when she came back here she was pale as a sheet, like she'd seen a ghost."

Tom didn't like the sound of what he was piecing together.

"Then I told her she could go because she's closed a lot recently and Carla was here. I did notice that the man was gone pretty soon after though."

She furrowed her brow, hands suddenly still in the meat.

"Her car is still here, isn't it?"

Tom nodded and said,

"Yes."

She looked at him.

"What's going on, Tom?"

"I'm not sure, but it's not good."

Right then, Mike walked in, worry marching across his face.

"Hey, Tom, Francie. Figure anything out?"

Tom told him what he knew, and Mike nodded his head, once, twice, three times, then said,

"We need to find her."

"How?"

Tom knew she was from New York, but that was about all.

"Have you texted her?"

He'd called her, but he'd been in too much of a worried hurry to text.

"Let's both text her. Short texts. And see if she answers."

Francie nodded at this, and added,

"I'll text her too."

"Good idea, Francie. Ask her why she's not at work."

She nodded, and went to the sink to clean her hands. Tom and Mike moved out to a booth in the dining area, because it was still the middle of the afternoon, and the dinner rush hadn't started yet. Both texted her, asking where she was and if she was okay. Then they sat there, staring at their phones. Mike broke the silence.

"It's safe to assume that if her dad came all the way here, he's going to bring her home."

"You think so?"

Mike nodded, said,

"I think if I were the kind of guy that he seems to be and I found out where my daughter was, I would come get her."

Tom's turn to nod.

"So he probably took her last night and headed home."

Mike shuddered at the danger Janelle could be in.

"Oh, Tom."

Tom nodded, and Mike didn't need to finish voicing his thought.

"Yeah. It's bad."

And they were silent. Moments later, simultaneously, their phones vibrated. Both had the same message.

Chi. Help.

Tom read it first.

"Chi? What's Chi? Chi who?"

"Chicago, probably."

Mike spoke with confidence.

"Chicago? How can she be in Chicago?"

"If her dad drove all night, they'd be close to Chicago by now. They'd probably even be further than Chicago, so he must have stopped somewhere."

Tom nodded, saying,

"What are we going to do?"

He couldn't gather his thoughts. Mike spoke without hesitation.

"Rescue her."

Tom's gentle manliness and Mike's hyper strength both swelled to action. Janelle needed them.

"Yes. You're right. How?"

"Well, she's in Chicago. She probably won't be for long. We need to get there."

"They'll keep moving?"

Mike nodded, saying,

"We should go."

Mike had always liked road trips. He had a fast car. Tom said,

"Alright. Can you take off work?"

Mike nodded, and asked,

"How soon can you be ready?"

Tom said,

"If we're really needing to hurry, I don't need anything. So, right now."

They stood up and went back to Francie, almost done with her meatloaf. Tom spoke.

"She's in Chicago. We're going to go get her."

He spoke with certainty. They were going to get her, and they would bring her back.

"Be careful, boys."

"Thanks, Francie. I'm going to leave my car here for a few days, if that's okay?"

She nodded.

"Fine, hon."

"You're an angel. We'll be in touch."

They walked out to Mike's car, got in, and zipped out of the parking lot, heading for the interstate like Janelle had less than 24 hours before, sad and scared and helpless.

CHAPTER TWENTY-FIVE

Janelle had curled into a ball in the corner of her seat and gone to sleep the night before. Long ago she'd learned that sleep was a most merciful escape, and she'd developed the knack for sleeping on command, giving herself no mercy and no choice but weary restlessness. Her father drove on and on. He was driving when she went to sleep, and when she woke up hours later, the sun was up. She assumed he'd stopped and slept for a while though, because they weren't much farther than they had been when she'd gone to sleep.

She hid her phone in her shirt before she went to sleep, and was glad she had, for her bag had been moved, and was unzipped where it'd been closed before. She situated herself, pulling her phone from her shirt in the process and putting it on the seat next to her right leg, hiding it from him. She'd put it on silent the night before, so he wouldn't be alerted if someone communicated with her. Tom hadn't gotten her text yet. Her father didn't speak to her, which was just as well. She had nothing to say.

Hours later, when Tom got off work, she guessed, he called her three times in a row. The third time she ended the call before the phone was done ringing.

"Give me a beer."

Her father sneered at her, raising his hand slowly. She handed him a can. He drank it quickly and signaled for another, smacking her lightly. She handed him another. They were close to Chicago, somewhere in central Illinois. She remembered stopping in Chicago on the bus on the way there. She'd liked it, but not as much as she liked Denver. Denver was more honest—open. Close to an hour later, her phone lit up. Tom and Mike and Francie had all texted her, Tom and Mike asking where she was and Francie asking why she wasn't at work. She picked up her phone, and her father glared.

"What are you doing?"

"My boss asked why I'm not at work."

"Tell her you're sick."

She nodded.

"I want to see it before you send it."

She nodded. She had no choice. She quickly texted Tom and Mike back together, then typed her text to Francie and held it up to show her dad. He was satisfied, adding,

"Don't ask any of your friends to come. It won't help."

He hated Denver. When she was growing up, whenever anyone said anything about Colorado he growled and complained and made angry faces. Her mother said it had to do with another woman. That's one of the reasons Janelle chose Denver—she hadn't thought he would come there to pick her up. A few minutes after she sent the texts, Tom and Mike both texted her.

We're coming.

Her heart filled with tears, but she hardened her face and stared at the snow-covered corn fields flying past. Mike and Tom were coming for her.

"I have to pee."

Her dad looked at her, unconcerned.

"Use a bottle. I do."

"No."

She refused. She would not. She knew he used a bottle, and threw it out the window. She'd seen him do it when she was little, and she'd heard him do it in the night, before she was asleep. Her mother had always sighed when he'd done it, but she could never make him change his habits.

"You will."

"I won't."

"Then you'll burst, because I'm not stopping."

He gripped the wheel with determination, and she sat silent in her misery. She'd had to use the bathroom for some time now, but she didn't want to speak to him, so the need was becoming imminent. She had one trick left. It could lose her everything, or gain her a little more time. She decided it was a gamble she needed to take.

"I'll call 9-1-1."

He glared.

"Fine. I'll stop at the side of the road."

"You'll stop at a civilized establishment with a real women's restroom."

And she held up her phone. He made a grab for it, but she had anticipated that and dodged him. At the next gas station, he pulled in and parked.

"Get out. I'm coming with you."

She didn't say anything, but climbed from her seat in the car when he unlocked her door. She was stiff and tired, and her left arm and her back hurt from where he'd hit her. They walked into the gas station, her father sending a fake grimace over to the cashier, Janelle heading straight for the tiny bathroom in the back. Her dad was right on her heels, and she realized he intended her to come into the bathroom with her.

"You may not."

"I will."

"You will not."

And she ran the last three steps, pulled the door open and closed and locked it behind her before he could do anything. Cognizant as he was, his reaction time was slower because of the alcohol. She peed, washed her hands, and looked at herself in the mirror. He was knocking on the door by this point. She was still wearing her work clothes, minus her apron, which she'd taken off. Her hair was messy, and there were shadows looped under her green gray eyes. She looked sad, she thought to herself. She unbuttoned her shirt and slipped the arm off so she could check her arm in the mirror. There were already bruises appearing. Her father had been knocking on the door this entire time. She sighed, and checked her phone. Mike and Tom hadn't texted her again, so she texted them.

Central Illinois. With my dad. He's driving tipsy.

Then, without thinking about it, she added,

Pray.

She didn't believe in praying, but surely if there was a God he wouldn't want her father to be hurting her. She slid her phone back down her shirt and pulled the door open abruptly, startling her father who stood with his fist raised to hit the door again.

"You took forever."

"I'm a girl. I can take a long time if I need to."

He scowled, but didn't touch her, because they were still in the gas station. She added,

"I'm cold. I need a sweatshirt."

He said,

"Ha. Should have dressed warmer. Your fault."

He walked behind her to the truck, and shut her door behind her, locking it, then walked around to his side and climbed in the cab. Janelle used the moment to hide her phone by her leg again, and minutes back on the road, Tom texted back.

Stall. Get away in Chi. XO.

Her father said,

"Give me another beer."

He cast his bloodshot eyes at her, and she said,

"You'll get drunk. It's not safe."

He pulled an oak rod from beside his seat, and before she could move them, he had slammed it down on her hands. The pain made her skin tingle.

"Give me a beer."

She bent down, and carefully clutched the can with her numb hands. He sighed in satisfaction.

Several hours later, after they'd passed Chicago, she broke her father's stony silence, saying,

"I need to pee again."

"You have problems, woman. You already did."

"I need to again."

He rolled his eyes at her.

"I'm also hungry."

"No."

"Yes."

And she held up her phone again, ready for blows, moving her arm beyond his reach.

"Buy food."

"Fine."

So, twenty minutes later, they pulled up at an Ohio rest area, a large circular building with large bathrooms and a few fast food joints.

"You know the drill."

He walked behind her, right up to the door of the bathroom.

"You have five minutes. Take longer than that and I come in there after you."

So she went in, heart racing. Five minutes to get away.

She peed and washed her hands. There was no option for getting out of the bathroom besides the door—no windows, nothing to hide behind or in, she thought. Then, a middle aged woman and her three teenage daughters came into the bathroom. Based on their conversation, they were on a road trip, it seemed, from Chicago to New Jersey. Janelle weighed the odds in the balance, and did the only thing she could do.

"Excuse me, ma'am?"

She spoke in a low voice, in case her father was straining his ears at the door.

"Yes?"

She looked nice, her daughters looked nice, and it was Janelle's only hope.

"I'm being kidnapped by my father and I need to get away."

The woman looked at her daughters, who looked at Janelle with eyes full of pity. They took in her already bruised hands, the circles under her eyes, her messy hair, and nodded. Janelle added,

"Will you help me?"

The woman exchanged looks with her daughters, and the oldest one nodded. She looked back at Janelle and said,

"Yes."

"He's standing outside of this bathroom. If I'm not out in five minutes he's coming in for me. That was three minutes ago."

The woman looked at Janelle then at her daughters.

"Lucy, give me your hoodie."

Lucy, who appeared to be the oldest, complied quickly. She took off her big black hoodie, showing a tight tank top.

"Put this on."

Janelle slid it over her head, tucking her hair into the back of it so it didn't come out.

"Take your glasses off."

Janelle did.

"And Lucy, switch shoes with her."

Janelle bent down and took off her black sneakers, exchanging them for Lucy's red converse. Just then, the five of them heard a loud male voice.

"Janelle."

She looked at them, frightened.

"That's you?"

She nodded at the woman.

"This is my only chance. He's a little drunk."

The woman nodded.

"Walk out hugging my waist like your life depends on it. Keep your head down on my chest, but try to look where you're walking. Lucy, walk out twenty seconds in front of us, and when you see her dad right outside the entrance, flirt with him like your life depends on it. Pull out all the stops. Get his back to the door of the bathroom. That's crucial. Drop something or break something and bend over and let your shirt come up or whatever. Don't let him touch you. Got it?"

The woman looked at her oldest daughter, Lucy, who nodded.

"Yeah, Ma."

"Now, you two, stand one on either side of me, and Elle, put your hand on her back like she's your sister. Both of you look sad and a little worried. We're going to march straight out and to the car. Lucy, only flirt with him till we're out the doors. Your father is out there, and I'll tell him to get you when I walk past. He'll probably come pull you off this guy and drag you to the car, yelling at you a little. It'll be okay. Ready?"

Her father's voice came echoing in.

"Janelle. You have one minute."

The girls nodded. Janelle prayed it would work. She never prayed— but it felt like a good time to start. She slid her hood up, and clung to the woman's waist.

"Lucy, go."

And Lucy walked out, swinging her hips. The four of them stood silently, waiting for her voice. In a moment, it came faintly, sweet and sugary.

"Hey, big guy. What're you doing here?"

His answer came mumbling out, and the woman motioned to her daughters.

"Elle, Mackenzie, now."

And they slowly walked out, Janelle clinging onto her for dear life. As they neared the door, the woman said,

"Moan a little."

Janelle was staring at her feet, concentrating on walking straight though she was bending over sideways. She heard Lucy saying things to her father that she never wanted to hear said to any respectable man. Even worse, her father was going right along with it. Janelle moaned quietly, and the woman began to walk a little faster. They'd passed the door of the bathroom, and her father, and they were halfway to the exit. Janelle saw a pair of male shoes in front of her, and heard the woman say,

"Wait about thirty seconds, then go pull her off of him."

The man must have trusted his wife. He stood there watching his oldest daughter flirt with a man at least twice her age, and his wife hold onto a person he'd never seen before. The woman kept marching. They walked through first one set of doors, then the next, straight through the parking lot, and up to a big white SUV.

"Quick, climb inside."

And Janelle did, followed by the two girls. The mother climbed into the front seat, and craning her neck back, looked at the entrance to the rest stop. There came her husband, holding Lucy by the elbow with a look on his face that did not bode well for any of them. He opened the car door crisply and closed it behind her, then walked around to the driver's side, climbed in, and looked back at the five of them.

"Please, will someone tell me what just happened?"

"Hold on, babe. Janelle, which car is his?"

Janelle looked around for his rusty red truck, and found it parked several spots away.

"That red truck."

"We're going to stay here and see what happens. Sit low in your seat. You can watch too, the windows are tinted, but keep your hood up and don't get too close to the glass. Here are your glasses."

Then they were silent. Janelle watched the entrance of the building intently, waiting for her father to storm out. Now he was probably marching into the bathroom—several moments later, discovering she wasn't there. He would look carefully, then march back out into the main lobby area. When he couldn't find her, he would come back out to the car. A few minutes later, he came stalking out of the building. He was angry, she could tell. He marched up to his car, looked in the windows, and slammed his fist on the door frame. He shouted, and started swearing profusely. There weren't many people at the rest area, but a mother with two small children led her sons to their car quickly.

There was also a man sitting in the car, and when her father started shouting he rolled down his window to watch the scene. Janelle could hear him, and hunkered down even smaller in her seat. It was her childhood, relived, only this time he wasn't hitting flesh, he was hitting metal. As she watched, he continued to swear and walked to the passenger side of the truck, opened the door, and yelled some more. Janelle sighed, the woman said,

"Oh my,"

The man said,

"What's going on?"

"Wait, honey. Wait a second."

Janelle's father stormed around his car, hitting it and swearing. Janelle saw the man in the car near him pull out his phone and quickly dial numbers. She guessed he was calling the police. She hoped against hope her father would drive away before he got picked up by the police. He was abusive. He was cruel, and negligent to her mother, and he hadn't done anything to love her in fifteen years. But he was her father, and somewhere in the very bottom of her heart, she didn't want him to be caught. She muttered, under her breath,

"Leave. Leave. Go. Drive away."

And suddenly, as if he'd heard her, he moved back to the driver's seat of the truck and got in. He was drunk now. The woman spoke.

"He's drunk."

"Yes."

Her husband still didn't know what was going on.

"You need to stop him before he kills someone."

He hesitated, and in that moment the truck roared to life and started to move.

"Go, Lee, go!"

She almost shoved her husband out of the car. By now the truck was moving, quickly, Janelle's father going straight to where he would turn right for the on ramp back onto the interstate. Lee was running towards the truck, but it seemed too late. Even if he could make it in time, there's not much a single man can do to stop a moving vehicle being driven by a drunken maniac. And then, suddenly, all five women in the car gasped. As if controlled by a cruel puppeteer, the red pickup truck, instead of turning right to get back on the interstate going east, turned left, and began to head towards the off ramp of the highway.

"He's going the wrong way down the off ramp."

The woman said it like she didn't believe it. He was moving, quickly now, towards oncoming traffic. Janelle watched, but it felt like a dream. A nightmare. He was getting closer and closer to the traffic, accelerating with every moment.

And then he was on the highway. They could see the road stretching out in front of him, and dozens of cars heading towards him. The first few dodged him and missed, as he drove in a relatively straight light down the busy road, but a semi-driver didn't have the time to swerve. The truck smashed into the grill of the semi, then bounced around and thudded up against the guard rails. It seemed like it took a lifetime for it to stop moving, but it was really a matter of moments. Lee stood frozen, staring at it, and Janelle sat in the Ford, mouth hanging open, staring at what was once her father's truck, reduced to a mangled mess on the side of the road. The semi stopped and the driver climbed down, and even from where she was, far away, Janelle could tell he was shaking.

Lee pulled his phone from his pocket, and presumably called 9-1-1. Then, he walked slowly over to the fence blocking the interstate from the rest area and climbed over it, walking along the shoulder to where the semi driver stood by the truck. They exchanged some words, then looked into the cab of the truck, that looked more like a compressed accordion. Janelle saw them shaking their heads. She sat in silence. The woman and her daughters looked at her, pitying her, wondering her story but too shocked to pry. Then the woman spoke.

"Honey, when the police come, are you going to tell them you're related?"

It was the last thing on Janelle's mind, but she realized it was an important question.

"Should I?"

The woman shrugged and said,

"It's up to you."

Fifteen minutes later, ambulances came shrieking up, and Janelle watched them pull the mangled frame of what was once her father from the car. He was dead. She watched in terror as they gently placed him on a stretcher and moved him to the ambulance. Lee came back to the car.

"I'm not sure what just happened or who he was or who you are, but were you related to him?"

"That was my dad."

"I'm so sorry."

She shrugged numbly.

"What do you need us to do?"

"My friends are on their way. It's fine if you go. Thank you for all you've done. You saved my life."

And she looked gratefully at the woman and her daughters, and at Lee.

"Are you sure you're going to be okay? We'll wait with you here till they get here?"

Janelle shook her head.

"I'll be fine. It's going to be a little while."

They made her give them her phone number, and the woman said,

"I'm going to call you every so often, okay dear?"

Janelle nodded, then climbed out of the car and walked slowly to a bench by the rest stop. It was cold, but the air cleared her mind. Her thoughts wandered aimlessly, and she felt powerless to take hold of any of them for longer than a moment. There were vague whisperings of other thoughts trying to work their ways to the forefront, but always was the nagging feeling that she was responsible. It came and went, teasing and flirting casually, and she sighed. Then she picked up her phone and called Tom. He answered right away.

"Janelle? Janelle? Are you alright? Talk to me—what happened? Where are you?"

She waited to speak till he had finished, then gathered her thoughts in silence.

"I'm at a rest stop in Ohio."

"Okay, good, good. We should be close before too long. Where's your dad? Are you okay? Are you safe?"

Again, she waited.

"I'm okay. My dad…"

She stopped. If she didn't say it, maybe it wouldn't be true. She didn't want to bring reality to life by explaining it, but Tom needed her to.

"Your dad?"

"Yeah, my dad's gone."

And with the words came the emotions, and with the emotions came the tears, streaming down her cold cheeks, falling one by one on her shirt front, faster and faster.

"Oh, Janelle."

He waited, then asked,

"What happened?"

"He drunk drove the wrong way into a semi on the freeway."

And what she knew would be her worst nightmare for the rest of her life played again and again in her mind. She heard Tom talking to someone on the other end of the phone, Mike she guessed.

"Drive faster—yeah, Ohio. We need to get there soon."

Then he came back to her, and said,

"Oh, Janelle."

"How far are you?"

"We're about twelve hours away. Mike drives fast though, so we'll hurry, okay?"

Dusk had begun, and she sighed.

"Okay."

"Here's what I want you to do. Go back inside, buy a cup of coffee, and sit at a table in the food court. I'm going to stay on the line with you until you've done it, okay?"

She nodded, realized he couldn't see her, and said,

"Okay."

Then she stood, wiping her tears with her hand, and realized she was still wearing the big sweatshirt—but the family had driven away. It was winter and she didn't have a coat, so she walked inside. She bought coffee, while Tom talked to her, telling her she was doing great and it was going to be okay. She sat down at a small table and stared at the empty chair across from her. It seemed to taunt her, chanting 'your fault,' 'your fault,' 'your fault'. She closed her eyes and squeezed more tears out, and Tom pulled her back.

"Janelle, stay with me, stay with me. It's going to be okay. Text me your location, then I'm going to hang up because I don't want your phone to die. We're coming, we'll be there soon. You are going to be okay."

He hung up and she sent her location, then sat, staring at the cup of coffee until it went cold. The tears had stopped, and now her mind felt like she'd left it outside in the snow—cold and frosted and tight. The minutes seemed to drag, and with every one she saw the truck, pressed flat against the air. And she saw her father's still form on the stretcher, being loaded into the ambulance. The hospital would call her mother when they looked at his identification—they probably already had. She kept waiting for the pain and dread of it to subside, but it wouldn't. Her mind rolled and rolled in circles, waiting hopelessly for relief. People came and went, and some stared at her, curled up in her chair, holding a cold cup of coffee like it was the last water on earth and she was in the desert. No one talked to her, and no one knew she'd just watched her father die. The hours crawled. She waited. Stood. Sat. Sighed. And when she felt like she couldn't wait another moment, she looked up, and it had only been two hours. And so she kept playing the game. Waiting. Finally, she crawled into a booth, put her head against the wall, and fell into a troubled sleep. Not because she was tired, but because she didn't want to be there and it was the only way she could get away. And when Mike and Tom got there hours later, close to dawn, that was how they found her; sleeping fitfully, tears streaming down her cheeks, knees pulled up to her chin. Tom sat down next to her, and gently touched her shoulder. She jerked awake, looked blearily at him, remembered everything that had happened, and started sobbing. He put his arms around her, holding her, then slid an arm under her legs, picked her up, and carried her out to Mike's car. It was the second time in so few months that she'd been picked up and carried when she couldn't walk, like a child who couldn't take life any more, like she'd never been cared for by her father. Tom addressed Mike.

"Do you have blankets in your car?"

"I don't think so."

"Buy two."

Mike nodded, and walked over to the small convenience area of the rest stop. Tom carried Janelle out to the car, opened the door, and climbed in with her on his lap. She wept, clinging to him like a child afraid of heights. He stroked her back gently.

"Shhhh, shhhh, you're okay."

Mike came back with the blankets, opened them, covered her with one and put the other in the back seat, then sat there as she cried. Men have never been comfortable with crying females, and it showed their care that they sat there as she wept. They loved her. She cried until she ran out of water, then opened her fists from where she'd been holding tightly to Tom's flannel, and revealed two wrinkled circles of material. She said,

"I'm really thirsty."

Tom looked over at Mike, who nodded.

"What do you want?"

"Anything. Water, lemonade, iced tea. Whatever."

So Mike left, and a few minutes later came back with three bottles of each. She saw them, and smiled sadly through the tears that were drying on her cheeks.

"Thanks, Mike."

"Pleasure."

He awkwardly patted her on the back. They sat in silence for some time, Janelle trying to breath slowly and reach equilibrium again, and the two men sitting there quietly trying to be comforting. When she seemed to be calm, Mike's practical side spoke.

"Where do you want to go?"

She sighed, then said,

"Home. I want to go home."

She paused, realized they didn't know which she meant, and said,

"Syracuse."

Mike nodded, and started the engine. She stayed in Tom's lap, and eventually fell asleep. Mike drove, seemingly never running out of energy, and Tom, after a long time of sitting in silence, said,

"She's so little."

She was clinging to him still, as if even in her sleep she was afraid to let go. Mike nodded.

"She is. Strong."

Tom nodded. Even guessing what she'd been through in the past 24 hours hurt his heart, and when he touched her left arm and she flinched, he sighed. There were bruises on her hands, and he was sure her arms would tell the same story. He clenched his fists. They'd seen the flattened truck when they drove up, and put two and two together, but when Tom saw the angry marks on her small delicate hands, he spoke.

"That man deserved what he got."

Mike didn't speak for a long time, then said,

"The Lord guides a man where he is to go. It was the end of that man's road." As if realizing that sounded too calm, he nodded emphatically and said, "But yes. He did." They drove on into the sunrise, on to Syracuse, where they woke Janelle up and asked her for her address. She'd slept on Tom's lap the entire trip, holding onto him tightly. She told them where she lived. It was late in the evening when they rolled into the driveway, and Tom gently lifted Janelle off of his lap onto the cement. She held onto the car, unsteady. He climbed out after her and gently led her up the walkway to the front door. She tried the handle first, but it was locked, so she knocked gently. Moments later, a small woman with bleached blonde hair came to the door. She looked exactly like Janelle, only older and careworn. She had hastily wiped her eyes before she'd come to the door, but they were telltale and red. When she saw Janelle, she gave a cry.

"My baby!"

And she pulled her into her arms and held her, as they both wept. Tom and Mike stood awkwardly back, scuffing their toes on the welcome mat and focusing their eyes on anything but the women.

Eventually she welcomed them into her house, a neat and ordered kitchen, and offered them coffee, through her tears. Neither of the women would let go of the other. Janelle's mother had gotten the call from the police early that morning, and though her life had been nothing but pain because of her husband, she loved him and mourned him. Janelle decided to stay home with her mother, and after many thanks and sympathy, Tom and Mike left to go sleep all day and night at a hotel, then drive back to Denver.

They climbed back into Mike's car, and Mike looked at Tom.

"That woman loved her husband."

He remembered the bruises he'd seen on her arms when her sleeves fell back. Tom added,

"Much more than he deserved."

Mike nodded, and said,

"Let that be a lesson to you. Treat your woman well, when you get her. She'll put up with more than you can even imagine."

Tom nodded, and each was silent. Too much to think about to speak.

CHAPTER TWENTY-SIX

So they returned home, each to his life, and the weeks passed. Spring came back slowly, and with it the flowers and the joy. After much deliberation and debate, and encouragement from Mary, Tom decided to go back to a community college and finish his degree. He applied, was accepted for the fall term, and called his family in delight.

Mike settled back into the routine of his life, putting his heart into his work and his church, missing his wife and working hard, in case he ever had an opportunity to get her back, or be loved by another. Each thought of Janelle often, for there was an emptiness in their threesome. She was gone. They missed her somber expression, her quirk, her laugh, her bristly blonde hair. They heard from her occasionally, to say that all was well, and she was recovering from the shock and her childhood fairly well. Then, one cool morning late in the summer, while Mike was in The Cup getting his coffee, he got a text. He pulled his phone out. It was a group message, to Tom as well.

"Tom, are you getting this?"

"I don't use my phone at work, you know that."

"Oh."

Mike did know that.

"Well, you should make an exception."

Tom raised his eyebrows, then found his phone in his bag and turned it on. Moments later, it dinged with a message from Janelle.

Going to school. In Denver. Coming back today. 6:45. Come get me.

Tom dropped the mug in his hand, and it clunked across the wood floor. He looked at Mike, who was grinning broadly.

Six forty-five found them standing at the gate of the airport, peering closely down the security lane, looking for the blond head that they'd come to know and love so well. And when it came walking down the lane towards them, Tom yelled and Mike bounced, and Janelle broke into a run, heading straight for their arms.

She was back. It was really only the beginning.

Made in the USA
Lexington, KY
27 October 2017